P9-DHC-300

DASH & LILY'S BOOK OF DARES

DASH & LILY'S BOOK OF DARES

Rachel Cohn & David Levithan

Alfred A. Knopf
New York

Special thanks to the Usual Suspects

THIS IS A BORZOI BOOK PUBLISHED BY ALFRED A. KNOPF

Grateful acknowledgment is made to Alfred A. Knopf, a division of Random House, Inc., for permission to reprint excerpts from "The Story of Our Lives" and "Keeping Things Whole," from *Selected Poems* by Mark Strand, copyright © 1979, 1980 by Mark Strand.

Visit us on the Web! www.randomhouse.com/teens

Educators and librarians, for a variety of teaching tools, visit us at www.randomhouse.com/teachers

Library of Congress Cataloging-in-Publication Data
Cohn, Rachel.
Dash & Lily's book of dares / by Rachel Cohn and David Levithan. — 1st ed.
p. cm.
Summary: Told in the alternating voices of Dash and Lily, two sixteen-year-olds carry on a wintry scavenger hunt at Christmastime in New York, neither knowing quite what—or who—they will find.
ISBN 978-0-375-86659-3 (trade) — ISBN 978-0-375-96659-0 (lib. bdg.) —
ISBN 978-0-375-89668-2 (e-book)
[1. Treasure hunt (Game)—Fiction. 2. Identity—Fiction. 3. New York (N.Y.)—Fiction.]
I. Levithan, David. II. Title. III. Dash and Lily's book of dares.
PZ7.C6665Das 2010
[Fic]—dc22
2009054084

The text of this book is set in 11.5-point Goudy and Hoefler Text.

Printed in the United States of America
October 2010
10 9 8 7 6 5 4 3 2 1

First Edition

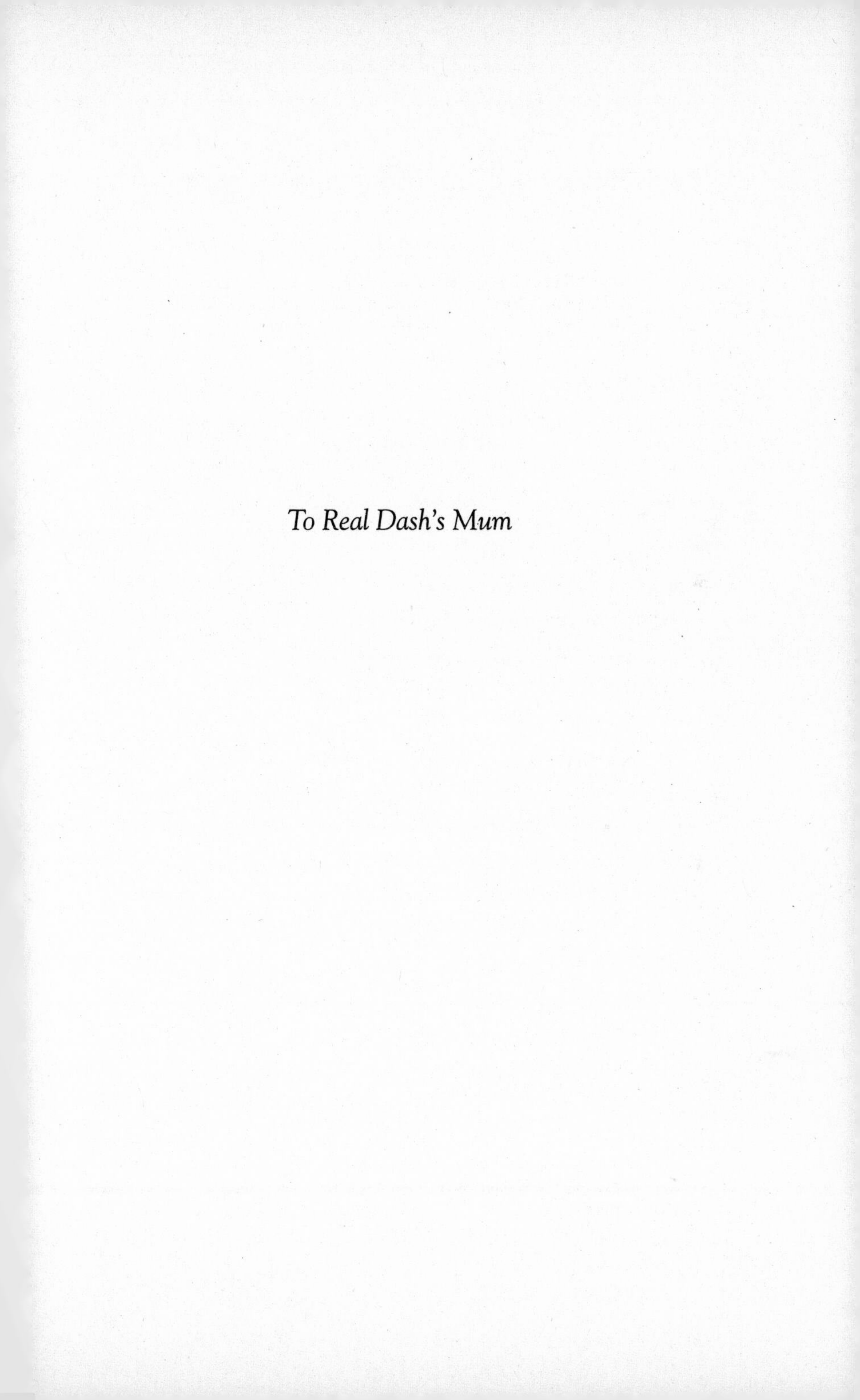

To Real Dash's Mum

one

–Dash–

December 21st

Imagine this:

You're in your favorite bookstore, scanning the shelves. You get to the section where a favorite author's books reside, and there, nestled in comfortably between the incredibly familiar spines, sits a red notebook.

What do you do?

The choice, I think, is obvious:

You take down the red notebook and open it.

And then you do whatever it tells you to do.

It was Christmastime in New York City, the most detestable time of the year. The moo-like crowds, the endless visits from hapless relatives, the ersatz cheer, the joyless attempts at joyfulness—my natural aversion to human contact could only intensify in this context. Wherever I went, I was on the wrong end of the stampede. I was not willing to grant "salvation" through any "army." I would never care about the whiteness of Christmas.

I was a Decemberist, a Bolshevik, a career criminal, a philatelist trapped by unknowable anguish—whatever everyone else was not, I was willing to be. I walked as invisibly as I could through the Pavlovian spend-drunk hordes, the broken winter breakers, the foreigners who had flown halfway across the world to see the lighting of a tree without realizing how completely pagan such a ritual was.

The only bright side of this dim season was that school was shuttered (presumably so everyone could shop ad nauseam and discover that family, like arsenic, works best in small doses . . . unless you prefer to die). This year I had managed to become a voluntary orphan for Christmas, telling my mother that I was spending it with my father, and my father that I was spending it with my mother, so that each of them booked nonrefundable vacations with their post-divorce paramours. My parents hadn't spoken to each other in eight years, which gave me a lot of leeway in the determination of factual accuracy, and therefore a lot of time to myself.

I was popping back and forth between their apartments while they were away—but mostly I was spending time in the Strand, that bastion of titillating erudition, not so much a bookstore as the collision of a hundred different bookstores, with literary wreckage strewn over eighteen miles of shelves. All the clerks there saunter-slouch around distractedly in their skinny jeans and their thrift-store button-downs, like older siblings who will never, ever be bothered to talk to you or care about you or even acknowledge your existence if their friends are around . . . which they always are. Some bookstores want you to believe they're a community center, like they need to host a cookie-making class in order to sell you some Proust. But the Strand leaves you completely on your own, caught between the warring forces of organization and idiosyncrasy, with idiosyncrasy winning every time. In other words, it was my kind of graveyard.

I was usually in the mood to look for nothing in particular when I went to the Strand. Some days, I would decide that the afternoon was sponsored by a particular letter, and would visit each and every section to check out the authors whose last names began with that letter. Other days, I would decide to tackle a single section, or would investigate the recently unloaded tomes, thrown in bins that never really conformed to alphabetization. Or maybe I'd only look at books with green covers, because it had been too long since I'd read a book with a green cover.

I could have been hanging out with my friends, but most of them were hanging out with their families or their Wiis. (*Wiis? Wiii?* What *is* the plural?) I preferred to hang out with the dead, dying, or desperate books—*used* we call them, in a way that we'd never call a person, unless we meant it cruelly. ("Look at Clarissa . . . she's such a *used* girl.")

I was horribly bookish, to the point of coming right out and saying it, which I knew was not socially acceptable. I particularly loved the adjective *bookish*, which I found other people used about as often as *ramrod* or *chum* or *teetotaler*.

On this particular day, I decided to check out a few of my favorite authors to see if any irregular editions had emerged from a newly deceased person's library sale. I was perusing a particular favorite (he shall remain nameless, because I might turn against him someday) when I saw a peek of red. It was a red Moleskine—made of neither mole nor skin, but nonetheless the preferred journal of my associates who felt the need to journal in non-electronic form. You can tell a lot about a person from the pages he or she chooses to journal on—I was strictly a college-ruled man myself, having no talent for illustration and a microscopic scrawl that made wide-ruled seem roomy. The blank pages were usually the most popular—I only had one friend, Thibaud, who went for the grid. Or at least he did until the guidance counselors confiscated his journals to prove that he had been plotting to kill our history teacher. (This is a true story.)

There wasn't any writing on the spine of this particular journal—I had to take it off the shelf to see the front, where there was a piece of masking tape with the words DO YOU DARE? written in black Sharpie. When I opened the cover, I found a note on the first page.

I've left some clues for you.
If you want them, turn the page.
If you don't, put the book back on the shelf, please.

The handwriting was a girl's. I mean, you can tell. That enchanted cursive.

Either way, I would've endeavored to turn the page.

So here we are.

1. Let's start with French Pianism.
I don't really know what it is,
but I'm guessing
nobody's going to take it off the shelf.
Charles Timbrell's your man.
88/7/2
88/4/8

Do not turn the page
until you fill in the blanks
(just don't write in the notebook, please).

____________________ ____________________

I can't say I'd ever heard of French pianism, although if a man on the street (wearing a bowler, no doubt) had asked me if I believed the French were a pianistic sort, I would have easily given an affirmative reply.

Because the bookstore byways of the Strand were more familiar to me than my own family home(s), I knew exactly where to start—the music section. It even seemed a cheat that she had given me the name of the author. Did she think me a simpleton, a slacker, a *numbskull*? I wanted a little credit, even before I'd earned it.

The book was found easily enough—easily enough, that is, for someone who had fourteen minutes to spare—and was exactly as I pictured it would be, the kind of book that can sit on the shelves for years. The publisher hadn't even bothered to put an illustration on the cover. Just the words *French Pianism: An Historical Perspective*, *Charles Timbrell*, then (new line) *Foreword by Gaby Casadesus*.

I figured the numbers in the Moleskine were dates—1988 must have been a quicksilver year for French pianism—but I couldn't find any references to 1988 . . . or 1888 . . . or 1788 . . . or any other '88, for that matter. I was stymied . . . until I realized that my clue giver had resorted to the age-old bookish mantra—*page/line/word*. I went to page 88 and checked out line 7, word 2, then line 4, word 8.

Are you

Was I what? I had to find out. I filled in the blanks (mentally, respecting the virgin spaces as she'd asked) and turned the page of the journal.

Okay. No cheating.
What bugged you about the cover of this book
(besides the lack of art)?

Think about it, then turn the page.

Well, that was easy. I hated that they'd used the construction *An Historical*, when it clearly should have been *A Historical*, since the *H* in *Historical* is a hard *H*.

I turned the page.

If you said it was the misbegotten phrase
"An Historical,"
please continue.

If not, please put this journal
back on its shelf.

Once more, I turned.

2. Fat Hoochie Prom Queen
64/4/9
119/3/8

__________________ __________________

No author this time. Not helpful.

I took *French Pianism* with me (we'd grown close; I couldn't leave her) and went to the information desk, where the guy sitting there looked like someone had slipped a few lithium into his Coke Zero.

"I'm looking for *Fat Hoochie Prom Queen*," I declared.

He did not respond.

"It's a book," I said. "Not a person."

Nope. Nothing.

"At the very least, can you tell me the author?"

He looked at his computer, as if it had some way to speak to me without any typing on his part.

"Are you wearing headphones that I can't see?" I asked.

He scratched at the inside of his elbow.

"Do you know me?" I persisted. "Did I grind you to a pulp in kindergarten, and are you now getting sadistic pleasure from this petty revenge? Stephen Little, is that you? Is it? I was much younger then, and foolish to have nearly drowned you in that water fountain. In my defense, your prior destruction of my book report was a completely unwarranted act of aggression."

Finally, a response. The information desk clerk shook his shaggy head.

"No?" I said.

"I am not allowed to disclose the location of *Fat Hoochie Prom Queen*," he explained. "Not to you. Not to anyone. And while I am not Stephen Little, you should be ashamed of what you did to him. *Ashamed*."

Okay, this was going to be harder than I'd thought. I tried to load Amazon onto my phone for a quick check—but there was no service anywhere in the store. I figured *Fat Hoochie Prom*

Queen was unlikely to be nonfiction (would that it were!), so I went to the literature section and began to scan the shelves. This proving fruitless, I remembered the teen literature section upstairs and went there straightaway. I skipped over any spine that didn't possess an inkling of pink. All my instincts told me *Fat Hoochie Prom Queen* would at the very least be dappled by pink. And lo and behold—I got to the M section, and there it was.

I turned to pages 64 and 119 and found:

going to

I turned the page of the Moleskine.

Very resourceful.

Now that you've found this in the teen section,
I must ask you:
Are you a teenage boy?

If yes, please turn the page.
If no, please return this to where you found it.

I was sixteen and equipped with the appropriate genitalia, so I cleared that hurdle nicely.

Next page.

3. The Joy of Gay Sex
(third edition!)
66/12/5
181/18/7

_______________ _______________

Well, there wasn't any doubt which section *that* would be in. So it was down to the Sex & Sexuality shelves, where the glances were alternately furtive and defiant. Personally, the notion of buying a used sex manual (of any sexuality) was a bit sketchy to me. Perhaps that was why there were four copies of *The Joy of Gay Sex* on the shelves. I turned to page 66, scanned down to line 12, word 5, and found:

cock

I recounted. Rechecked.

Are you going to cock?

Perhaps, I thought, *cock* was being used as a verb (e.g., *Please cock that pistol for me before you leave the vestibule*).

I moved to page 181, not without some trepidation.

Making love without noise is like playing a muted piano—fine for practice, but you cheat yourself out of hearing the glorious results.

I'd never thought a single sentence could turn me off so decisively from both making love *and* playing the piano, but there it was.

No illustration accompanied the text, mercifully. And I had my seventh word:

playing

Which left me with:

Are you going to cock playing

That didn't seem right. Fundamentally, as a matter of grammar, it didn't seem right.

I looked back at the page in the journal and resisted the urge to turn forward. Scrutinizing the girlish scrawl, I realized I had mistaken a 5 for a 6. It was page 66 (the junior version of the devil's number) that I was after.

be

Much more sensical.

Are you going to be playing—

"Dash?"

I turned to find Priya, this girl from my school, somewhere between a friend and acquaintance—a *frequaintance*, as it were. She had been friends with my ex-girlfriend, Sofia, who was now in Spain. (Not because of me.) Priya had no personality traits that I could discern, although in all fairness, I had never looked very hard.

"Hi, Priya," I said.

She looked at the books I was holding—a red Moleskine, *French Pianism*, *Fat Hoochie Prom Queen*, and, open to a rather graphic drawing of two men doing something I had heretofore not known to be possible, *The Joy of Gay Sex* (third edition).

Apprising the situation, I figured some explanation was in order.

"It's for a paper I'm doing," I said, my voice rife with fake intellectual assurance. "On French pianism and its effects. You'd be amazed at how far-reaching French pianism is."

Priya, bless her, looked like she regretted ever saying my name.

"Are you around for break?" she asked.

If I'd admitted I was, she might have been forthcoming with an invitation to an eggnog party or a group excursion to the holiday film *Gramma Got Run Over by a Reindeer*, featuring a black comedian playing all of the roles, except for that of a female Rudolph, who was, one assumed, the love interest. Because I withered under the glare of an actual invitation, I was a firm believer in preventative prevarication—in other words, lying early in order to free myself later on.

"I leave tomorrow for Sweden," I replied.

"Sweden?"

I did not (and do not) look in any way Swedish, so a family holiday was out of the question. By way of explanation, I simply said, "I love Sweden in December. The days are short . . . the nights are long . . . and the design completely lacks ornament."

Priya nodded. "Sounds fun."

We stood there. I knew that according to the rules of conversation, it was now my turn. But I also knew that refusal to conform to these rules might result in Priya's departure, which I very much wanted.

After thirty seconds, she could stand it no longer.

"Well, I gotta go," she said.

"Happy Hanukkah," I said. Because I always liked to say the wrong holiday, just to see how the other person would react.

Priya took it in stride. "Have fun in Sweden," she said. And was gone.

I rearranged my books so the red journal was on top again. I turned to the next page.

The fact that you are willing to stand there
in the Strand with The Joy of Gay Sex
bodes well for our future.

However, if you already own this book
or would find it useful in your life,
I am afraid our time together
must end here.
This girl can only go boy-girl,
so if you're into

boy-boy, I completely support that,
but don't see where I'd fit into the picture.

Now, one last book.
4. What the Living Do, by Marie Howe
23/1/8
24/5/9, 11, 12, 13, 14, 15

______ ______ ______
______ ______ ______ ______?

I headed immediately to the poetry section, completely intrigued. Who was this strange reader of Marie Howe who'd summoned me? It seemed too convenient that we should both know about the same poet. Really, most people in my circle didn't know any poets at all. I tried to remember talking about Marie Howe with someone—anyone—but came up blank. Only Sofia, probably, and this wasn't Sofia's handwriting. (Plus, she was in Spain.)

I checked the *H*s. Nothing. I went through the whole poetry section. Nothing. I was about to scream in frustration when I saw it—at the very top of the bookshelf, at least twelve feet from the floor. A slight corner peeking out—but I knew from its slimness and dark plum color that it was the book I was looking for. I pulled over a ladder and made the perilous climb. It was a dusty ascent, the out-of-reach heights clouded with disinterest, making the air harder to breathe. Finally, I had the volume in my hand. I couldn't wait—I quickly turned to pages 23 and 24 and found the seven words I needed.

for the pure thrill of unreluctant desire

I nearly fell off the ladder.

Are you going to be playing for the pure thrill of unreluctant desire?

I was, to put it mildly, aroused by the phrasing.

Carefully, I stepped back down. When I hit the floor again, I retrieved the red Moleskine and turned the page.

So here we are.
Now it's up to you,
what we do (or don't) do.

If you are interested in continuing this conversation,
please choose a book, any book, and
leave a slip of paper with your email address inside of it.
Give it to Mark, at the information desk.

If you ask Mark any questions about me,
he will not pass on your book.
So no questions.

Once you have given your book to Mark,
please return this book to the shelf
where you found it.

If you do all these things,
you very well might hear from me.
Thank you.
Lily

Suddenly, for the first time that I could recall, I was looking forward to winter break, and I was relieved that I was not, in fact, being shipped out to Sweden the next morning.

I didn't want to think too hard about which book to leave—if I started to second-guess, it would only lead to third-guessing and fourth-guessing, and I would never leave the Strand. So I chose a book rather impulsively, and instead of leaving my email address inside, I decided to leave something else. I figured it would take a little time for Mark (my new friend at the information desk) to give the book to Lily, so I would have a slight head start. I handed it to him without a word; he nodded and put it in a drawer.

I knew the next step was for me to return the red notebook, to give someone else a chance of finding it. Instead, I kept it. And, furthermore, I moved to the register to buy the copies of *French Pianism* and *Fat Hoochie Prom Queen* currently in my hands.

Two, I decided, could play this game.

two

(Lily)

December 21st

I love Christmas.

I love everything about it: the lights, the cheer, the big family gatherings, the cookies, the presents piled high around the tree, the *goodwill to all.* I know it's technically *goodwill to all men,* but in my mind, I drop the *men* because that feels segregationist/elitist/sexist/generally bad *ist*. *Goodwill* shouldn't be just for men. It should also apply to women and children, and all animals, even the yucky ones like subway rats. I'd even extend the goodwill not just to living creatures but to the dearly departed, and if we include them, we might as well include the undead, those supposedly mythic beings like vampires, and if they're in, then so are elves, fairies, and gnomes. Heck, since we're already being so generous in our big group hug, why not also embrace those supposedly inanimate objects like dolls and stuffed animals (special shout-out to my Ariel mermaid, who presides over the shabby chic flower power pillow on my bed—love you, girl!). I'm sure Santa would agree. *Goodwill to all.*

I love Christmas so much that this year I've organized my own caroling society. Just because I live in the gentrified bohemia of the East Village does not mean I consider myself too cool and sophisticated for caroling. To the contrary. I feel so strongly about it that when *my own family members* chose to disband our caroling group this year because everyone was "traveling" or was "too busy" or "has a life" or "thought you would have grown out of it by now, Lily," I did some old-fashioned problem solving. I made my own flyer and put it up in cafés around my street.

Hark!

You there, closet caroler!
Care to herald some holiday song?
Really? Me too! Let's talk.*
Yours sincerely, Lily

No creeps need apply; my grandpa knows everyone in the neighborhood and you will incur much shunning should you be anything less than sincere in your response.*
Thx again, yours most truly, Lily

****Sorry to be so cynical, but this is New York.**

That flyer was how I formed my Christmas caroling troupe this year. There's me, Melvin (computer guy), Roberta (retired high school choir teacher), Shee'nah (cross-dressing part-time choreographer/part-time waiter) and his boi Antwon (assistant manager at Home Depot), angry Aryn (vegan riot grrrl

NYU film student), and Mark (my cousin—because he owes Grandpa a favor and that's the one Grandpa called in). The carolers call me Third-Verse Lily because I'm the only one who remembers past the second verse of any Christmas song. Besides Aryn (who doesn't care), I'm also the only one not of legal drinking age, so with the amount of hot chocolate laced with peppermint liquor that my merry caroling troupe passes round from Roberta's flask, it's no surprise I'm the only one who remembers the third verse.

Truly He taught us to love one another.
His law is love and His gospel is peace.
Chains he shall break, for the slave is our brother.
And in His name all oppression shall cease.
Sweet hymns of joy in grateful chorus raise we,
With all our hearts we praise His holy name.
Christ is the Lord! Then ever, ever praise we,
His power and glory ever more proclaim!

Hallelujah, third verse!

In all honesty, I should admit I have researched much of the scientific evidence refuting G-d's existence, as a result of which I suspect I am a true believer in him the way I am in Santa. But I will unhesitatingly, and joyfully, *O-Holy-Night* his name between Thanksgiving and Christmas Eve, with the mutual understanding that as of Christmas Day, once the presents are opened, my relationship with him goes on hiatus until I camp out for best viewing of the Macy's parade the following year.

I would like to be the person who stands outside Macy's

during the holiday season wearing a cute red outfit and ringing a bell to chime in donations for the Salvation Army, but Mom said no. She said those bell people are possibly religious freaks, and we are holiday-only lapsed Catholics who support homosexuality and a woman's right to choose. We do not stand outside Macy's begging for money. We don't even *shop* at Macy's.

I may go begging for change at Macy's simply as a form of protest. For the first time in, like, the history of ever—that is, all of my sixteen years—our family is spending Christmas apart. My parents abandoned me and my brother for Fiji, where they're celebrating their twenty-fifth wedding anniversary. When they got married, my parents were poor graduate students who couldn't afford a proper honeymoon vacation, so they've gone all out for their silver anniversary. It seems to me that wedding anniversaries are meant for their children to celebrate with them, but apparently I am the minority opinion on this one. According to everyone besides me, if my brother and I tag along on their vacation, it won't be as "romantic." I don't see what's so "romantic" about spending a week in a tropical paradise with your spouse whom you've already seen almost every day for the past quarter century. I can't imagine anyone ever wanting to be alone with me that much.

My brother, Langston, said, "Lily, you don't understand because you've never been in love. If you had a boyfriend, you'd understand." Langston has a new boyfriend and all I understand from that is a sorry state of co-dependence.

And it's not entirely true that I've never been in love. I had a pet gerbil in first grade, Spazzy, whom I loved passionately. I will never stop blaming myself for bringing Spazzy to show-and-tell at school, where Edgar Thibaud let open his cage when I wasn't looking and Spazzy met Jessica Rodriguez's cat Tiger and, well, the rest is history. Goodwill to Spazzy up in gerbil heaven. Sorry sorry sorry. I stopped eating meat the day of the massacre, as penance for Spazzy. I've been a vegetarian since age six, all for the love of a gerbil.

Since I was eight, I have been in literary love with the character Sport from *Harriet the Spy.* I've kept my own Harriet-style journal—red Moleskine notebooks that Grandpa buys me at the Strand—since I first read that book, only I don't write mean observations about people in my journals like Harriet sometimes did. Mostly I draw pictures in it and write memorable quotes or passages from books I've read, or recipe ideas, or little stories I make up when I'm bored. I want to be able to show grown-up Sport that I've tried my darnedest not to make sport out of writing mean gossip and stuff.

Langston has been in love. Twice. His first big romance ended so badly that he had to leave Boston after his freshman year of college and move back home till his heart could heal; the breakup was that bad. I hope I never love someone so much that they could hurt me the way Langston was hurt, so wounded all he could do was cry and mope around the house and ask me to make him peanut butter and banana sandwiches with the crusts cut off, then play Boggle with him, which of course I always did, because I usually do whatever Langston wants me to do. Langston eventually recovered and now he's in love again. I think this new one's okay. Their first date was at the symphony. How mean can a guy be who likes Mozart? I hope, at least.

Unfortunately, now that Langston has a boyfriend again, he has forgotten all about me. He has to be with Benny *all the time.* To Langston, our parents and Grandpa being gone for Christmas is a gift, and not the outrage it is to me. I protested to Langston about him basically granting Benny a permanent state of residence in our house over the holidays. I reminded him that if Mom and Dad were going to be away at Christmas, and Grandpa would be at his winter apartment in Florida, then it was Langston's responsibility to keep me company. I was there for him in his time of need, after all.

But Langston repeated, "Lily, you just don't understand. What you need is someone to keep you occupied. You need a boyfriend."

Well sure, who *doesn't* need a boyfriend? But realistically, those exotic creatures are hard to come by. At least a quality one. I go to an all-girls school, and meaning no disrespect to my sapphic sisters, but I have no interest in finding a romantic companion there. The rare boy creatures I do meet who aren't either related to me or who aren't gay are usually too attached to their Xboxes to notice me, or their idea of how a teenage girl should look and act comes directly from the pages of *Maxim* magazine or from the tarty look of a video game character.

There's also the problem of Grandpa. Many years ago, he owned a neighborhood family grocery store on Avenue A in the East Village. He sold the business but kept the corner block building, where he had raised his family. My family lives in that building now, along with Grandpa in the fourth-floor "penthouse" apartment, as he calls the converted space that was once an attic studio. There's a sushi restaurant on the ground floor where the grocery store once was. Grandpa has presided over the neighborhood as it went from low-income haven for immigrant families to yuppie enclave. Everybody knows him. Every morning he joins his buddies at the local Italian bakery, where these huge, burly guys drink espresso from dainty little cups. The scene is very *Sopranos* meets *Rent.* It means that because everyone looks affectionately upon Grandpa, they're all looking out for Grandpa's pet—me, the baby of the family, the youngest of his ten grandchildren. The few local boys so far who've expressed an interest in me have all been quickly "persuaded" that I'm too young to date, according to Langston. It's like I wear an invisible cloak of unavailability to cute boys when I walk around the neighborhood. It's a problem.

So Langston decided to make it his project to (1) give me a project to keep me occupied so he could have Benny all to himself over Christmas and (2) move that project to west of First Avenue, away from Grandpa's protection shield. Langston took the latest red Moleskine notebook that Grandpa bought me and, together with Benny, mapped out a series of clues to find a companion just right for me. Or so they said. But the clues could not have been further removed from who I am. I mean, French pianism? Sounds possibly naughty. *The Joy of Gay Sex*? I'm blushing even thinking about that. Definitely naughty. *Fat Hoochie Prom Queen*? Please. I'd include *hoochie* as a most un-goodwill type of curse word. You'd never hear me utter the word, much less read a book with that word in its title.

I thought the notebook was seriously Langston's stupidest idea ever until Langston mentioned *where* he was going to leave it—at the Strand, the bookstore where our parents used to take us on Sundays and let us roam the aisles like it was our personal playground. Furthermore, he'd placed it next to my personal anthem book, *Franny and Zooey.* "If there's a perfect guy for you anywhere," Langston said, "he'll be found hunting for old Salinger editions. We'll start there."

If it had been a regular Christmas season, where my folks were around and our normal traditions carried on, I never would have agreed to Langston's red notebook idea. But there was something so empty about the prospect of a Christmas Day without opening presents and other, less important forms of merrymaking. Truthfully, I'm not exactly a popularity magnet at school, so it wasn't like I had alternate choices of companionship over the holidays. I needed something to look forward to.

But I never thought anyone—much less a prospect from that highly coveted but extremely elusive Teenage Boy Who Actually Reads and Hangs Out at the Strand species—would actually find the notebook and respond to its dares. And just as I never thought my newly formed Christmas caroling society would abandon me after only two nights of street caroling to take up Irish drinking songs at a pub on Avenue B, I never thought someone would actually figure out Langston's cryptic clues and return the favor.

Yet there it was on my phone, a text from my cousin Mark confirming such a person might exist.

`Mark: Lily, you have a taker at the Strand. He left you something in return. I left it there for you in a brown envelope.`

I couldn't believe it. I texted back: `WHAT DID HE LOOK LIKE?!?!?`

Mark answered: `Snarly. Hipster wannabe.`

I tried to imagine myself befriending a snarly hipster wannabe boy, and I couldn't see it. I am a nice girl. A quiet girl (except for the caroling). I get good grades. I am the captain of my school's soccer team. I love my family. I don't know anything about what's supposed to be "cool" in the downtown scene. I'm pretty boring and nerdy, actually, and not in the ironic hipster way. It's like if you picture Harriet the Spy, eleven-year-old tomboy wunderkind spy, and then picture her a few years later, with boobs she hides under a school oxford uniform shirt that she wears even on non-school days, along with her brother's discarded jeans, and add to her ensemble some animal pendant necklaces for jewelry, worn-out Chucks on her feet, and black-rimmed nerd glasses, then you've pictured me. Lily of the Field, Grandpa calls me sometimes, because everyone thinks I am so sweet and delicate.

Sometimes I wonder what it would feel like to venture to the darker side of the lily-white spectrum. Maybe.

I sprinted over to the Strand to retrieve whatever the mysterious notebook taker had left behind for me. Mark was gone, but he'd scrawled a message on the envelope he'd left behind for me: *Seriously, Lily. Dude snarls a lot.*

I ripped open the package, and . . . what?!?! Snarl had left me a copy of *The Godfather,* along with a delivery menu for Two Boots Pizza. The menu had dirty footprints embedded on it, indicating perhaps it had been on the floor at the Strand. To go along with the unsanitary theme, the book wasn't even a new copy of *The Godfather,* but a tattered used copy that smelled like cigarette smoke and had pages that were crinkled and a binding that was at death's door.

I called Langston to decipher this nonsense. No answer.

Now that our parents had messaged us that they'd arrived in Fiji paradise safely, Benny was probably officially moved in, the door to Langston's room locked, his phone off.

I had no choice but to go grab a slice and ponder the red notebook alone. What else could I do? When in doubt, ingest carbs.

I went to the Two Boots location on the delivery menu, on Avenue A just above Houston. I asked the person at the counter, "Do you know a snarly boy who likes *The Godfather*?"

"I *wish* I did," the counter person said. "Plain or pepperoni?"

"Calzone, please," I said. Two Boots makes weird Cajun-flavored pizzas. Not for me and my sensitive digestive system.

I sat at a corner booth and flipped through the book Snarl had left for me but could find no viable clues. *Well,* I thought, *I guess this game is over as soon as it's started.* I was too Lily white to figure it out.

But then the menu that had been tucked inside the book dropped to the ground, and out of it peeked a Post-it note I hadn't noticed before. I picked up the Post-it note. It was definitely a boy's scrawl: moody, foreign, and barely legible.

Here's the scary part. I *could* decipher this message. It contained a poem by Marie Howe, a personal favorite of my mother's. Mom is an English professor specializing in twentieth-century American lit, and she regularly tortured Langston and me with poetry passages instead of bedtime stories when we were kids. My brother and I are frighteningly well-versed in modern American poetry.

The note was a passage from my mother's favorite of Marie Howe's poems, too, and it was a poem I had always liked because it contained a passage about the poet seeing herself in the window glass of a corner video store, which never failed to strike me as funny, imagining some mad poet wandering the streets and spying herself in a video store window reflected next to, perhaps, posters of Jackie Chan or Sandra Bullock or someone super-famous and probably not at all poet-y. I liked Moody Boy even more when I saw that he'd underlined my favorite part of the poem:

I am living. I remember you.

I had no idea how Marie Howe and Two Boots Pizza and *The Godfather* could possibly be connected. I tried calling Langston again. Still no answer.

I read and re-read the passage. *I am living. I remember you.* I don't really get poetry, but I had to give the poetess credit: nice.

Two people sat in the booth next to me, setting down some rental videos on their table. That's when I realized the connection: *say the window of the corner video store.* This particular Two Boots location also had a video store attached to it.

I dashed over to the video section like it was the bathroom after I'd accidentally ingested some Louisiana hot sauce on top of my calzone. I immediately went to where *The Godfather* was. The movie wasn't there. I asked the clerk where I'd find it. "Checked out," she said.

I returned to the *G* section anyway and found, misshelved, *The Godfather III.* I opened up the case and—*yes!*—another Post-it note, in Snarl's scrawl:

Nobody ever checks out Godfather III. Especially when it's misfiled. Do you want another clue? If so, find Clueless. Also misfiled, where sorrow meets pity.

I returned to the clerk's counter. "Where does sorrow meet pity?" I asked, fully expecting an existential answer.

The clerk didn't look up from the comic book she was reading under the counter. "Foreign documentaries."

Oh.

I went to the foreign documentaries section. And yes, next to a film called *The Sorrow and the Pity* was a copy of *Clueless*! Inside the case for *Clueless* was another note:

I didn't expect you to make it this far. Are you also a fan of depressing French films about mass murder? If so, I like you already. If not, why not? Do you also despise les films de Woody Allen? If you want your red Moleskine notebook back, I suggest you leave instructions in the film of your choice with Amanda at the front desk. Please, no Christmas movies.

I returned to the front desk. "Are you Amanda?" I asked the clerk girl.

She looked up, raising an eyebrow. "I am."

"May I leave something for someone with you?" I asked. I almost added, *Wink wink,* but I couldn't bring myself to be that obvious.

"You may," she said.

"Do you have a copy of *Miracle on 34th Street*?" I asked her.

three

–Dash–

December 22nd

"Is this a joke?" I asked Amanda. And the way she looked at me, I knew that I was the joke.

Oh, the impertinence! I should have known better than to mention Christmas movies. Clearly, no invitation was too small for Lily's sarcasm. And the note:

> *5. Look for the warm woolen mittens*
> *with the reindeer on them, please.*

Could there be any doubt what my next destination was supposed to be?

Macy's.

Two days before Christmas Eve.

She might as well have gift-wrapped my face and pumped the carbon dioxide in. Or hung me on a noose of credit card receipts. A department store two days before Christmas Eve is like a city in a state of siege—wild-eyed consumers battling in the aisles over who gets the last sea horse snow globe to give to their respective great-aunt Marys.

I couldn't.

I wouldn't.

I had to.

I tried to distract myself by debating the difference between *wool* and *woolen*, then expanding it to include *wood* vs. *wooden* and *gold* vs. *golden*. But this distraction only lasted the time it took to walk the stairs from the subway, since when I emerged on Herald Square, I was nearly capsized by the throngs and their shopping bags. The knell of a Salvation Army bell ringer added to the grimness, and I had no doubt that if I didn't escape soon, a children's choir would pop up and carol me to death.

I walked inside Macy's and faced the pathetic spectacle of a department store full of shoppers, none of whom were shopping for themselves. Without the instant gratification of a self-aimed purchase, everyone walked around in the tactical stupor of the financially obligated. At this late date in the season, all the fallbacks were being used. Dad was getting a tie, Mom was getting a scarf, and the kids were getting sweaters, whether they liked it or not. I had done all of my shopping online from 2 a.m. to 4 a.m. on the morning of December 3; the gifts now sat at their respective houses, to be opened in the new year. My mother had left me gifts to open in her house, while my father had slipped me a hundred-dollar bill and told me to go to town with it. In fact, his exact words were, "Don't spend it all on booze and women"—the implication being, of course, that I should spend at least *some* of it on booze and women. Had there been a way to get a gift certificate for booze and women, I was sure he would have made his secretary run out and get me one over her lunch break.

The salespeople were so shell-shocked that a question like "Where do I find the warm woolen mittens with reindeer on them?" didn't seem the least bit strange. Eventually, I found myself in Outer Garments, wondering what, short of an earplug, would count as an Inner Garment.

I had always felt that mittens were a few steps back on the evolutionary scale—why, I wondered, would we want to make ourselves into a less agile version of a lobster? But my disdain for mittens took on a new depth when looking at Macy's (*Macy's's?*) holiday offerings. There were mittens shaped like gingerbread men and mittens decorated in tinsel. One pair of mittens simulated the thumb of a hitchhiker; the destination was, apparently, the North Pole. In front of my very eyes, a middle-aged woman took a pair off the rack and placed them in the pile she'd grown in her arms.

"Really?" I found myself saying aloud.

"Excuse me?" she said, irritated.

"Aesthetic and utilitarian considerations aside," I said, "those mittens don't particularly make sense. Why would you want to hitchhike to the North Pole? Isn't the whole gimmick of Christmas that there's home delivery? You get up there, all you're going to find is a bunch of exhausted, grumpy elves. Assuming, of course, that you accept the mythical presence of a workshop up there, when we all know there isn't even a pole at the North Pole, and if global warming continues, there won't be any ice, either."

"Why don't you just fuck off?" the woman replied. Then she took her mittens and got out of there.

This was the miracle of the season, the way it put the *fuck off* so loud in our hearts. You could snap at strangers, or snap at the people closest to you. It could be a *fuck off* for a slight reason—*You took my parking space* or *You questioned my choice of mittens* or *I spent sixteen hours tracking down the golf club you wanted and you gave me a McDonald's gift certificate in return*. Or it could bring out the *fuck off* that'd been lying in wait for years. *You always insist on cutting the turkey even though I'm the one who spent hours cooking it* or *I can't spend one more holiday pretending to be in love with you* or *You want me to inherit your love for booze and women, in that order, but you're more of a role anti-model than a father*.

This was why I shouldn't have been allowed in Macy's. Because when you turn a short span of time into a "season," you create an echo chamber for all of its associations. Once you step in, it's hard to escape.

I started shaking hands with all the reindeer mittens, certain that Lily had hidden something inside one of them. Sure enough, the fifth shake brought a crumple. I pulled out the slip of paper.

6. *I left something under the pillow for you*.

Next stop: bedding. Personally, I preferred the word *bedding* when it was a verb, not a noun. *Can you show me the bedding section?* could not compare to *Are you bedding me? Seriously, are we going to bed each other?* In truth, I knew these sentences worked better in my head than anywhere else—Sofia never really understood what I was saying, although I usually chalked that up to her not being a native speaker. I even encouraged her to throw some obscure Spanish wordplay my way, but she never knew what I was talking about when I talked about that, either.

She was pretty, though. Like a flower. I missed that.

When I got to the bedding section, I wondered if Lily appreciated how many beds there were for me to probe. They could house a whole orphanage in here, with a few extra beds for the nuns to fool around in. (*Pull my wimple! PULL MY WIMPLE!*) The only way I was going to be able to do this was to divide the floor into quadrants and move clockwise from north.

The first bed was a paisley print with four pillows propped up on it. I immediately launched my hand underneath them, looking for the next note.

"Sir? Can I help you?"

I turned and saw a bed salesman, his look half amused and half alarmed. He looked a lot like Barney Rubble, only with the remnants of a spray tan that would have been unavailable in the prehistoric age. I sympathized. Not because of the spray tan—I'd never do shit like that—but because I figured being a bed salesman was a job of biblically bad paradox. I mean, here he was, forced to stand for eight or nine hours a day, and the whole time he's surrounded by beds. And not only that, he's surrounded by shoppers who see the beds and can't help but think, *Man, I'd love to lie down on that bed for a second.* So not only does he have to stop himself from lying down, but he has to stop everyone else from doing it, too. I knew if I were him, I would be desperate for human company. So I decided to take him into my confidence.

"I'm looking for something," I said. I glanced at his ring finger. Bingo. "You're a married man, right?"

He nodded.

"Well, here's the thing," I said. "My mother? She was looking at bedding and she totally dropped her shopping list under one of the pillows. So now she's upstairs in cutlery, upset that she can't remember what to get anyone, and my dad is about to blow his last fuse, because he likes shopping about as much as he likes terrorism and the estate tax. So he sent me down here to find the list, and if I don't find it quick, there's going to be a major meltdown on floor five."

Super-tan Barney Rubble actually put his finger on his temple to help him think.

"I might remember her," he said. "I'll go look under those pillows if you want to look under these. Just *please* be careful to put the pillows back in their place and avoid mussing the sheets."

"Oh, I will!" I assured him.

I decided if I were ever to get into booze and women, my line would be *Excuse me, madam, but I would really love to bed and muss you. . . . Are you perchance free this evening?*

Now, at the risk of saying something legally actionable, I have to remark: It was amazing the things I found underneath the pillows at Macy's. Half-eaten candy bars. Baby chew toys. Business cards. There was one thing that could have been either a dead jellyfish or a condom, but I pulled my fingers back before I found out for sure. Poor Barney actually let out a little scream when he found a decomposed rodent; it was only after he ran away for a quick burial and thorough disinfecting that I found the slip of paper I was looking for.

7. I dare you to ask Santa for your next message.

No. No fucking no no no.

If I hadn't appreciated her sadism, I would've headed straight for the hills.

But instead, I headed straight for Santa.

It wasn't as easy as that, though. I got down to the main floor and Santa's Wonderland, and the line was at least ten classrooms long. Children lolled and fidgeted while parents talked on cell phones or fussed with strollers or teetered like the living dead.

Luckily, I always travel with a book, just in case I have to wait on line for Santa, or some such inconvenience. More than a few of the parents—especially the dads—gave me strange looks. I could see them doing the mental math—I was way too old to believe in Santa, but I was too young to be after their children. So I was safe, if suspicious.

It took me forty-five minutes to get to the front of the line. Kids were whipping out lists and cookies and digital cameras, while I just had *Vile Bodies*. Finally, it was my turn. I saw the girl in front of me wrapping up, and I started to move forward.

"One second!" a dictatorial rasp commanded.

I looked down to find the least satisfying cliché in Christmas history: a power-mad elf.

"HOW OLD ARE YOU?" he barked.

"Thirteen," I lied.

His eyes were as pointy as his stupid green hat.

"I'm sorry," he said, his voice not sorry at all, "but twelve is the limit."

"I promise I won't take long," I said.

"TWELVE IS THE LIMIT!"

The girl had finished her stint with Santa. It was my turn. By all rights, it was my turn.

"I just have to ask Santa one thing," I said. "That's all."

The elf body-blocked me. "Get out of the line now," he demanded.

"Make me," I replied.

The whole line was paying attention now. Kids' eyes were wide with fear. Most of the dads and some of the moms were getting ready to jump me if I tried anything.

"I need security," the elf said, but I couldn't tell who he was talking to.

I walked forward, knocking his shoulder with my thigh. I was almost at Santa when I felt a tug on my ass—the elf had grabbed the back pocket of my jeans and was trying to pull me back.

"Get. Off. Of. Me," I said, kicking back.

"You're NAUGHTY!" the elf screamed. "Very NAUGHTY!"

We'd caught Santa's attention. He gave me the once-over, then chuckled out, "Ho ho ho! What seems to be the problem?"

"Lily sent me," I said.

From somewhere behind the beard, he figured it out. Meanwhile, the elf was about to pull down my pants.

"Ho! Ho! Ho! Get off of him, Desmond!"

The elf let go.

"I'm calling security," he insisted.

"If you do," Santa murmured, "you'll be back to folding hand towels so fast you won't even have time to take the bells off your boots or your balls out of your elfy boxer briefs."

It was a very good thing that the elf wasn't packing any of his toy-carving tools at that point, because it might have been a very different day at Macy's if he had.

"Well, well, well," Santa said once the elf had retreated. "Come and sit on my lap, little boy."

This Santa's beard was real, and so was his hair. He wasn't fucking around.

"I'm not really a little boy," I pointed out.

"Get on my lap, then, *big boy*."

I walked up to him. There wasn't much lap under his belly. And even though he tried to disguise it, as I went up there, I swear he adjusted his crotch.

"Ho ho ho!" he chortled.

I sat gingerly on his knee, like it was a subway seat with gum on it.

"Have you been a good little boy this year?" he asked.

I didn't feel that I was the right person to determine my own goodness or badness, but in the interest of speeding along this encounter, I said yes.

He actually wobbled with joy.

"Good! Good! Then what can I bring you this Christmas?"

I thought it was obvious.

"A message from Lily," I said. "That's what I want for Christmas. But I want it right now."

"So impatient!" Santa lowered his voice and whispered in my ear. "But Santa does have a little something for you"—he shifted a little in his seat—"right under his coat. If you want to have your present, you'll have to rub Santa's belly."

"What?" I asked.

He gestured with his eyes down to his stomach. "Go ahead."

I looked closely and saw the faint outline of an envelope beneath his red velvet coat.

"You know you want it," he whispered.

The only way I could survive this was to think of it as the dare it was.

Fuck off, Lily. You can't intimidate me.

I reached right under Santa's coat. To my horror, I found he wasn't wearing anything underneath. It was hot, sweaty, fleshy, hairy . . . and his belly was this massive obstacle, blocking me from the envelope. I had to lean over to angle my arm in order to reach it, the whole time having Santa laugh, "Oh ho ho, ho ho oh ho!" in my ear. I heard the elf scream, "What the hell!" and various parents start to shriek. Yes, I was feeling up Santa. And now the corner of the envelope was in my hand. He tried to jiggle it away from me, but I held tight and yanked it out, pulling some of his white belly hair with me. "OW ho ho!" he cried. I jumped off his lap. "Security's here!" the elf proclaimed. The letter was in my hand, damp but intact. "He touched Santa!" a young child squealed.

I ran. I bobbed. I weaved. I propelled myself through the tourists until I was safe in menswear, sheltered in a changing room. I dried my hand and the envelope on a purple velour tracksuit that someone had left behind, then opened it to reveal Lily's next words.

> 8. *That's the spirit!*
> *Now, all I want for Christmas*
> *(or December 22nd)*
> *is your best Christmas memory.*
> *I also want my red notebook back,*
> *so leave it, with your memory included,*
> *in my stocking on the second floor.*

I opened to the first available blank page in the Moleskine and started to write.

My best Christmas was when I was eight. My parents had just split up, and they told me I was really lucky, because this year I was going to get two Christmases instead of one. They called it Australian Christmas, because I would get presents at my mom's place one evening and at my dad's place the next morning, and it would be okay because they would both be Christmas Day in Australia. This sounded great to me, and I honestly felt lucky. Two Christmases! They went all out, too. Full dinners, all the relatives from each side at each Christmas. They must have split my Christmas list down the middle, because I got everything I wanted, and no duplication. Then my father, on the second night, made the big mistake. I was up late, way too late, and everyone else had gone home. He was drinking something brown-gold—probably brandy—and he pulled me to his side and asked me if I liked having two Christmases. I told him yes, and he told me again how lucky I was. Then he asked me if there was anything else I wanted.

I told him I wanted Mom to be with us, too. And he didn't blink. He said he'd see what he could do. And I believed him. I believed I was lucky, and I believed two Christmases were better than one, and I believed even though Santa wasn't real, my parents could still perform magic. So that's why it was my best Christmas. Because it was the last one when I really believed.

Ask a question, get the answer. I figured if Lily couldn't understand that, there wasn't any reason to continue.

I found the spot on the second floor where they were selling the personalized Christmas stockings, making a wide berth around the Santa stand and all of the security guards. Sure enough, there was a hook of Lily stockings, right before LINAS and LIVINIA. I'd leave the red notebook there . . .

. . . but first I had to go to the AMC to buy Lily a ticket to the next day's 10 a.m. showing of *Gramma Got Run Over by a Reindeer*.

four

(Lily)

December 23rd

I have never gone to a movie by myself. Usually when I see a movie, it's with my grandpa, or my brother and parents, or lots of cousins. The best is when we all go at once, like an army of interrelated popcorn zombies who laugh the same laughs and gasp the same gasps and aren't so germ-phobic with each other that we won't share a ginormous Coke with one straw. Family is useful like that.

I planned to insist that Langston and Benny accompany me to the 10 a.m. showing of *Gramma Got Run Over by a Reindeer.* I figured it was their responsibility to take me, since they started this whole thing. I woke them up promptly at 8 a.m. to let them know and to give them enough time to figure out their ironic T-shirts and tousled I-don't-care-but-actually-I-care-too-much hairstyles before we headed out for the day.

Only Langston threw his pillow at me when I tried to get him up. He didn't budge from bed.

"Get out of my room, Lily!" he grumbled. "Go to the movies by yourself!"

Benny rolled over and looked at the clock next to Langston's bed. "*Ay, mamacita,* it's what o'clock in the morning? Eight? *Merde merde merde,* and during Christmas break, when it's like the law to sleep in till noon? *Ay, mamacita . . .* GO BACK TO SLEEP!" Benny rolled over onto his stomach and placed his pillow over his head to get started right away, I guess, on dreaming in Spanglish.

I was pretty tired myself, since I'd gotten up at 4 a.m. to make my mystery snarly friend a special present. I wouldn't have minded taking a nap on the floor next to Langston like when we were kids, but I suspected if I suggested such a thing on this particular morning, in this particular company, Langston would repeat his standby refrain:

"Did you hear me, Lily? GET OUT OF MY ROOM!"

He actually did say that. I wasn't imagining he might say it.

"But I'm not allowed to go to the movies by myself," I reminded Langston. At least, that was the rule when I was eight. Mom and Dad had never clarified whether the rule had been amended as I'd aged.

"Of course you're allowed to go to the movies by yourself. And even if you're not, I'm in charge while Mom and Dad are gone, and I hereby authorize you. And the sooner you leave my room, the sooner your curfew gets bumped from eleven p.m. to midnight."

"My curfew is ten p.m. and I'm not allowed to be outside alone late at night."

"Guess what? Your new curfew is no curfew, and you can stay out as long as you want, with whomever you want, or be alone, I don't care, just make sure your phone is turned on so

I can call you to make sure you're still alive. And feel free to get wasted drunk and fool around with boys and—"

"LA LA LA LA LA," I said, my hands over my ears to block out Langston's dirty talk. I turned around to step out of his room but leaned back in to ask, "What are we making for pre–Christmas Eve dinner? I was thinking we could roast some chestnuts and—"

"GET OUT!" Langston and Benny both yelled.

So much for day before the day before Christmas Eve cheer. When we were little, the Christmas countdown began a week in advance and always started with either Langston or me greeting each other at breakfast by saying, "Good morning! And happy day before the day before the day before the day before Christmas!" And so on until the real day.

I wondered what kind of monsters lurked in theaters to prey on people sitting by themselves because their brothers wouldn't get out of bed to take them to the movies. I figured I'd better get mean real fast so I could be prepared for any dangerous scenario. I got dressed, wrapped my special present, then stood in front of the bathroom mirror, where I practiced making scary faces that would ward off any movie monsters preying upon single-seated persons.

As I practiced my meanest face—tongue wagging out, nose crinkled, eyes at a most hateful glare—I saw Benny standing behind me in the bathroom hallway. "Why are you making kitten faces in the mirror?" he asked, yawning.

"They're *mean* faces!" I said.

Benny said, "Look, that *outfit* you're wearing is gonna scare *papi* off more than your mean kitten face. *What* are you wearing, Little Miss *Quinceañera* Gone Batshit?"

I looked down at my outfit: oxford uniform school shirt tucked into a knee-length lime-green felt material skirt with a reindeer embroidered on it, candy-cane-colored swirled stockings, and beat-up Chucks on my feet.

"What's the matter with my outfit?" I asked, smiling upside down into a . . . *shudder* . . . frown. "I think my outfit is very festive for the day before the day before Christmas. And for a movie about a reindeer. Anyway, I thought you went back to sleep."

"Bathroom break." Benny inspected me head to toe. "No," he said. "The shoes don't work. If you're gonna go with that outfit, you might as well go *all* out. C'mon."

He took my hand and dragged me to the closet in my room. He perused through the heaps of Converse sneakers. "You don't got no other types of shoes?" he said.

"Only in our old dress-up-clothes trunk," I said, joking.

"Perfect," he said.

Benny darted over to the old trunk in the corner of my room, pulling out tulle tutus, yards of muumuus, #1 FAN baseball caps, fireman hats, princess slippers, platform shoes, and an alarming number of Crocs, until finally he grabbed for our Great-aunt Ida's retired tasseled majorette boots, with taps still on the toes and heels. "These fit you?" Benny asked.

I tried them on. "A little big, but I guess." The boots spiced up my candy-cane-colored stockings nicely. I liked.

"Awesome. They'll go great with your winter hat."

My winter head-warming accessory of choice is a vintage red knit hat with pom-poms dangling down from the ears. It's "vintage" in the sense of being a hat I made for my fourth-grade school Christmas pageant production of *A Christmas*

Carol(ing) A-go-go, the Dickens-inspired disco musical I had to heavily lobby our school principal to allow to be staged. Some people are so rigidly secular.

My outfit complete, I walked outside toward the subway. I almost returned inside to change my shoes from the majorette boots to my old familiar Chucks, but the tapping noises from my feet hitting the pavement were comfortingly festive, so I didn't, even though the boots were too big and my feet kept almost walking right out of them. (*These boots were made for . . . slipping out of . . . la la la . . . ha ha ha.*)

I had to acknowledge that despite my excitement to follow the trail of mystery snarl, any boy who left me a ticket to see *Gramma Got Run Over by a Reindeer* would unlikely turn out to be a keeper. The title, quite simply, offended me. Langston says I should have a better sense of humor about these things, but I don't see what's so funny about the idea of a reindeer going after one of our senior friends. It is a known fact that reindeers are herbivores who subsist on plant life and shun meat, so I hardly think they'd be gunning for someone's gramma. It upset me to think about a reindeer harming Gramma, because we all know that if that happened in the real world and not in the movies, then the Wildlife Service would go hunting for that reindeer and do away with the poor antlered guy when it was probably Gramma's fault getting in his way like that! She always forgets to wear her glasses and osteoporosis hunches her walk and slows her down. She's like a walking bull's-eye for dear ol' Bambi!

I figured the whole point of bothering going to the movie at all would be to possibly get a look at mystery boy. But the dares he'd left inside my stocking with the Moleskine notebook, on a Post-it note placed onto the movie ticket, had said:

DON'T read what I wrote in the notebook until you're at the theater.
DO write down your worst Christmas memory in the notebook.
DON'T leave out the most horrific details.
DO leave the notebook behind for me, behind Mama's behind.
Thank you.

I believe in honor. I didn't read the notebook ahead of time, which would be like peeking in your parents' closet to see your Christmas present stash, and I vowed to hold off reading it until after the movie.

As prepared as I'd been to dislike *Gramma Got Run Over by a Reindeer,* I was completely unprepared for what I'd find at the cinema. Outside the theater showing this particular movie, there were rows of strollers in uniform formation against the wall. Inside was complete pandemonium. The 10 a.m. show, apparently, was the Mommy and Me viewing, where moms could bring their babies and toddlers to watch really inappropriate movies while the little ones babbled and burped and cried to their hearts' content. The theater was a cacophony of "Wah wah" and "Mommy, I want . . ." and "No!" and "Mine!" I barely had a chance to pay attention to the movie, what with having Goldfish crackers and Cheerios thrown in my hair from the aisles behind me, watching Legos hurl through the air, and unsticking Great-aunt Ida's taps from the sippy cup liquid spillage on the floor.

Children frighten me. I mean, I appreciate them on a cute

aesthetic level, but they're very demanding and unreasonable creatures and often smell funny. I can't believe I ever was one. Hard to believe, but I was more put off by the movie theater than the movie. I only made it through twenty minutes of watching the black comedian man playing a fat mama on the screen while rows of mommies tried to negotiate with their toddlers in the seats before I couldn't take it any longer.

I got up from my seat and went outside the movie theater to get some peace and quiet in the lobby so I could finally read the notebook. But two mommies returning from taking their toddlers to the potty accosted me before I could dig in.

"I just *love* your boots. They're *adorable*!"

"*Where* did you get that hat? *Adorable!*"

"I AM NOT ADORABLE!" I shrieked. "I'M JUST A LILY!"

The mommies stepped back. One of them said, "Lily, please tell your mommy to get you an Adderall prescription," as the other *tsk-tsk'd.* They quickly hustled their tykes back into the cinema and away from the Shrieking Lily.

I found a hiding place behind a huge, standing cardboard cutout advertisement for *Gramma Got Run Over by a Reindeer*. I sat down cross-legged behind the cutout and opened the notebook. Finally.

His words made me so sad.

But they made me especially glad I'd gotten up at four that morning to make him cookies. Mom and I had been making the dough all month and storing it in the freezer, so all I'd had to do was thaw out the various flavors, place them in the cookie press, and bake. Voilà! I made a cornucopia tin of spritz cookies in all the available flavors (a strong affirmation of faith that Snarl would be worthy of such efforts): chocolate snowflake, eggnog, gingerbread, lebkuchen spice, mint kiss, and pumpkin. I'd decorated the spritz cookies with appropriate sprinkles and candies according to each one's flavor and wrapped a bow around the cookie tin.

I took out my headphones and tuned my iPod to Handel's *Messiah* so I could concentrate on writing. I resisted the urge to mock-conduct with the pen in my hand. Instead, I answered Mystery Boy's question.

My only bad Christmas was the year I was six.

That was the year that my pet gerbil died in a horrible incident at show-and-tell at school about a week before Christmas break.

I know, I know, it sounds funny. It wasn't. It was actually a gruesome massacre.

I'm sorry, but despite your DON'T request, I must leave out the horrific details. The memory is still that vivid and upsetting to me.

The part that really scarred me—separate from the guilt and loss of my pet, of course—was that I earned a nickname after the incident. I had screamed like heck when it happened, but my rage, and grief, were so big, and real, even to such a little person, that I couldn't make myself STOP screaming. Anyone at school who tried to touch or talk to me, I just screamed. It was like basic instinct. I couldn't help myself.

That was the week I became known at school as Shrilly. That name would stay with me through elementary and middle school, until my parents finally moved me to a private school for high school.

But that particular Christmas was my first week as Shrilly. That holiday, I mourned not only the loss of my gerbil but also that bizarre kind of innocence that kids have, believing they can always fit in.

That was the Christmas I finally understood what I'd heard family members whisper in worry about me: that I was too sensitive, too delicate. Different.

It was the Christmas I realized Shrilly was the reason I didn't get invited to birthday parties, or why I always got picked last for teams.

It was the Christmas I realized I was the weird girl.

When I finished writing my answer, I stood up. I realized I had no idea what Mystery Boy had meant by telling me to leave the notebook behind Mama's behind. Was I supposed to leave it on the stage in front of the screen showing the movie?

I looked over to the concession stand, wondering if I should ask for help. The popcorn looked especially yummy, so I went to get some, nearly knocking over the cardboard cutout in my hungry stomach's sudden urgency. That's when I saw it: Mama's behind. I was already behind it. The cardboard cutout was a picture of the black man playing fat Mama, whose rear end was particularly huge.

I wrote new instructions into the notebook and placed it behind Mama's behind, where no one would likely see it except for the one who came looking for it. I left the red Moleskine along with the box of cookies and a tourist postcard that had been stuck to a piece of gum on the floor in the movie theater. The postcard was from Madame Tussauds, my favorite Times Square tourist trap.

I wrote on the postcard:

What do you want for Christmas?

No, really, don't be a smart aleck. What do you really really really supercalifragiwant?

*Please leave information about that, along with the notebook, with the security lady watching over Honest Abe.**

Thank you.
Yours sincerely,
Lily

**PS Don't worry, I promise the security guard won't try to feel you up like Uncle Sal at Macy's might have. I assure you that wasn't sexual so much as he's genuinely just a huggy kind of person.*

PPS What is your name?

five

–Dash–

December 23rd

The doorbell rang at around noon, just when *Gramma Got Run Over* should have been getting out. So my first (admittedly irrational) thought was that somehow Lily had tracked me down. Her uncle in the CIA had run my fingerprints, and they were here to arrest me for impersonating someone worthy of Lily's interest. I took a practice run for the perp walk as I headed over to the peephole. Then I peeped, and instead of finding a girl or the CIA, I saw Boomer shifting from side to side.

"Boomer," I said.

"I'm out here!" he called back.

Boomer. Short for Boomerang. A nickname given to him not for his propensity to rebound after being thrown, but for his temperamental resemblance to the kind of dog who chases after said boomerang, time after time after time. He also happened to be my oldest friend—old in terms of how long we'd known each other, certainly not in maturity. We had a pre-Christmas ritual dating back to when we were seven of going to the movies together on the twenty-third. Boomer's tastes hadn't changed much since then, so I was pretty sure which movie he was going to choose.

Sure enough, as soon as he bounded through the door, he cried, "Hey! You ready to go see *Collation*?"

Collation was, of course, the new Pixar animated movie about a stapler who falls helplessly in love with a piece of paper, causing all of his other office-supply friends to band together to win her over. Oprah Winfrey was the voice of the tape dispenser, and an animated version of Will Ferrell was the janitor who kept getting in the young lovers' way.

"Look," Boomer said, emptying his pockets, "I've been getting Happy Meals for weeks. I have all of them except Lorna the lovable three-hole punch!"

He actually put the plastic toys in my hands so I could examine them.

"Isn't this the three-hole punch?" I asked.

He slapped his forehead. "Dude, I thought that was the expandable file folder, Frederico!"

As fate would have it, *Collation* was playing at the same theater to which I'd sent Lily. So I could keep my playdate with Boomer and still intercept Lily's next message before any rascals or rapscallions got to it.

"Where's your mom?" Boomer asked.

"At her dance class," I lied. If he'd had any inkling that my parents were out of town, he would've been on the horn to his mom so fast that I would've been guaranteeing myself a Very Boomer Christmas.

"Did she leave you money? If not, I can probably pay."

"Don't you worry, my guileless pal," I said, putting my arm around him before he could even take his coat off. "Today, the movie's on me."

I wasn't going to tell Boomer about my other errand, but there was no getting rid of him when I ducked behind Gramma's cardboard booty to find the loot.

"Are you okay?" he asked. "Did you lose your contact lens?"

"No. Someone left something for me here."

"Ooh!"

Boomer was not a big guy, but he tended to take up a lot of space, because he was always jittering around. He kept peering over cardboard Gramma's shoulder, and I was sure it was only a matter of time before the minimum-wage popcorn staff would evict us.

The red Moleskine was right where I'd left it. There was also a tin at its side.

"This is what I was looking for," I told Boomer, holding up the journal. He grabbed for the tin.

"Wow," he said, opening the lid and looking inside. "This must be a special hiding place. How funny is it that someone would leave cookies in the same place that your friend left the notebook?"

"I think the cookies are from her, too." (This was confirmed by a Post-it on the top of the notebook that read: *The cookies are for you. Merry Xmas! Lily.*)

"Really?" he said, picking a cookie out of the tin. "How do you know?"

"I'm just guessing."

Boomer hesitated. "Shouldn't your name be on it?" he asked. "I mean, if it's yours."

"She doesn't know my name."

Boomer immediately put the cookie back in the tin and closed the lid.

"You can't eat cookies from someone who doesn't know your name!" he said. "What if there are, like, razor blades inside?"

Kids and parents were streaming into the theater, and I knew we'd have front-row seats to *Collation* if we didn't move a little faster.

I showed him the Post-it. "You see? They're from Lily."

"Who's Lily?"

"Some girl."

"Ooh . . . a girl!"

"Boomer, we're not in third grade anymore. You don't say, 'Ooh . . . a girl!' "

"What? You fucking her?"

"Okay, Boomer, you're right. I liked 'Ooh . . . a girl!' much more than that. Let's stick with 'Ooh . . . a girl!' "

"She go to your school?"

"I don't think so."

"You don't think so?"

"Look, we'd better get a seat or else there won't be any seats left."

"Do you like her?"

"I see someone took his persistence pills this morning. Sure, I like her. But I don't really know her yet."

"I don't do drugs, Dash."

"I know that, Boomer. It's an expression. Like putting on your thinking cap. There isn't an actual thinking cap."

"Of course there is," Boomer said. "Don't you remember?"

And yes, suddenly I *did* remember. There were two old ski

hats—his blue, mine green—that we'd used as thinking caps back when we were in first grade. This was the strange thing about Boomer—if I asked him about his teachers up at boarding school this past semester, he'd have already forgotten their names. But he could remember the exact make and color of every single Matchbox car with which we'd ever played.

"Bad example," I said. "There are definitely such things as thinking caps. I stand corrected."

Once we found our seats (a little too much toward the front, but with a nice coat barrier between me and the snot-nosed tyke on my left), we dove into the cookie tin.

"Wow," I said after eating a chocolate snowflake. "This puts the *sweet* in *Sweet Jesus*."

Boomer took bites of all six varieties, contemplating each one and figuring out the order in which he would then eat them. "I like the brown one and the lighter brown one and the almost-brown one. I'm not so sure about the minty one. But really, I think the lebkuchen spice one is the best."

"The what?"

"The lebkuchen spice one." He held it up for me. "This one."

"You're making that up. What's a lebkuchen spice? It sounds like a cross between a Keebler elf and a stripper. *Hello, my name ees Lebkuchen Spice, and I vant to show you my cooooookies. . . .*"

"Don't be rude!" Boomer protested. As if the cookie might be offended.

"Sorry, sorry."

The pre-movie commercials started, so while Boomer paid rapt attention to the "exclusive previews" for basic-cable crime shows featuring stars who'd peaked (not too high) in the eighties,

I had a chance to read what Lily had written in the journal. I thought even Boomer would like the Shrilly story, although he'd probably feel really bad for her, when I knew the truth: It was so much cooler to be the weird girl. I was getting such a sense of Lily and her twisted, perverse sense of humor, right down to that classic *supercalifragiwant*. In my mind, she was Lebkuchen Spice—ironic, Germanic, sexy, and offbeat. And, *mein Gott*, the girl could bake a damn fine cookie . . . to the point that I wanted to answer her *What do you want for Christmas?* with a simple *More cookies, please!*

But no. She warned me not to be a smart-ass, and while that answer was totally sincere, I was afraid she would think I was joking or, worse, kissing up.

It was a hard question, especially if I had to batten down the sarcasm. I mean, there was the beauty pageant answer of world peace, although I'd probably have to render it in the beauty pageant spelling of *world peas*. I could play the boo-hoo orphan card and wish for my whole family to be together, but that was the last thing I wanted, especially at this late date.

Soon *Collation* was upon us. Parts of it were funny, and I certainly appreciated the irony of a film distributed by Disney bemoaning corporate culture. But the love story was lacking. After all the marginally feminist Disney heroines of the early to mid-nineties, this heroine was literally a blank piece of paper. Granted, she could fold herself into a paper airplane in order to take her stapler boyfriend on a romantic glide around a magical conference room, and her final rock-paper-scissors showdown with the hapless janitor showed brio of a sort . . . but I couldn't fall for her the way that Boomer and the stapler and most of the kids and parents in the audience were falling for her.

I wondered if what I really wanted for Christmas was to find someone who'd be the piece of paper to my stapler. Or, wait, why couldn't *I* be the piece of paper? Maybe it was a stapler I was after. Or the poor mouse pad, who was clearly in love with the stapler but couldn't get him to give her a second look. All I'd managed to date so far was a series of pencil sharpeners, with the exception of Sofia, who was more like a pleasant eraser.

I figured the only way for me to really find the meaning of my own personal Christmas needs was to leg on over to Madame Tussauds. Because what better barometer could there be than a throng of tourists taking photos of wax statues of public figures?

I knew Boomer would be game for a field trip, so after the stapler and the piece of paper were safely frolicking over the end credits (to the dulcet tones of Celine Dion piping "You Supply My Love"), I shanghaied him from the lobby to Forty-second Street.

"Why are there so many people out here?" Boomer asked as we bobbed and weaved roughly forward.

"Christmas shopping," I explained.

"Already? Isn't it early to be returning things?"

I really had no sense of how his mind worked.

The only time I had ever been in Madame Tussauds was the previous year, when three friends and I had tried to collect the world record for most suggestive posings with wax statues of B-list celebrities and historical figures. To be honest, it gave me the heebie-jeebies to go down on so many wax figures—especially Nicholas Cage, who already gave me the heebie-jeebies in real life. But my friend Mona wanted it to be a part of her senior project. The guards didn't seem to mind, as long as there was no physical contact. Which made me expound upon one of my earlier theories, that Madame Tussaud had been a true madam, and had started her whole operation with a waxwork whorehouse somewhere near Paris, Texas. Mona loved this theory, but we could find no proof, and thus it did not transform into true scholarship.

A wax replica of Morgan Freeman was guarding the entrance, and I wondered if this was some kind of cosmic payback—that every time an actor with a modicum of talent sold his soul to be in a big Hollywood action picture of no redeeming social value, his sellout visage was struck in wax and placed outside Madame Tussauds. Or maybe the people at Madame Tussauds figured that everyone loved Morgan Freeman, so who wouldn't want to pose with him for a quick snapshot before stepping inside?

Weirdly, the next two wax figures were Samuel L. Jackson and Dwayne "the Rock" Johnson, confirming my sellout theory, and also making me wonder whether Madame Tussauds was deliberately keeping all the black statues in the lobby. Very strange. Boomer didn't seem to notice this. Instead, he was acting as if he were having real celebrity sightings, exclaiming with glee every time he saw someone—"Wow, it's Halle Berry!"

I wanted to scream bloody murder over the price of admission—I made a note to tell Lily that the next time she wanted me to fork over twenty-five bucks to see a wax statue of Honest Abe, she should slip some cash into the journal to cover my expenses.

Inside, it was a total freak show. When I'd visited before, it had been nearly empty. But clearly the holidays had caused a lot of family-time desperation, so there were all sorts of crowds around the unlikeliest of figures. I mean, was Uma Thurman really worth jostling for? Jon Bon Jovi?

To be honest, the whole place depressed me. The wax figures were lifelike, for sure. But, hell, you say *wax* and I think *melt*. There's some kind of permanence to a real statue. Not here. And not only because of the wax. You had to know that in some corner of this building, there was a closet full of discarded statues, the people whose spotlight had come and gone. Like the members of *NSYNC whose initials weren't JT; or all the Backstreet Boys and Spice Girls. Were people really buddying up to the Seinfeld sculpture anymore? Did Keanu Reeves ever stop by his own statue, just to remember when people cared?

"Look, Miley Cyrus!" Boomer called, and at least a dozen preteen girls followed him over to gawk at this poor girl frozen in an awkward (if lucrative) adolescence. It didn't even look like Miley Cyrus—there was something a little off, so it looked like Miley Cyrus's backwater cousin Riley, dressing up and trying to pretend to be Miley. Behind her, the Jonas Brothers were frozen mid-jam. Didn't they have to know that the Closet of Forgotten Statues would call to them someday?

Of course, before I found Honest Abe, I needed to figure out what I wanted for Christmas.

A pony.

An unlimited MetroCard.

A promise that Lily's uncle Sal would never be allowed to work around children again.

A swank lime-green couch.

A new thinking cap.

It seemed I was incapable of coming up with a serious answer. What I really wanted for Christmas was for Christmas to go away. Maybe Lily would understand this . . . but maybe she wouldn't. I'd seen even the hardest-edge girls go soft for Santa. I couldn't fault her for believing, because I had to imagine it was nice to have that illusion still intact. Not the belief in Santa, but the believe that a single holiday could usher in goodwill toward man.

"Dash?"

I looked up, and there was Priya, with at least two younger brothers in tow.

"Hey, Priya."

"Is this her?" Boomer asked, somehow diverting his attention long enough from the Jackie Chan display to make it awkward for me.

"No, this is Priya," I said. "Priya, this is my friend Boomer."

"I thought you were in Sweden," Priya said. I couldn't tell if she was irritated at me or irritated at the way one of her brothers was stretching out her sleeve.

"You were in Sweden?" Boomer asked.

"No," I said. "The trip got called off at the last minute. Because of the political unrest."

"In Sweden?" Priya seemed skeptical.

"Yeah—isn't it strange how the *Times* isn't covering it? Half the country's on strike because of that thing the crown prince said about Pippi Longstocking. Which means no meatballs for Christmas, if you know what I mean."

"That's so sad!" Boomer said.

"Well, if you're around," Priya said, "I'm having people over the day after Christmas. Sofia will be there."

"Sofia?"

"You know she's back in town, right? For the holidays."

I swear, it looked like Priya was enjoying this. Even her pipsqueak brothers seemed to be enjoying this.

"Of course I knew," I lied. "I just—well, I thought I was going to be in Sweden. You know how it is."

"It starts at six. Feel free to bring your friend here." The brothers started to tug on her again. "I'll see you then, I hope."

"Yeah," I said. "Sure. Sofia."

I hadn't meant to say that last word aloud. I wasn't even sure Priya heard it, she was whisked away so fast by the running tugs on her clothing.

"I liked Sofia," Boomer said.

"Yeah," I told him. "So did I."

It seemed a little strange to have two run-ins with Priya while on my Lily chase—but I had to dismiss it as coincidence. I didn't see how she or Sofia could possibly fit into what Lily was doing. Sure, it could be one big practical joke, but the thing about Sofia and her friends was that while they were always practical, they were never jokers.

Naturally, the next consideration was: Did I want Sofia for Christmas? Wrapped in a bow. Under the tree. Telling me how frickin' great I was.

No. Not really.

I'd liked her, sure. We'd been a good couple, insofar as that our friends—well, her friends more than mine—had created this mold of what a couple should be, and we fit into it just fine. We were the fourth couple tacked onto the quadruple date. We were good board game partners. We could text each other to sleep at night. She'd only been in New York for three years, so I got to explain all kinds of pop cultural references to her, while she'd tell me stories about Spain. We'd made it to third base, but got stuck there. Like we knew the catcher would tag us out if we tried to head home.

I'd been relieved (a little) when she'd told me she had to move back to Spain. We'd pledged we'd keep in touch, and that had worked for about a month. Now I read the updates on her online profile and she read mine, and that's what we were to each other.

I wanted to want something more than Sofia for Christmas.

And was that Lily? I couldn't really tell. For sure, the last thing I was going to write to her was *All I want for Christmas is you*.

"What do I want for Christmas?" I asked Angelina Jolie. Her full lips didn't part with an answer.

"What do I want for Christmas?" I asked Charlize Theron. I even added, "Hey, nice dress," but she still didn't reply. I leaned over her cleavage and asked, "Are they real?" She didn't make a move to slap me.

Finally, I turned to Boomer.

"What do I want for Christmas?"

He looked thoughtful for a second, then said, "World peace?"

"Not helpful!"

"Well, what's in your Amazonian hope chest?" Boomer asked.

"My WHAT?"

"You know, on Amazon. Your hope chest."

"You mean my wish list?"

"Yeah, that."

And just like that, I knew what I wanted. Something I had always wanted. But it was so unrealistic it hadn't even made it to my wish list.

I needed a bench to sit down on, but the only one I could see already had Elizabeth Taylor, Hugh Jackman, and Clark Gable perched atop it, waiting for a bus.

"I just need a sec," I told Boomer before I ducked behind Ozzy Osbourne and his whole family (circa 2003) to write in the Moleskine.

No smart-assness (assy-smartness?) here.

The truth?

What I want for Christmas is an OED. Unabridged.

Just in case you are not a word nerd like myself:

O = Oxford

E = English

D = Dictionary

Not the concise one. Not the one that comes on CDs. (Please!) No.

Twenty volumes.

22,000 pages.

600,000 entries.

Pretty much the English language's greatest achievement.

It's not cheap—almost a thousand dollars, I think. Which is, I admit, a lot for a book. But, criminy, what a book. It's the complete genealogy of every word we use. No word is too grand or too infinitesimal to be considered.

Deep down, you see, I long to be arcane, esoteric. I would love to confound people with their own language.

Here's a riddle for you:

My name is a connector of words.

I know that's a childish tease—the truth is, I'd love to let the mystery remain, if only for a little longer. I bring it up solely to emphasize the point—that even though my parents had no idea (and I'm sure my father would have worked willfully against it), somehow they pegged me with my very name to know that while some fellows would find their creature comfort in sport or pharmacy or sexual conquest, I was destined to get that from words. Preferably read or written.

Please note: In case you happen to be an heiress, hoping to bestow a Christmas wish on a lonesome mystery boy/linguistic rabblerouser—I actually don't want to get the OED as a gift, as much as I would love to have one. I actually want to earn it, or at least to earn the money (through words, in some way) to get it. It will be even more special then.

This is about as far as I can go without some sarcasm creeping in. But before it does, I must say, with utmost sincerity, that your cookies are good enough to bring some of these wax statues back to life. Thanks for that. I once made corn muffins for a fourth-grade project on Williamsburg and they came out like baseballs. So I'm not sure how to reciprocate . . . but, believe me, I shall.

I was worried I was being a little too much of a word nerd . . . but then I figured a girl who left a red Moleskine in the stacks of the Strand would understand.

Then came the hard part. The next assignment.

I looked over to the Osbournes (they were a surprisingly short family, at least in wax) and saw Boomer fist-pounding with President Obama.

Stovepiping over the rest of the politicians was Honest Abe, looking like the European tourists taking his picture were worse company than John Wilkes Booth. Next to Abe was a figure I pegged as Mary Todd . . . until she moved, and I realized it was the guard I was supposed to seek. She looked like an older, less bearded version of fondle-friendly Uncle Sal. There was, it seemed, no limit to the number of relatives Lily could employ.

"Hey, Boomer," I said. "How would you feel about doing something for me at FAO Schwarz?"

“The toy store?” he asked.

“No, the apothecary.”

He looked at me blankly.

“Yes, the toy store.”

“Awesome!”

I just had to be sure he was free on Christmas Eve. . . .

six

(Lily)

December 24th

I woke up on Christmas Eve morning, and my first instinct was sheer excitement: *Yay! It's finally the day before Christmas—the day before the best day of the year!* My second reaction was pitiful remembrance: *Ugh, and with no one here to share it with.* Why had I ever agreed to allow my parents to go on their twenty-five-years-delayed honeymoon? Such a brand of selflessness was not meant for Christmastime.

Grandpa's calico cat, Grunt, seemed to agree with me about the day starting out less than auspiciously. The cat aggressively rubbed himself across the front of my neck, draping his head over my shoulder, then growled his signature grunt directly into my ear to indicate, "Get out of bed and feed me already, person!"

Since Langston was lost to Benny, I had spent the night in my special "Lily pad," in Grandpa's apartment. The Lily pad is an ancient, afghan-draped chaise that sits underneath a skylight built into the attic apartment that Grandpa turned into his retirement home after he sold his business on the ground floor and my family moved into the third-floor apartment, where Grandpa and Grandma once raised my mom and my uncles. Grandma died right before I was born, which is maybe why I am Grandpa's special girl. I was named after her, and I arrived into the downstairs just as Grandpa was transitioning upstairs. So while he'd lost one Lily, he'd gained back another. Grandpa said he decided to renovate the upstairs apartment for his later-in-life bachelor digs because climbing the stairs every day would keep him young.

I take care of Grandpa's cat, Grunt, when Grandpa goes to Florida. Grunt's an ornery cat, but lately I like him more than Langston. So long as I feed him and don't smother his furry head in too many unwanted kisses, Grunt would never toss me aside for some boy. Grunt's as close to my own animal as I'm allowed to have in our living space.

When I was little, we had two rescue cats, named Holly and Hobbie, who disappeared very suddenly. They both died from feline leukemia, only I didn't understand that at the time. I was told that Holly and Hobbie had graduated to "college" and that's why I didn't see them anymore. Holly and Hobbie went off to college only a couple years after the gerbil incident, so I guess I understand why the real reason was kept secret from me. But it would have saved everyone a lot of grief if they'd been honest at the time. Because when I was eight and went with Grandpa to visit my cousin Mark, who was a freshman at Williams College, I spent the whole weekend darting through alleys and peering inside every bookcase crevice I found in the library, looking for my cats. That's when Mark had to break it to me, in the very public dining hall no less, why the poor little things were not, in fact, at Mark's college, or at any college, other than the big one up in the sky. Begin Shrilly incident, stage 2. Let's just say Williams College probably would appreciate me not applying there next year.

In the years since, I have petitioned at various times to adopt a kitten, a turtle, a dog, a parrot, and a lizard, but all requests have been denied. And yet I allowed my parents to go on holiday at Christmas, guilt free. Who was the wronged party here? I ask.

I like to think of myself as an optimistic person, especially at the holidays, but I couldn't deny the cold, hard suckage that this Christmas had sunk to. My parents were away in Fiji, Langston was all into Benny, Grandpa was in Florida, and most of the cousins were spread far and wide away from Manhattan. December 24—what should have been the Most Exciting Day Before the Really Most Exciting Day of the Year—appeared to be one big blah.

It would have been helpful at this point, I suppose, if I had some girlfriends to hang out with, but I'm comfortable as a nobody at school, except on the soccer field, where I am a superstar. Strangely, my saved-many-a-game goalie skills have never translated into popularity. Respect, yes. Movie invitations and after-school socializing, no. (My dad is the vice principal at my school, which probably doesn't help—it's a political risk to befriend me, I suspect.) My athletic ability mixed with my complete social apathy are what got me elected captain of the soccer team. I'm the only person who gets along with everyone, by way of not being friends with anyone.

On Christmas Eve morning, I decided maybe I should

work on this deficiency as my New Year's resolution. A less Shrilly, more Frilly plan. Learn to be more girl friendly so I'd have some backup on important holidays should my family ever abandon me again.

I wouldn't have minded someone special to spend Christmas with.

But all I had was a red Moleskine notebook.

And even Nameless He of the Notebook Game, while he was intriguing me to an extreme that was causing my body to feel all tingly every time I was alerted that the notebook had been returned to She Who *Has* Politely Told Her Name, was also a cause for concern. When not one, not two, but three relatives (Cousin Mark at the Strand, Uncle Sal at Macy's, and Great-aunt Ida at Madame Tussauds), independent of each other, all used the same word—*snarl*—to describe the notebook's mystery boy, who thinks he's too "esoteric" and "arcane" to tell me something as simple as his name, I had to wonder why I was bothering with this charade. No one had even bothered to mention whether he's cute.

Is it wrong that I long for that idealistic, pure kind of love like in that animated movie *Collation*? Oh, how I yearn to be the piece of paper gliding the stapler around the conference room, treating it to amazing visions of city skyscraper skylines and annual reports with rosy earnings forecasts, while avoiding the villainous starfish intercom phone on the boardroom table, Dante, voiced by Christopher Walken, the corporate raider who's secretly planning a hostile takeover of the company. Secretly, I want to be held prisoner by Dante and rescued by a heroic Swingline. I guess I want to be . . . stapled. (Is that crude of me? Or anti-feminist? I don't mean to be.)

Snarl is probably no dreamy stapler, but I think I might like Snarl anyway. Even if he is too pretentious to tell me his name.

I like that he wants an *OED* for Christmas. That's so geeky. I wonder how he would react if he knew that I actually know a way I could give him what he wants, and for free. But he'd have to prove worthy. If he can't even tell me his name, I don't know.

My name is a connector of words.

What was *that* supposed to mean?!?!? I'm not Einstein here, Snarl. Or Train Man (connector of Amtrak and Metro North?), whoever you are. Conductor? Is that your name?

The only other thing I want for Christmas, besides the OED, is for you to tell me what you really want for Christmas. But not a thing. More like a feeling. Something that can't be bought in a store or gift-wrapped in a pretty box. Please write it in the notebook and deposit it with the worker bees in the Make Your Own Muppet department at FAO Schwarz at noon on Christmas Eve. Good luck. (And yes, evil genius, you should consider FAO Schwarz on the day before Christmas payback for Macy's.)

Conductor Snarl should consider himself lucky that this year turned out to be the Christmas of Suck. Because normally on this day, I would be (1) helping Mom chop and peel food for Christmas dinner the following night while we listened to Christmas music and sang along, (2) helping Dad wrap presents and organize the mountains of gifts around the tree, (3) wondering if I should put a sedative in Langston's water bottle so he'd fall asleep early and then have no problem getting up at five the next morning to open presents with me,

(4) wondering if Grandpa will like the sweater I knit him (poorly, but I get better each year, and he still wears them anyway, unlike Langston), and (5) hoping and praying I was going to get a BRAND-NEW BIKE, or any other Major Gift of Comparable Extravagance, the following morning.

I got shivers when I re-read that Snarl called me "evil genius." Even though I am anything but, the compliment was so personal. Like he'd been thinking about me. *Me* me, and not just notebook me.

After I fed Grunt, I headed toward the glass screen door that opened to the rooftop garden outside Grandpa's apartment so I could water the plants. From my warm perch inside the glass door, I looked out at the cold city, north toward the Empire State Building, which would be lit at night in green and red for Christmas, then I looked east toward the Chrysler Building in Midtown, closer to where FAO Schwarz was, should I decide to accept the dare. (Of course I would. Who was I kidding? Shrilly play hard to get with an assignment in a red Moleskine deposited for her at Madame Tussauds? Hardly.)

I noticed my old sleeping bag on the ground outside, the sleeping bag in which Langston and I used to snuggle up on Christmas Eve when we were super-little so that Dad could, in his words, "zipper up the excitement until dawn on Christmas morning." I saw Langston and Benny curled up together in the sleeping bag now, with the blue comforter from Langston's bed on top of them.

I went outside. They were just waking up.

"Happy Christmas Eve!" I chirped. "Did you two sleep out here last night? I didn't hear you come in. You must have been freezing! Let's make a big breakfast this morning, what do you say? Eggs and toast and pancakes and . . ."

"Orange juice," Langston coughed. "Please, Lily. Go to the corner store and get us some fresh orange juice."

Benny, too, coughed. "And some echinacea!"

"Sleeping outside in the dead of winter not such a smart idea, huh?" I said.

"Seemed romantic under the stars last night," Langston sighed. Then sneezed. Again. And again, this time with a full-on hacking cough. "Make us some soup, please please please, Lily Bear?"

It seemed to me that, in allowing himself to get sick, my brother had finally, and totally, ruined Christmas. All hope for any semblance of a decent Christmas was now gone. It further seemed to me, since he made the choice to sleep outside with his boyfriend last night instead of play Boggle with his Lily Bear as she specifically asked him to do and which she specifically used to do for him during his time of need, that Langston sicko would have to deal with this crisis on his own.

"Make your own soup," I told the boys. "And get your own OJ. I have an errand to run in Midtown." I turned to go back inside and leave the boys to their nasty new colds. Suckahs. That ought to teach them not to go out clubbing when they could stay home and Boggle with me.

"You'll be sorry next year when you're living in Fiji and I'm still in Manhattan where I can order food and juice from the bodega at the corner and have it delivered to me anytime I want!" Langston exclaimed.

I swiveled back around. "Excuse me? What did you just say?"

Langston pulled the comforter over his head. "Nothing. Never mind," he said from underneath.

Which meant it was seriously something.

"WHAT ARE YOU TALKING ABOUT, LANGSTON?" I said, feeling a Shrilly panic moment coming on.

Benny popped his head under the covers, too. I heard him say to Langston, "You have to tell her now. You can't leave her hanging like that once you slipped."

"SLIPPED ON WHAT, LANGSTON?" I almost was ready to cry. But I'd decided to try to be less Shrilly for New Year's, and even though that was still a week away, I felt like I had to get started sometime. Now was as good a time as any. I stood strong, shaking—but not crying.

Langston's head re-emerged from underneath the comforter. "Mom and Dad are in Fiji for their second honeymoon, but also to spend time visiting a boarding school there. A place that's offered Dad a headmaster's job for the next two years."

"Mom and Dad would never want to live in Fiji!" I fumed. "Vacation paradise, maybe. But people don't *live* there."

"Lots of people live there, Lily. And this school caters to kids like Dad was, who have parents in the diplomatic service, like in Indonesia and Micronesia—"

"Stop it with all these *-esia*s!" I said. "Why would the diplomatic parents send their kids to a stupid school in Fiji?"

"It's a pretty amazing school, from what I've heard. It's for parents who don't want to send their kids to schools in the places where they're posted, but also want to not send them so far away as to the States or the UK. For them, it's a good alternative."

"I'm not going," I announced.

Langston said, "It would be a good opportunity for Mom, too. She could take a sabbatical and work on her research and her book."

"I'm not going," I repeated. "I like living here in Manhattan. I'll live with Grandpa."

Langston threw the comforter over his head again.

Which could only mean there was more to the story.

"WHAT?!?!?" I demanded, now feeling truly scared.

"Grandpa is proposing to Glamma. In Florida."

Glamma, as she likes to be known, is Grandpa's Florida girlfriend—and the reason he had abandoned us at Christmas. I said, "Her name is Mabel! I will never call her Glamma!"

"Call her whatever you want. But she's probably soon going to be Mrs. Grandpa. When that happens, my guess is he will move down there permanently."

"I don't believe you."

Langston sat up so I could see his face. Even sick, he was pathetically sincere. "Believe me."

"How come no one told me?"

"They were trying to protect you. Not cause you concern until they knew for sure these things would happen."

This was how Shrilly was born, from people trying so hard to "protect" me.

"PROTECT THIS!" I shouted, lifting my middle finger to Langston.

"Shrilly!" he admonished. "That's so unlike you."

"What *is* like me?" I asked.

I stormed away from the garden rooftop, snarled at poor ol' Grunt, who was licking his paws after breakfast, and continued my storming, to downstairs, to *my* apartment, to *my* room, in *my* city, Manhattan. "No one's moving me to Fiji," I muttered as I got dressed to go out.

I couldn't think about this Christmas catastrophe. I just couldn't. It was too much.

I felt especially grateful now having the red Moleskine to confide in. Just knowing a Snarl was on the other side to read it—to possibly care—inspired my pen to move quickly in answer to his question. As I waited for the subway en route to Snarl's Midtown destination, I had plenty of free time on the bench at the Astor Place station, since the notoriously slow 6 train seemed to take its usual forever to arrive.

I wrote:

What I want for Christmas is to believe.

I want to believe that, despite all the evidence to the contrary, there is reason to hope. I write this while a homeless man is sleeping on the ground under a dirty blanket a few feet away from the bench where I'm sitting at the Astor Place subway stop, on the uptown side, where I can see across the tracks to the Kmart entrance on the downtown side. Is this relevant? Not really, except that when I started to write this to you, I noticed him, then stopped writing long enough to dash over to the Kmart to buy the man a bag of "fun size" Snickers bars, which I slipped underneath his blanket, and that made me extra sad because his shoes are all worn out and he's dirty and smelly and I don't think that bag of Snickers is going to make much difference to this guy, ultimately. His problems are way bigger than a bag of Snickers can resolve. I don't understand how to process this stuff sometimes. Like, here in New York, we see so much grandeur and glitz, especially this time of year, and yet we see so much suffering, too. Everyone else on the platform here is just ignoring this guy, like he doesn't exist, and I don't know how that's possible. I want to believe it's not crazy of me to hope he will wake up and a social worker will take him to a shelter for a warm shower, meal, and bed, and the social worker will then help him find a job and an apartment and . . . See? It's just too much to process. All this hoping for something—or someone—that's maybe hopeless.

I'm having a hard time processing what I am supposed to believe, or if I'm even supposed to. There is too much information, and I don't like a lot of it.

And yet, for some reason that all scientific evidence really should make impossible, I feel like I really do hope. I hope that global warming will go away. I hope that people won't be homeless. I hope that suffering will not exist. I want to believe that my hope is not in vain.

I want to believe that even though I hope for things that are so magnanimous (good OED word, huh?), I am not a bad person because what I really want to believe in is purely selfish.

I want to believe there is a somebody out there just for me. I want to believe that I exist to be there for that somebody.

Remember in Franny and Zooey (which I assume you've read and loved, considering the location where you found the Moleskine in the Strand) how Franny was this girl from the 1950s who freaked out over what's the meaning of life because she thought it was embedded in a prayer someone told her about? And even though neither her brother Zooey nor her mom understood what Franny was going through, I think I really did. Because I would like the meaning of life explained to me in a prayer, and I would probably flip out, too, if I thought the possibility of attaining this prayer existed, but was out of my reach of understanding. (Especially if being Franny meant I'd also get to wear lovely vintage clothes, although I'm dubious on whether I'd want the Yale boyfriend named Lane who's possibly a bit of a prick but people admire me for going out with him; I think I'd rather be with someone more . . . er . . . arcane.) At the end of the book, when Zooey calls Franny pretending to be their brother Buddy, trying to cheer her up, there's a line where he talks about Franny going to the phone and becoming "younger with each step" as she walked, because she's making it to the other side. She's going to be okay. At least that's what I took it to mean.

I want that. The getting younger with each step, because of anticipation, in hope and belief.

Prayer or not, I want to believe that, despite all evidence to the contrary, it is possible for anyone to find that one special person. That person to spend Christmas with or grow old with or just take a nice silly walk in Central Park with. Somebody who wouldn't judge another for the prepositions they dangle, or their run-on sentences, and who in turn wouldn't be judged for the snobbery of their language etymology inclinations. (Gotcha with the word choices, right? I know, sometimes I surprise even myself.)

Belief. That's what I want for Christmas. Look it up. Maybe there's more meaning there than I understand. Maybe you could explain it to me?

I had continued writing in the notebook when the train came, and finished my entry just as it arrived at Fifty-ninth and Lex. As the zillions of people, along with me, poured out of the train and up into Bloomingdale's or the street, I concentrated hard on not thinking about what I was determined not to think about.

Moving. Change.

Except I wasn't thinking about that.

* * *

I dodged Bloomingdale's, walking straight toward FAO Schwarz, where I realized what Snarl had meant by "payback." A line down the street outside the store greeted me—a line just to get *into* the store! I had to wait twenty minutes just to reach the door.

But no matter what, I love Christmas, really really really I do, don't care if I am sardined in between two million panicky Christmas shoppers, nope, don't care at all, I loved every moment of the experience once I got inside—the jingle bells playing from the speakers, the heart-racing excitement at seeing all the colorful toys and games in such a larger-than-life setting. Aisle after aisle and floor after floor of dense fun^{fun} experience. I mean, Snarl must know me well already, perhaps on some psychic level, if he'd sent me to FAO Schwarz, only the mecca of everything that was Great and Beautiful about the holidays. Snarl must love Christmas as much as me, I decided.

I went to the information counter. "Where will I find the Make Your Own Muppet Workshop?" I asked.

"Sorry," the counter person said. "The Muppet Workshop is closed for the holidays. We needed the space for the *Collation* action figure displays."

"There are action figures for paper and staplers?" I asked. How had I not known to include these on my list to Santa?

"Yup. Just a hint: You might have better luck finding the Fredericos and the Dantes at Office Max on Third Ave. They sold out here the first day they went on sale. But you didn't hear that from me."

"But please," I said. "There has to be a Muppet workshop here today. The Moleskine said so."

"Excuse me?"

"Never mind," I sighed.

I worked my way past the Candy Shoppe and Ice Cream Parlor and Barbie Gallery, upstairs past all the boy toys of guns and Lego warlands, through the mazes of people and products, until I finally landed in the *Collation* corner. "Please," I said to the salesclerk. "Is there a Muppet workshop here?"

"Hardly," she spat. "That's in *April*." She said this with all the contempt of *Well, duh, who* doesn't *know that?*

"Sorry!" I said. I hoped someone's parents sent *her* to Fiji next Christmas.

I was about to give up and leave the store, my belief in the Moleskine defeated, when I felt a tap on my shoulder. I turned around and saw a girl who looked college age, dressed like Hermione Potter. I assumed she was a store employee.

"Are you the girl looking for the Muppet workshop?" she asked.

"I am?" I said. Don't know why I said it like a question, other than I wasn't sure I wanted Hermione knowing my business. I've always resented Hermione, because I wanted to be her so badly and she never seemed to appreciate as much as I thought she should that she got to be her. She got to live at Hogwarts and be friends with Harry and kiss Ron, which was supposed to happen to me.

"Come with me," Hermione demanded. Since it would be dumb not to do what a smarty like Hermione instructed, I let her guide me to the farthest, darkest corner of the store, where the stuff no one cared about anymore, like Silly Putty and Boggle games, was. She stopped us at a giant rack of stuffed giraffes and tapped on the wall behind the animals. Suddenly the wall opened, because it was in fact a door camouflaged by the giraffes (*giraffe-o-flaged*?–must *OED* that term).

I followed Hermione inside to a small closet-like room where a worktable with Muppet heads and parts (eyes, noses, glasses, shirts, hair, etc.) was set up. A teenage boy who looked like a human Chihuahua—excitably compact yet larger than life—sat at a card table, apparently waiting for me.

"You're HER!" he said, pointing to me. "You don't look at all like I expected even if I didn't really imagine how you'd look!" His voice even sounded like a Chihuahua's, quivery and hyperactive at the same time, but somehow endearing.

My mother always taught me it was impolite to point.

Since she was in Fiji on her own covert mission and wouldn't be here to scold, I pointed back at the boy. "I'm ME!" I said.

Hermione shushed us. "Please lower your voices and be discreet! I can only let you have the room for fifteen minutes." She inspected me suspiciously. "You don't smoke, do you?"

"Of course not!" I said.

"Don't try anything. Think of this closet as an airline lavatory. Go about your business, but know that smoke detectors and other devices are monitoring."

The boy said, "Terrorist alert! Terrorist alert!"

"Shut up, Boomer," Hermione said. "Don't scare her."

"You don't know me well enough to call me Boomer," Boomer (apparently) said. "My name's John."

"My instructions said *Boomer*, Boomer," said Hermione.

"Boomer," I interrupted. "Why am I here?"

"Do you have a notebook to return to someone?" he asked.

"I might. What's his name?" I asked.

"Forbidden information!" Boomer said.

"Really?" I sighed.

"Really!" he said.

I looked to Hermione, hoping to invoke some girl power solidarity. She shook her head at me. "Nuh-uh," she said. "Not getting it out of me."

"Then what's the point of all this?" I asked.

"It's the Make Your Own Muppet point!" Boomer said. "Designed just for you. Your special friend. Arranged this for you."

My day had been seriously suck so far, and despite the seemingly good intentions, I wasn't sure I felt like playing. I've never desired a cigarette in my life, but suddenly I wanted to light one up, if only to set off the alarm that might get me out of this situation.

There was too much not to think about. I was tired from not thinking about it all. I wanted to go home and ignore my brother and watch *Meet Me in St. Louis* and cry when sweet little Margaret O'Brien bashes the snowman to bits (best part). I wanted to not think about Fiji or Florida or anything—or anyone—else. If "Boomer" wouldn't reveal Snarl's name or probably anything else about him, what was the point of my being here?

As if he knew I might need a morale boost, Boomer handed me a box of Sno-Caps. My favorite movie candy. "Your friend," Boomer said. "He sent this for you. As a deposit on a later gift. Potentially."

Okay okay okay, I'd play. (*Snarl sent me candy! Oh, how I might love him!*)

I sat down at the worktable. I decided to make a Muppet that looked like how I imagined Snarl looked. I chose a blue head and body, some black fur styled like an early Beatles hairdo, some Buddy Holly black glasses (not unlike my own), and a purple bowling shirt. I glued on a pink Grover nose shaped like a fuzzy golf ball. Then I cut some red felt to shape the lips like a snarl, and placed that onto the mouth position.

I remembered when I was ten—not too long ago, now that I thought about it—and loved going to the American Girl store beauty parlor to get my doll's hair fixed up, and how one time I asked the store manager if I could possibly design my own American Girl. I'd already figured my girl out—LaShonda Jones, a twelve-year-old roller boogie champion from Skokie, Illinois, circa 1978. I knew her history and what clothes she'd wear and everything. But when I asked the store manager if they would help me create LaShonda right there inside the American Girl palace, the manager looked at me with such an expression of sacrilege you'd have thought I was a junior revolutionary politely asking if I might blow up Mattel, Hasbro, Disney, and Milton Bradley headquarters at the same time.

Even if his name was classified information, I wanted to hug Snarl. He'd inadvertently made one of my secret dreams come true—allowing me to build my own doll while in a toy mecca headquarters.

"Do you play soccer?" Hermione asked me while she folded away the clothes I didn't use for my Muppet. Her folding was so expert I wondered if she was a store employee on loan from the Gap.

"Yeah," I said.

"Thought so," she said. "I'm a freshman at college now, but last year, when I was a senior, I think my high school played yours. I remember you because your team's not that great, but you're such a power goalie it didn't matter much that the rest of your team seemed more interested in touching up their lip gloss than playing, because you were so determined not to let the other side score. You're a captain, right? So was I."

I was about to ask Hermione what school she played for when she dropped this one on me: "You're different than Sofia. But maybe more interesting-looking. Is that your school uniform shirt you're wearing underneath that reindeer cardigan? Weird. Sofia wears the most gorgeous clothes. From Spain. Do you speak Catalan?"

"No."

I said no in Catalan, but since the word sounds the same in English, Hermione didn't notice.

I was starting to wonder what language they spoke in Fiji.

"Time's up!" Hermione said.

I held up the Muppet. "I christen thee Snarly," I told it. I handed Snarly over to the guy named Boomer. "Please give this to He of the Unknowable Name." I also handed over the red Moleskine. "This too. And don't read the notebook, Boomer. It's personal."

"I won't!" Boomer promised.

"I think he will," Hermione murmured.

I had so many questions.

Why can't I know his name?

What does he look like?

Who the heck is Sofia and why does she speak Catalan?

What am I even doing here?

I figured I would get answers in the notebook, if Snarl decided to continue our game.

Since Grandpa wasn't here this year to take me to my favorite Christmas sight—the way way *waaaayyyyy* over-the-top decorated houses in Dyker Heights, Brooklyn, which this time every year were lit up to such an extreme that the neighborhood was probably visible from space—I figured the least Snarl could do would be to show up himself and tell me about the experience. I'd already dared him to in the notebook, leaving him a street name in Dyker Heights and these words: *The Nutcracker House.*

I realized I wanted to add something to the instructions I'd written in the notebook, so I tried to take it back from Boomer.

"Hey!" he said, trying to block me from my own Moleskine. "That's mine."

"It's not yours," Hermione said. "You're just the messenger, Boomer."

Soccer captains look out for one another.

"I just want to add something," I told Boomer. I gently tried to extract the notebook from Boomer's grip, but he wasn't letting go. "I'll give it back. Promise."

"Promise?" he said.

"I just said 'Promise'!" I said.

Hermione said, "She said 'Promise'!"

"Promise?" Boomer repeated.

I was starting to see how John got his name.

Hermione snatched the notebook from Boomer's grip

and handed it over to me. "Hurry, before he freaks. This is a lot of responsibility for him."

Quickly, after the words *The Nutcracker House,* I added a line to the instructions:

Do bring Snarly Muppet. Or don't.

seven

–Dash–

December 24th/December 25th

Boomer refused to tell me a thing.

"Was she tall?"

He shook his head.

"So she was short?"

"No—I'm not telling you."

"Pretty?"

"Not telling."

"Hellaciously homely?"

"I wouldn't tell you even if I knew what that meant."

"Was her blond hair blocking her eyes?"

"No—wait, you're trying to trick me, aren't you? I'm not saying anything except that she wanted me to give this to you."

Along with the notebook, there was . . . a Muppet?

"It looks like Animal and Miss Piggy had sex," I said. "And this was the spawn."

"My eyes!" Boomer cried. "My eyes! I can't stop seeing it now that you've said it!"

I looked at the clock.

"You should probably get home before they start serving dinner," I said.

"Will your mom and Giovanni be home soon?" he asked.

I nodded.

"Christmas hug!" he called out. And immediately I was enmeshed in what could only be called a Christmas hug.

I knew this was supposed to raise the temperature of my cockles. But nothing associated with the culture of Christmas could really do that for me. Not in a humbug sense—I still hugged Boomer like I meant every last squeeze. But mostly I was ready to have the apartment to myself again.

"So I'll see you the day after Christmas for that party, right?" Boomer asked. "Is that the twenty-seventh?"

"The twenty-sixth."

"I should write it down."

He grabbed a pen off the table by our door and wrote *THE 26TH* on his arm.

"Don't you have to write down what's on the twenty-sixth?" I asked.

"Oh, no. I'll remember that. It's your girlfriend's party!"

I could have corrected him, but I knew I'd only have to do it again later.

Once Boomer was safely out of the building, I luxuriated in the silence. It was Christmas Eve, and I had nowhere to be. I kicked off my shoes. Then I kicked off my pants. Amused by this, I took off my shirt. And my underwear. I walked from room to room, naked as the day I was born, only without the blood and amniotic fluid. It was strange—I'd been home alone plenty of times before, but I'd never walked around naked. It was a little chilly, but it was also kind of fun. I waved to the neighbors. I had some yogurt. I put on my mom's copy of the *Mamma Mia* soundtrack and spun around a little. I did some light dusting.

Then I remembered the notebook. It didn't feel right to open the Moleskine naked. So I put my underwear back on. And my shirt (unbuttoned). And my pants.

Lily deserved some respect, after all.

It pretty much blew me away, what she had written. Especially the part about Franny. Because I'd always had a soft spot for Franny. Like most of Salinger's characters, she wouldn't be such a fuckup, you felt, if these fucked-up things didn't keep happening to her. I mean, you never wanted her to end up with Lane, who was a douche bag, only without the vinegar. If she ended up going to Yale, you wanted her to burn the place down.

I knew I was starting to confuse Lily with Franny. Only, Lily wouldn't fall for Lane. She'd fall for . . . Well, I had no idea who she'd fall for, or if he happened to resemble me.

We believe in the wrong things, I wrote, using the same pen Boomer had used on his arm. *That's what frustrates me the most. Not the lack of belief, but the belief in the wrong things. You want meaning? Well, the meanings are out there. We're just so damn good at reading them wrong.*

I wanted to stop there. But I went on.

It's not going to be explained to you in a prayer. And I'm not going to be able to explain it to you. Not just because I'm as ignorant and hopeful and selectively blind as the next guy, but because I don't think meaning is something that can be explained. You have to understand it on your own. It's like when you're starting to read. First, you learn the letters. Then, once you know what sounds the letters make, you use them to sound out words. You know that c-a-t leads to cat and d-o-g leads to dog. But then you have to make that extra leap, to understand that the word, the sound, the "cat" is connected to an actual cat, and that "dog" is connected to an actual dog. It's that leap, that understanding, that leads to meaning. And a lot of the time in life, we're still just sounding things out. We know the sentences and how to say them. We know the ideas and how to present them. We know the prayers and which words to say in what order. But that's only spelling.

I don't mean this to sound hopeless. Because in the same way that a kid can realize what "c-a-t" means, I think we can find the truths that live behind our words. I wish I could remember the moment when I was a kid and I discovered that the letters linked into words, and that the words linked to real things. What a revelation that must have been. We don't have the words for it, since we hadn't yet learned the words. It must have been astonishing, to be given the key to the kingdom and see it turn in our hands so easily.

My hands were starting to shake a little. Because I hadn't known that I knew these things. Just having a notebook to write them in, and having someone to write them to, made them all rise to the surface.

There was the other part of it, too—the *I want to believe there is a somebody out there just for me. I want to believe that I exist to be there for that somebody.* That was, I had to admit, less a concern to me. Because the rest of it seemed so much bigger. But I still had enough longing for that concept that I didn't want to dispel it completely. Meaning: I didn't want to tell Lily that I felt we'd all been duped by Plato and the idea of a soulmate. Just in case it turned out that she was mine.

Too much. Too soon. Too fast. I put down the notebook, paced around the apartment. The world was too full of wastrels and waifs, sycophants and spies—all of whom put words to the wrong use, who made everything that was said or written suspect. Perhaps this was what was so unnerving about Lily at this moment—the trust that was required in what we were doing.

It is much harder to lie to someone's face.

But.

It is also much harder to tell the truth to someone's face.

Words failed me, insofar as I wasn't sure I could find the words that wouldn't fail her. So I put the journal down and pondered the address she'd given me (I had no idea where Dyker Heights was) and the ghastly Muppet that had accompanied it. *Do bring Snarly Muppet*, she'd written. I liked the ring of the *do bring*. Like this was a comedy of manners.

"Can you tell me what she's like?" I asked Snarly.

He just snarled back. Not helpful.

My cell phone rang—Mom, asking me how Christmas Eve at Dad's place was. I told her it was fine and asked her if she and Giovanni were having a traditional Christmas Eve dinner. She giggled and said no, there wasn't a turkey in sight, and she was just fine with that. I liked the sound of her giggle—kids don't really hear their parents giggle enough, if you ask me—and I let her get off the phone before she felt the urge to pass it over to Giovanni for some perfunctory salutations. I knew my dad wouldn't call until actual Christmas Day—he only called when the obligation was so obvious even a gorilla would get it.

I imagined what it would be like if my lie to my mom was actually the truth—that is, if I was with Dad and Leeza right then, at some "yoga retreat" in California. Personally, I felt yoga was something to retreat *from*, not *toward*, so the mental image involved me sitting cross-legged with an open book in my lap while everyone else did the Spread-Eagle Ostrich. I'd vacationed with Dad and Leeza exactly once in the two or so years they'd been together, and that had involved a redundantly named "spa resort" and me walking in on them while they were kissing with mud masks on. That had been more than enough for this lifetime, and the three or four after.

Mom and I had decorated the tree before she and Giovanni had left. Even though I wasn't into Christmas, I did get some satisfaction from the tree—every year, Mom and I got to take out our childhoods and scatter them across the branches. I hadn't said anything, but Mom had known that Giovanni deserved no part in this—it was just her and me, taking out the palm-sized rocking chair that my great-grandmother had made for my mother's dollhouse and dangling it from a bow, then taking the worn-out washcloth from when I was a baby, its lion face still peering through the cartoon woods, and balancing it on the pine. Every year we added something, and this year I'd made my mother laugh when I'd brought out one of my younger self's most prized possessions—a mini Canadian Club bottle that she'd drained quickly on a flight to see my paternal grandparents, and that I'd then proceeded to hold (in amazement) for the rest of the vacation.

It was a funny story, and I wanted to tell it to Lily, the girl I barely knew.

But I left the notebook where it was. I knew I could have buttoned my shirt, put my shoes back on, and headed to the mysterious Dyker Heights. But my gift to myself this Christmas Eve was a full retreat from the world. I didn't turn on the TV. I didn't call any friends. I didn't check my email. I didn't even look out the windows. Instead, I reveled in solitude. If Lily wanted to believe there was a somebody out there just for her, I wanted to believe that I could be somebody in here just for me. I made myself dinner. I ate slowly, trying to take the time to actually taste the food. I picked up *Franny and Zooey* and enjoyed their company again. Then I tangoed with my bookshelf, dipping in and out again, in and out again—a Marie Howe poem, then a John Cheever story. An old E. B. White essay, then a passage from *Trumpet of the Swans*. I went into my mother's room and read some of the pages she'd dog-eared—she always did that when she read a sentence that she liked, and each time I opened the book, I had to try to figure out which sentence was the one that had impressed itself upon her. Was it the Logan Pearsall Smith quote "The indefatigable pursuit of an unattainable perfection, even though it consist in nothing more than in the pounding of an old piano, is what alone gives a meaning to our life on this unavailing star" from page 202 of J. R. Moehringer's *The Tender Bar* or, a few lines down, the more simple "Being alone has nothing to do with how many people are around"? From Richard Yates's *Revolutionary Road*, was it "He had admired the ancient delicacy of the buildings and the way the street lamps made soft explosions of light green in the trees at night" or "The place had filled him with a sense of wisdom hovering just out of reach, of unspeakable grace prepared and waiting just around the corner, but he'd walked himself weak down its endless blue streets and all the people who knew how to live had kept their tantalizing secret to themselves"? On page 82 of Anne Enright's *The Gathering*, was it "But it is not just the sex, or remembered sex, that makes me think I love Michael Weiss from Brooklyn, now, seventeen years too late. It is the way he refused to own me, no matter how much I tried to be owned. It was the way he would not take me, he would only meet me, and that only ever halfway." Or was it "I think I am ready for that now. I think I am ready to be met"?

I spent hours doing this. I didn't say a word, but I wasn't conscious of my silence. The sound of my own life, my own internal life, was all that I needed.

It felt like a holiday, but that had nothing to do with Jesus or the calendar or what anyone else in the world was doing.

Before I went to bed, I got back into my usual routine—opening up the (sadly, abridged) dictionary next to my bed and trying to find a word I could love.

> **li•ques•cent,** *adj.* 1. becoming liquid; melting. 2. tending toward a liquid state.

Liquescent. I tried to say myself to sleep with it.

It was only as I was drifting off that I realized what I'd done:

In opening the book at random, I'd only landed a few pages long of *Lily*.

I hadn't left any milk and cookies out for Santa. We didn't have a chimney; there wasn't even a fireplace. I had submitted no list, and had not received any certifications of my niceness. And yet, when I woke up around noon the next day, there were still presents from my mother waiting for me.

I unwrapped them one by one underneath the tree, since I knew that was how she'd want me to do it. I felt pangs for her then—just for these ten minutes, just so I could give her presents, too. There wasn't anything surprising beneath the wrapping paper—a number of books I'd wanted, a gadget or two to add some diversity, and a blue sweater that didn't look half bad.

"Thanks, Mom," I said to the air. Because it was still too early to call her time zone.

I lost myself immediately in one of the books, only emerging when the phone rang.

"Dashiell?" my father intoned. As if someone else with my voice might be answering the phone at my mother's apartment.

"Yes, Father?"

"Leeza and I would like to wish you a merry Christmas."

"Thank you, Father. And to you, as well."

[awkward pause]

[even more awkward pause]

"I hope your mother isn't giving you any trouble."

Oh, Father, I love it when you play this game.

"She told me if I clean all the ashes out of the grate, then I'll be able to help my sisters get ready for the ball."

"It's Christmas, Dashiell. Can't you give that attitude a rest?"

"Merry Christmas, Dad. And thanks for the presents."

"What presents?"

"I'm sorry—those were all from Mom, weren't they?"

"Dashiell . . ."

"I gotta go. The gingerbread men are on fire."

"Wait—Leeza wants to wish you a merry Christmas."

"The smoke's getting pretty thick. I really have to go."

"Well, merry Christmas."

"Yeah, Dad. Merry Christmas."

It was, I figured, at least an eighth my fault for picking up the phone in the first place. But I'd just wanted to get it over with, and now here it was—very over. I gravitated toward the red notebook and almost started venting there—but then I felt like I didn't want to burden Lily with what I was feeling, not right now. That would just be passing the unfairness along, and Lily would be even more powerless to stop what had happened than I had been.

It was only five o'clock, but it was already dark outside. I decided the time had come for me to head to Dyker Heights.

This involved me taking the D train farther than I'd ever taken the D train before. After the frenzied crowds of the past week, the city was almost blank on Christmas Day. The only things open were ATMs, churches, Chinese restaurants, and movie theaters. Everything else was dark, sleeping the season off. Even the subway seemed like it had been hollowed out—only a few scattered people on the platform, a thin row of passengers on the seats. Yes, there were signs it was Christmas—little girls delighting in their frocks and little boys looking imprisoned by their little suits. Eye contact was often met with friendliness instead of hostility. But for a place that had been overrun with tourists, there was nary a guidebook in sight, and all the conversations were kept quiet. I read my book from Manhattan into Brooklyn. But then, when the D train emerged from the ground, I shifted so I could stare out the window, stealing glimpses of family windows as we chugged past.

I still didn't know how I was going to find the Nutcracker House. When I got to the subway stop, however, I had some idea. A disproportionate number of passengers had gotten off with me, and they all seemed to be heading in the same direction—clusters of families, couples holding hands, old people making pilgrimage. I followed.

At first, it seemed like there was something strange in the

air, giving it a halo of electricity, like in Times Square. Only, we were nowhere near Times Square, so it didn't make much sense . . . until I started to see the houses, each one more electrified than the next. These were not Christmas light dilettantes here. This was a spectacular spectacular of lawn and house ornamentation. For as far as the eye could see, every house was ringed with lights. Lights of every color, lights of every shape. Outlines of reindeer and Santa and his sleigh. Boxes with ribbon, toy teddy bears, larger-than-life dolls—all strung together from Christmas lights. If Joseph and Mary had lit the manger like this, it would've been seen all the way in Rome.

Observing it all, I felt such contradictory feelings. On the one hand, it was an astonishing misuse of energy, a testament to the ingenious wastefulness that American Christmas inspires. On the other hand, it was amazing to see the whole community lit up like this, because it made it feel very much like a community. You could imagine everyone taking out their lights on the same day and having a block party while they put them all up. The children walked around transfixed by the sights, as if their neighbors had suddenly become purveyors of an exquisite magic. There was as much conversation swirling around as there was light—none of it involved me, but I was glad to have it around.

The Nutcracker House was not hard to find—the nutcracker soldiers held sentry at least fifteen feet into the sky as the Rat King threatened the festivities and Clara danced through the night. I looked for a scroll in her hand, or a card on the top of one of the light-strung presents. Then I saw it on the ground—a light-dappled walnut the size of a basketball that had been cracked open just far enough to reach into.

The note I found inside was brief and clear.

Tell me what you see.

So I sat on the curb and told her about the contradictions, about the waste and the joy. Then I told her that I preferred the quiet demonstrations of a well-stocked bookshelf to the voltage of this particular street. Not that one was wrong and the other was right—it was just a matter of preference. I told her that I was glad Christmas was over, and then I told her why. I looked around some more, tried to see everything, just so I could tell it to her. The yawn of a three-year-old, tired despite his happiness. The elderly couple from the train who'd finally completed the walk to the block—I imagined they'd been doing this for years, and that they saw both the houses in front of them and all the houses from the past. I imagined each of their sentences started with the phrase *Remember the time*.

Then I told her what I didn't see. Namely, that I didn't see her.

You could be standing a few feet away—Clara's dance partner, or across the street taking a picture of Rudolph before he takes flight. I could have sat next to you on the subway, or brushed beside you as we went through the turnstiles. But whether or not you are here, you are here—because these words are for you, and they wouldn't exist if you weren't here in some way. This notebook is a strange instrument—the player doesn't know the music until it's being played.

I know you want to know my name. But if I told you my name, even just the first name, you'd be able to go online and find all of these inaccurate, incomplete depictions of me. (If my name were John or Michael, this would not be a problem.) And even if you swore up and down that you wouldn't check, the temptation would always be there. So I'd like to remain at that one delicate remove, so you can get to know me without the distraction of other people's noise. I hope that's okay.

The next assignment on the do (or don't) list is time sensitive—meaning, it would be best if you did it this very evening. Because at this club that changes names every month or so (I gave her the address), there is an all-nighter that is about to start. The theme (seasonally appropriate) is the Seventh Night of Hanukkah. The opener is some "jewfire" band (Ezekial? Ariel?), and at about two in the morning, this gay Jewish dancepop/indie/punk band called Silly Rabbi, Tricks Are for Yids will go on. Between the opener and the main act, look for the writing on the stall.

An all-nighter at a club wasn't exactly my scene, so I knew I had a phone call or two to make before the plan would be complete. I quickly slipped the Moleskine into the walnut and took Snarly Muppet out of my backpack.

"Watch over this, will you?" I asked it.

And then I left it there, a small sentry among the nutcrackers.

eight

(Lily)

December 25th

I decided to give myself a Christmas present this year. I decided to spend the day only speaking to animals (real and stuffed), select humans as necessary so long as they weren't my parents or Langston, and a Snarl in a red Moleskine notebook—if he returned it to me.

When I was old enough to read and write, my parents gave me an eraser board that I kept in my room at all times. The idea was that when frustrated, I, Lily, should write down words on the board to express my feelings instead of letting she-devil Shrilly express them through shrieking. It was supposed to be a therapeutic tool.

I brought the eraser board out of retirement on Christmas morning when my parents phoned in for a video chat. I almost didn't recognize them on the computer screen. The betrayers looked so healthy, tan, and relaxed. Completely not Christmasy.

"Merry Christmas, Lily darling!" Mom said. She was sitting

on the balcony of their cabana or whatever it was, and I could see the ocean lapping behind her. She looked ten years younger than when she left Manhattan a week earlier.

Dad's glowing face wormed onto the screen next to Mom's, blocking my ocean view.

"Merry Christmas, Lily darling!" he said.

I scribbled onto the eraser board and held it up to the computer screen for them to see: *Merry Christmas to you, too.*

Mom and Dad both frowned at the sight of the eraser board.

"Uh-oh," Mom said.

"Uh-oh," Dad said. "Is Lily Bear feeling a bit unsettled today? Even though we've been preparing you for our anniversary trip since last Christmas, and you *assured* us you would feel okay having just this one Christmas without us?"

I erased my last statement and replaced it with: *Langston told me about the boarding school job.*

Their faces fell.

"Put Langston on!" Mom demanded.

I wrote, *He's sick in bed. Asleep right now.*

Dad said, "What's his temperature?"

101.

Mom's peeved face turned concerned. "Poor baby. On Christmas Day, too. It's just as well we all agreed not to open presents until we get home on New Year's Day. It wouldn't be any fun with him sick in bed, now would it?"

I shook my head. *Are you moving to Fiji?*

Dad said, "We haven't decided anything. We'll talk about it as a family when we get home."

Rapidly, my hands erased and re-scribbled.

It makes me UPSET that you didn't tell me.

Mom said, "I'm sorry, Lily bear. We didn't want to make you upset before there was anything to really be upset about."

SHOULD I BE UPSET?

My hand started to feel tired from the erasing and writing. I almost wished my voice wasn't being so obstinate.

Dad said, "It's Christmas. Of course you shouldn't be upset. We'll make this decision as a family—"

Mom interrupted him. "There's some chicken soup in the freezer! You can thaw it for Langston in the microwave."

I started to write: *Langston deserves to be sick.* But I erased that and wrote, *Okay. I'll make him some.*

Mom said, "If his temperature goes up any more, I'm going to need you to take him to the doctor. Can you do that, Lily?"

My voice broke free. "Of course I can do that!" I snapped. Geez, how old did they think I was? Eleven?

The eraser board, and my conviction, were both mad at my voice's betrayal.

Dad said, "I'm sorry this Christmas is turning out not so swell, sweetheart. I promise you we'll make it up to you on New Year's Day. You take good care of Langston today and then have a nice Christmas dinner at Great-aunt Ida's tonight. That will make you feel better, right?"

My silence returned in the form of my head nodding up and down.

Mom said, "What have you been doing with your time, dear?"

I had no desire to tell her about the notebook. Not because I was UPSET about Fiji. But because it, and he, seemed to be the best part of Christmas so far. I wanted to keep them all for myself.

I heard a moan from my brother's room. *"Lilllllllllllyyyy . . ."*

For the sake of expediency, I typed a message to my parents rather than speak or write it on the eraser board.

```
    Your sick son is calling to me from his
sickbed. I must anon. Merry Christmas,
parents. I love you. Please let's not move
to Fiji.
```

"We love you!" they squealed from their side of the world.

I signed off and walked toward my brother's room. I stopped first at the bathroom to extract a disposable mask and gloves from the emergency preparedness kit to place over my mouth and hands. No way was I getting sick, too. Not with a red notebook possibly coming back my way.

I went into Langston's room and sat down next to his bed. Benny had decided to be sick at his own apartment, which I appreciated, since tending to not one but two patients on Christmas Day might have tipped me over the edge. Langston hadn't touched the orange juice or saltines I left for him a few hours earlier, the last time he called *"Lilllllllllllyyyy . . ."* to me from his room, at about the approximate time when on a normal Christmas morning we should have been ripping through our gifts.

"Read to me," Langston said. "Please?"

I wasn't speaking to Langston that day, but I would read to him. I picked up the book at the point where we'd left off the night before. I read aloud from *A Christmas Carol.* "'It is a fair, even-handed, noble adjustment of things, that while there is infection in disease and sorrow, there is nothing in the world so irresistibly contagious as laughter and good-humour.'"

"That's a nice quote," Langston said. "Underline it and fold down the page for me, will you?" I did as instructed. I can never decide what I think about my brother and his book passage quotes. Sometimes it's annoying that I can never open a book in our home and not find some part of it that Langston has annotated. I'd like to figure out what I think about the words myself without having to see Langston's handwritten comments, like *lovely* or *pretentious BS* next to it; on the other hand, sometimes it's interesting to find his notes and to read them back and try to decipher why that particular passage intrigued or inspired him. It's a cool way of getting inside my brother's brain.

A text message came through on Langston's phone. "Benny!" he said, grabbing for it. Langston's thumbs went into hyper-motion in response. I knew Mr. Dickens and I were finished for the time being.

I left his room.

Langston hadn't even bothered to ask if we should exchange presents. We'd promised our parents we would wait for New Year's Day to do our gift exchanges, but I was willing to cheat, if asked.

I returned to my own room and saw I had five voice mails on my phone: two from Grandpa, one from Cousin Mark, one from Uncle Sal, and one from Great-aunt Ida. The great Christmas merry-go-round of phone calls had begun.

I didn't listen to any of the messages. I turned my phone off. I was on strike this Christmas, I decided.

When I told my parents last year I didn't mind if we celebrated Christmas late this year, I obviously hadn't meant it. How had they not figured that out?

This should have been a real Christmas morning of tearing through presents and eating a huge breakfast and laughing and singing with my family.

I was surprised to realize there was something I wanted more than that, though.

I wanted the red notebook back.

With nothing to do and no one to hang out with, I lay on my bed and wondered how Snarl's Christmas was going. I imagined him living in some swank artists' loft in Chelsea, with a super-hip mom and her super-cool new boyfriend and they had, like, asymmetrical haircuts and maybe spoke German. I imagined them sitting around their Christmas hearth drinking hot cider and eating my lebkuchen spice cookies while the turkey roasted in the oven. Snarl was playing the trumpet for them, wearing a beret, too, because suddenly I wanted him to be a musical prodigy who wore a hat. And when he finished playing his piece, which he composed for them as a Christmas present, they cried and said, *"Danke! Danke!"* The piece was so perfect and beautiful, his playing so exquisite, even Snarly Muppet seated by the hearth clapped its Muppet hands, a Pinocchio come to life from the sound of such sweet trumpeting.

Since I couldn't speak to Snarl myself and find out how his Christmas was going, I decided to get dressed and take a walk in Tompkins Square Park. I know all the dogs there. Because of the prior gerbil and cat incidents, my parents long ago mandated that it was better for me not to have my own pets since I get too attached. They compromised by allowing me to take on dog-walking jobs in the neighborhood, so long as they or Grandpa knew the owners. This compromise has worked out nicely over the last couple years, as I have gotten to spend quality dog time with loads more dogs than I would have gotten to know if I'd had my own, and I am also quite wealthy now.

The weather was weirdly warm and sunny for a Christmas Day. It felt more like June than December, yet another sign of the wrongness of this particular Christmas Day. I sat down on a bench while people walked by with their dogs, and I cooed, "Hi, puppy!" to all the dogs I didn't know, and I cooed, "Hi, puppy!" to all the dogs I did know, but to those dogs, I pet them and fed them bone-shaped dog biscuits I'd baked the night before, using red and green food coloring so the biscuits would appear festive. I didn't talk except as necessary to the humans, but I listened to them, and found out all the ways in which the Christmases of everyone else in the neighborhood were not sucking this year like mine was. I saw their new sweaters and hats, their new watches and rings, heard about their new TVs and laptops.

But all I could think about was Snarl. I imagined him surrounded by doting parents and the exact presents he wanted today. I pictured him opening up gifts of moody black turtlenecks, and angry novels by angry young men, and ski equipment just because I'd like to think there's a possibility we might one day go skiing together even though I don't know how to ski, and not one single English-Catalan dictionary.

Had Snarl gone to Dyker Heights yet? Since I'd turned my phone off and left it at home, the only way to find out would be to go see Great-aunt Ida, who was on my talk-to list for the day.

Great-aunt Ida lives in a town house on East Twenty-second Street near Gramercy Park. My family of four lives in a small, cramped East Village apartment (with no pets, grrr . . .) that my academic parents can afford only because Grandpa owns the building; our whole apartment is about the size of one floor of Great-aunt Ida's house, which she occupies all by herself. She never married or had her own kids. She was a fabulously successful art gallery owner in her day; she did so well for herself she could afford to buy her own house in Manhattan. (Though Grandpa always points out that she bought that house when the city was in economic turmoil, and the prior occupants practically paid Great-aunt Ida to take it off their hands. Lucky lady!) Her fancy house in her fancy neighborhood doesn't mean Great-aunt Ida's gone all snobby, though. She's so not snobby, in fact, that even though she has lots of money, she still works one day a week at Madame Tussauds. She said she needs something to do, and she likes hanging out with celebrities. Secretly I think she is writing a tell-all book about what happens between the wax people when no one's looking.

Langston and I call Great-aunt Ida Mrs. Basil E. because of the book we loved when we were kids, *From the Mixed-up Files of Mrs. Basil E. Frankweiler.* That book's Mrs. Basil E. is a rich old lady who sets the sister and brother in the book out on a treasure hunt in the Metropolitan Museum of Art of New York. When we were kids, our Mrs. Basil E. used to take Langston and me on museum adventures on school holidays when our parents had to work. The days always ended with a trip for giant ice cream sundaes. How great is a great-aunt who lets her niece and nephew have ice cream for dinner? *Truly* great, in my opinion.

Great-aunt Ida/Mrs. Basil E. wrapped me in a giant Christmas hug when I arrived at her apartment. I loved how she always smells like lipstick and classy perfume. She always wears a proper ladies' suit, too, even on Christmas Day, when she should be lounging around in her pj's.

"Hello, Lily bear," Mrs. Basil E. said. "I see you found my old majorette boots from my high school days at Washington Irving High."

I leaned into her for another hug. I love her hugs. "Yes." I nodded into her shoulder, grateful for it. "I found them in our old dress-up-clothes trunk. At first they were too big on me, but I put on a thick pair of socks over my tights, so they're comfy now. They're my new favorite boots."

"I like the gold tinsel you added to the tassels," she said. "Are you going to let me go anytime before New Year's?"

Reluctantly, I released my arms from around her.

"Now please take my boots off," she said. "I don't want the taps on the soles scratching my wood floors."

"What's for dinner?" I asked.

Mrs. Basil E.'s tradition is to have tons of people over for Christmas dinner, and enough food for a ton more.

"The usual," she said.

"Can I help?" I asked.

"Right this way," she said, turning toward the kitchen.

But I didn't follow her.

She turned around. "Yes, Lily?" she asked.

"Did he return the notebook?"

"Not yet, dear. But I'm sure he will."

"What does he look like?" I asked her, once again.

"You'll have to find out for yourself," she said. Aside from being snarly, Snarl must not be a total monster, because if he was, no way would Mrs. Basil E. have signed on as an accessory to the latest installment.

Into the kitchen we went.

Mrs. Basil E. and I cooked and sang till six while workers around us did the same, preparing the grand house for its grand feast. I kept wanting to shriek, *WHAT IF HE DOESN'T RETURN THE NOTEBOOK?* But I didn't. Because my great-aunt didn't seem too concerned. Like she had faith in him, and so should I.

Finally, at seven that night—perhaps the loooongest wait of my life ever—the Dyker Heights contingent of the family arrived. Uncle Carmine and his wife and their massive brood came in loaded with presents.

I didn't bother to open mine. Uncle Carmine still thinks I'm eight and gives me American Girl doll accessories. Which I still love, by the way, but it's not exactly like there's a mystery about what's inside his wrapped gift boxes for me. So I asked him, "Do you have it?"

Uncle Carmine said, "It'll cost you." He turned his cheek to me. I gave his cheek a Christmas kiss. The toll paid, he pulled the red notebook from his goody bag of presents and handed it to me.

Suddenly I didn't see how I could survive one more second without absorbing the latest contents in the notebook. I needed to be alone.

"Bye, everyone!" I chirped.

"Lily!" Mrs. Basil E. scolded. "You can't possibly think you're leaving."

"I forgot to tell you I'm not really talking to anyone today! I'm more or less on strike! So I wouldn't be very good company! And since Langston's sick at home, I should probably check on him." I threw her a kiss from my hand. "Mwahhh!"

She shook her head. "That child," she said to Carmine. "Kooky." She threw her hands up in the air before throwing me back an air kiss. "What should I tell the caroling friends you invited here to dinner tonight?"

"Tell them merry Christmas!" I called out as I left.

Langston was asleep again when I got home. I filled his water glass and left some Tylenols by his bed and went to my own room to read the notebook in private.

At last I had it—the Christmas present I'd wanted all along, but hadn't realized. His words.

I felt a sense of longing for him such as I've never experienced in my lifetime for any person, or even for any pet.

It seemed weird to me that he'd spent his Christmas alone . . . and had seemed to like it. He hadn't seemed to think anyone should feel sorry for him about that, either.

I had spent my Christmas mostly alone for the first time in my life, too.

I had felt rather sorry for myself.

But it hadn't been so terrible, actually.

In the future, I decided I would tackle the solitude thing more enthusiastically, so long as solitude meant I could also walk in the park and pet a few dogs and pass them treats.

What did you get for Christmas? he asked me in the notebook.

I wrote:

We didn't do presents this year at Christmas. We're saving it for New Year's. (Long story. Maybe you'd like to hear it in person sometime?)

But I couldn't concentrate on writing in the notebook. I wanted to live inside it, not write in it.

What kind of girl did Snarl think I was, sending me to a music club in the middle of the night?

My parents would never let me go.

But they weren't here to say no.

I returned to the notebook. *I liked what you said, my nameless new friend. Are we that? Friends? I hope so. Only for a friend would I consider going out at TWO IN THE MORNING on Christmas night—or any night, for that matter. It's not that I'm afraid of the dark, so much as . . . I don't really go out that much. In that teenager kind of way. Is that okay?*

I'm not sure how this Being a Teenager thing is supposed to work. Is there an instruction manual? I think I have the moody muscle installed, but I don't flex it that often. More times I feel so filled with LOVE for the people I know—and even more so for the dogs I walk in Tompkins Square Park—that I feel like I could well up like a giant balloon and fly away. Yes, that much love. But other teenagers? Historically, I haven't always related so much. In seventh grade, my parents made me join my school's soccer team to force me to socialize with other girls my age. It turns out I was pretty good at soccer, but not so great at the socializing part. Don't worry—it's not like I am a complete freak of nature that nobody talks to. It's more like the other girls talk to me, but after a while they'll sort of look at me like, "HUH? What did she just say?" Then they go off into their groups, where I'm pretty sure they speak a secret language of popularity, and I go back to kicking the ball by myself and having imaginary conversations with my favorite dogs and literary characters. Everyone wins.

I don't mind being the odd girl out; it's kind of a relief, maybe. In the language of soccer, however, I am highly fluent. That's what I like about sports. No matter if everyone playing the game speaks completely different languages, on the field, or the court, wherever they are playing, the language of moves and passes and scores is all the same. Universal.

Do you like sports? I don't imagine you being the sporty type. I KNOW! Your name is Beckham, isn't it?

I'm not sure you will get this notebook back tonight. I'm not sure I can accept your latest mission. It's only because my parents are away that I can even consider it. I've never been to a late-night music club before. And going out by myself in the middle of the night, in the middle of Manhattan? Wow. You must have a lot of faith in me. Which I appreciate. Even if I'm not sure I share it.

I stopped writing so I could take a nap. I wasn't sure I had it in me to accept Snarl's task, but if I did, I'd need to rest first.

I dreamt about Snarl. In my dream, Snarl's face was Eminem's, and he was singing "My name is . . ." over and over while holding up the red notebook to reveal a new page displaying different names.

My name is . . . Ypsilanti.

My name is . . . Ezekiel.

My name is . . . Mandela.

My name is . . . Yao Ming.

At one in the morning, my alarm went off.

Snarl had infiltrated my subconscious. The dream was obviously a sign: he was too enticing too resist.

I checked in with Langston (passed out cold), then put on my best Christmas party frock, a gold-colored crushed velvet mini-dress. I was surprised to discover I'd developed more boobage and hippage since I wore the dress the previous Christmas, but decided not to care how snug it was. The club would probably be dark. Who'd notice me? I completed the outfit with red tights and Mrs. Basil E.'s majorette boots with the gold-tinseled tassels. I put my red knit hat with the poms-poms dangling from the ears on my head but pulled out some strands of blond hair from the front to cover one of my eyes so I could look a little mysterious for once. I whistled to hail a cab.

Snarl must have had me under some kind of spell because sneaking out in the middle of the night, on Christmas night no less, to a dive club on the Lower East Side was about the last dare that pre-notebook Lily ever would have taken on. But somehow, knowing the Moleskine was tucked away in my bag, containing our thoughts and clues, our imprints to each other, somehow that made me feel safe, like I could have this adventure and not get lost and not call my brother to save me. I could do this on my own, and not freak out that I had no idea what waited for me on the other side of this night.

"Merry Christmas. Tell me something that's a drag."

The bouncer she-man's request at the door to the club would have confused me before Thanksgiving, but because of meeting Shee'nah through my caroling group a few weeks ago, I understood the system.

Shee'nah, who is a proud member of this "new now next wave of fabulosity" in the downtown club scene, had explained the drag-on ladies as being "not quite drag queens, not quite dragons, there for you to drag your woes to."

And so, to a very large, very gold-lamé-dress-wearing club bouncer who had a dragon's mask on her head, I whined, "I didn't get any presents for Christmas."

"Sister, this is a Hanukkah show. Who cares about your Christmas presents? Come on, do me better. What's your drag?"

"There may or may not be a person of unknowable name and face inside that club who may or may not be looking for me."

"Bored."

The door did not budge open.

I leaned into the drag-on lady and whispered, "I've never been kissed. In that certain way."

Drag-on lady's eyes widened. "Seriously? With those boobs?"

Gosh! Ex-squeamish me?

I covered my chest with my hands, ready to bolt.

"You *are* serious!" the drag-on lady said, finally opening the door to me. "Get in there already! And mazel tov!"

I kept my arms covering my chest as I entered the club. Inside, all I could see was screaming-thrashing-moshing crazy people. It smelled like beer and puke. It was as close an approximation to hell as I could imagine. Immediately I wished to return outside and pass the night chatting with the drag-on lady, and hearing everyone else's tales of woe at the door.

Was Snarl playing some kind of cosmic joke on me, sending me to such a dump?

I was scared, frankly.

If I'd ever been intimidated trying to make conversation

with a posse of lip-glossed sixteen-year-old girls at school, they were child's play in comparison to the formidable group of club folks.

Meet [*dramatic drumroll, please*] the punky hipsters.

I was easily the youngest person there, and the only person there by herself, so far as I could tell. And for a Hanukkah party, no one was dressed appropriately. I seemed to be the only person there dressed festively. Everyone else was in skinny jeans and crappy T-shirts. Like teenage girls, the hipsters congregated in cooler-than-you packs, wearing bored expressions on their faces, but unlike the teenage girls I knew, I didn't think any of them wanted to ask to copy my math homework or play soccer. The hipsters' sneers in my direction immediately dismissed me as Not One of Them. I can't say I wasn't grateful about that.

I wanted to go home to the safety of my bed and to my stuffed animals and to my people I'd known my whole life. I had nothing to say to anybody, and fervently prayed that no one there would have anything to say to me. I was starting to hate Snarl for throwing me into this lion's den. The worst punch I'd swung him was Madame Tussauds. But wax people don't pass judgment and say to each other "*What* is that girl wearing? Are there *taps* on her boots?" when I walk by. I don't think.

Ah, but . . . the music. When the band of young Hasidic punk boys took the stage—a guitar player, a bass player, some horns, some violins, and, strangely, no drummer—and let loose their explosion of sounds, then I understood Snarl's master plan.

The band played a style I'd heard before, when one of my cousins married a Jewish musician. At their wedding reception, a klezmer band played, which Langston told me was like a kind of Jewish punk-jazz fusion. The music at this club was like if you mixed the horah dance with Green Day playing a Mardi Gras parade? The guitar and bass provided the sound's foundation, while the horns riffed with the violins, and the band members' voices laughed and wept and sang all at once.

It was clown insane. I *loved* it. My arms removed themselves from protecting my chest. I needed to *move*! I danced my *tuchus* off, not caring what anyone thought. I twirled in the middle of the mosh, thrashed my hair around, and jumped like I was on a pogo stick. I tapped my boot taps on the floor like I was part of the music, too, not caring what anyone thought.

Apparently, the wildly dancing hipsters thought the same as me about the music, dancing around me like we were in a punk horah dance. Maybe klezmer music was a universal language, like soccer. I couldn't believe how much I enjoyed myself.

I realized that Snarl had given me what I asked for as a Christmas present. Hope and belief. I'd always hoped but never believed that I could have such an adventure on my own. That I could own it. And love it. But it had happened. The notebook had made it so.

I was sad when the band's set ended, but also glad. My heart rate needed to come down. And it needed to find its next message.

While the opening band left the stage, I went to the bathroom, as instructed.

May I just say, if I ever have to return to that bathroom in my lifetime, I'm bringing a bottle of Clorox.

I took a paper towel from the sink and placed it on the toilet to sit down on; no way would I use that toilet. There was writing all over the stall wall—trails of graffiti and quotes, messages to lovers and friends, to exes and enemies. It was almost like a wailing wall—the punked-out place to puke out your heart. If it wasn't so filthy and smelly, it could almost have doubled as a museum art installation—so many words and feelings, so many diverse styles of scribbling, with messages written in Magic Marker, different-colored pens, eyeliner, nail polish, glitter pens, and Sharpies.

I related most to this scrawled line:

BECAUSE I'M SO UNCOOL AND SO AFRAID

I thought, *Good for you, Uncool and So Afraid. You made it here anyway. Maybe that's half the battle?*

I wondered what happened to that person. I wondered if I could leave him or her a red notebook to find out.

My favorite scrawl was written in black Magic Marker. It said:

The Cure. For the Exes. I'm sorry, Nick. Will you kiss me again?

Because suddenly, on the night-(horah-)mare after Christmas, as I sat on a filthy toilet in a stinky bathroom, dripping in sweat from dancing, I really really wanted that certain someone to kiss. In a way I'd never wished for in my life. It wasn't about the fantasy. That was now replaced with hope and belief that it could happen, for real.

(I've never kissed anyone for real, in a romantic way,

before. I hadn't lied to the drag-on lady. I don't think my pillow counts.

(Should I confess this to Snarl in the notebook? Full disclosure, so he had a fair chance to run?

(Nah.)

There were so many messages on the bathroom wall that I might never have found his, except I recognized his handwriting. The message was a few lines down from the Cure kiss message. He'd painted a strip of white paint as background, then alternated the words in blue and black Magic Marker—a nice Hanukkah-themed message, I guessed. So Snarl was secretly a sentimentalist. Or maybe part Jewish?

The message said:

> *Please return the notebook to the handsome gumshoe wearing the fedora hat.*

Well, just dreidel me *verklempt.*

Was Snarl *here?*

Or was I going to meet a kid named Boomer again?

I stepped back out into the club. In all the black jeans and black T-shirts and bad lighting, I finally identified two men in a corner by the bar wearing fedora hats, although one had a yarmulke pinned over it. Both guys wore sunglasses. I noticed the one not wearing the yarmulke lean down and scrape a piece of gum from his shoe with a paper clip. (I think he used a paper clip. Gosh, I hope he didn't use his fingernail—gross.)

In the club's darkness, it was impossible to make out their faces.

I pulled out the notebook, then changed my mind and put it in my purse for safekeeping, in case I had the wrong guys. If they were the right guys, shouldn't they be saying something to me like, *Hey, we're here for the notebook*?

They shot me their glazed, punky hipster glares instead.

I was struck mute, panic-afflicted.

I ran out of the club as fast as I could.

Mortifyingly, I ran right out of one of my boots. Really. I'd neglected to wear socks over my tights so the too-big boots would fit properly, and like a Shrilly Cinderella at the indie-gayjewfire ball, I slipped right out of one of my boots.

No way was I going back for it.

Only when the cab dropped me off at home and I took out my wallet to pay the driver did I realize:

I'd left the gumshoe a boot and no notebook.

The notebook was still in my purse.

I'd given Snarl no clues how to find me back.

nine

–Dash–

December 26th

I was woken up at eight in the morning by a banging on the door. I stumbled into the front hallway, squinted into the peep-hole, and found Dov and Yohnny peering back at me, fedoras askew.

"Hey, guys," I said after I opened the door. "Isn't it a little early for you?"

"Haven't gone to sleep yet!" Dov said. "We're all Red Bullish and Diet Coked–up, if you know what I mean."

"Can we crash here?" Yohnny asked. "I mean, soon. Like, in two minutes."

"How could I turn you away?" I asked. "How was the show?"

"You should've stayed," Dov said. "Silly Rabbi was awesome. I mean, they're no Fistful of Assholes, but they're about eighteen times better than Ozrael. And let me tell you, your girl busted some moves, man."

I smiled. "Really?"

"She put the *ho* in *horah*!" Dov exclaimed.

Yohnny shook his head. "It was more like the *rah*. I mean, she was more like the *rah*."

Dov hit Yohnny on the shoulder with what looked like a boot.

"Bitch, I'm talking here!" Dov cried.

"Someone's not getting to break the glass tonight," Yohnny muttered.

I stepped in. "Guys! Do you have something for me?"

"Yeah," Dov said, holding out the boot. "This."

"What is it?" I asked.

Dov looked at me flatly. "What is it? Well, let's see . . ."

Yohnny said, "There wasn't any notebook. I mean, she held it out to Dov, but then she ran away with it. Only, she lost her boot in the process. Don't ask me how—it seems to defy the law of physics for a foot to fall out of a boot. So maybe she wanted to leave it behind for you."

"Cinderella!" Dov cried. "Let down your hair!"

"Yeah," Yohnny went on, "I think it's time for bed. Mind if we crawl into a cave?"

"You can use my mom's room," I said. Then I took the boot from Dov and looked inside.

"No notebook," Yohnny said. "I thought that, too. I even checked the floor, which was not a pleasant experience. I can honestly say, if the notebook had fallen out, it wouldn't have gotten far—it would've stuck right where it landed."

"Ew. Sorry. I mean, thanks." I led them to my mom's room. It felt a little wrong to loan out her bed, but it was also Giovanni's bed, and I loved the idea of casually mentioning to him that two clubbed-out gay unorthodox Jews had caved there together while he was gone. I removed the bedspread while Yohnny kept Dov propped up; just the sight of a sleeping place had drained all the Red Bull from his veins.

"What time do you want a wake-up call?" I asked.

"You going to Priya's party tonight?" Yohnny said.

I nodded.

"Well, wake us up a little before that."

Delicately, Yohnny removed his hat, then Dov's. I bid them good night, even though the morning was just getting started.

I examined the boot. I pondered it. I searched for secret messages etched into the leather. I removed the insole to see if there was a note underneath. I asked the boot questions. I played with its tassel. I felt that Lily had outriddled me.

If she hadn't left anything, I would've thought, *Wow. That's it. It's over.* But the boot was a clue, and if there was a clue, that meant the mystery was still intact.

I decided to retrace my steps. I knew Macy's had probably opened early for the day after Christmas, so I called them right away . . . and was put on hold for fifteen minutes.

Finally, an exasperated voice answered, "Macy's—how may I help you?"

"Hi," I said. "I was wondering if Santa was still there."

"Sir, it's the day after Christmas."

"I know—but is there any way to track down Santa?"

"Sir, I don't have time for this."

"No, you don't understand—I really need to have a word with the man who was Santa four days ago."

"Sir, I appreciate your desire to speak to Santa, but this is our busiest day of the year and I have other calls I must attend to.

Maybe you should just write him a letter—do you need the address?"

"One North Pole?" I guessed.

"Precisely. Have a nice day, sir."

And then she hung up.

The Strand, of course, didn't open early for the day after Christmas. I had to wait until nine-thirty to get through to someone there.

"Hi," I said, "I was wondering if Mark was around?"

"Mark?" a bored male voice asked.

"Yeah. Works at the information desk."

"There are about twenty of us named Mark. Can you be more specific?"

"Dark hair. Glasses. Ironic detachment. Scruff."

"That doesn't narrow it down."

"He's a little heavier than the rest of you?"

"Oh, I think I know the Mark you mean. He's not here today. Let me see—yeah, he's on tomorrow."

"Could you tell me his last name?"

"I'm sorry," the guy said, pleasantly enough, "but we don't disclose personal information to stalkers. If you want to leave a message, I can get it to him tomorrow."

"No, it's okay."

"I thought so."

So, not much progress there. But at least I knew he'd be around the next day.

As a last resort, I left Dov and Yohnny asleep in my mom's bed and ponied up another twenty-five bucks to hang with the waxed-out celebrities. But the woman guard was nowhere to be found, as if she'd been moved into the back room with the statues of the cast of *Baywatch*.

When I got back to the apartment, I decided to write to Lily anyway.

I fear you may have outmatched me, because now I find these words have nowhere to go. It's hard to answer a question you haven't been asked. It's hard to show that you tried unless you end up succeeding.

I stopped. It wasn't the same without the notebook. It didn't feel like a conversation. It felt like I was talking to silence.

I wished I had been there to see her dancing. To witness her there. To get to know her that way.

I could have looked up all the Lilys in Manhattan. I could have shown up on the doorsteps of all the Lilys of Brooklyn. I might have scoured the Lilys of Staten Island, sifted through the Lilys of the Bronx, and treated the Lilys of Queens like royalty. But I had a feeling I wasn't supposed to find her that way. She was not a needle. This was not a haystack. We were people, and people had ways of finding each other.

I could hear the sounds of sleep coming from my mom's bedroom—Dov snoring, Yohnny murmuring. I called Boomer to remind him of the party, then reminded myself who was going to be there.

Sofia. It was strange she hadn't told me she would be in town, but it wasn't that strange. We'd had the easiest breakup imaginable—it hadn't even felt like a breakup, just a parting. She had been going back to Spain, and nobody had expected us to stay together through that. Our love had been liking; our feelings had been ordinary, not Shakespearean. I still felt fondness for her—*fondness*, that pleasant, detached mix of admiration and sentiment, appreciation and nostalgia.

I tried to prepare myself for the inevitable conversation. The awkward teetering. The simple smiles. In other words, a return to our old ways. No sharp shocks of chemistry, just the low hum of knowing our place. We'd had her going-away party at Priya's, too, and I remembered it now. Even though we'd already had the talk about things ending when she left, I was still put in the boyfriend position; standing next to her for so many goodbyes made me feel the goodbye a little more deeply within myself. By the time most of the people had left, the feelings of fondness were nearly overwhelming me—not just a fondness for her, but a fondness for our friends, our time together, and the future with her that I'd never quite wanted.

"You look sad," she told me. We were alone in Priya's bedroom, only a few coats left on the bed.

"You look exhausted," I told her. "Exhausted from the goodbyes."

She nodded and said yes—a little redundancy I'd always noticed in her without ever saying something about it. She'd nod and say yes. She'd shake her head and say no.

If it hadn't been over, I might have hugged her. If it hadn't been over, I might have kissed her. Instead, I surprised both of us by saying, "I'm going to miss you."

It was one of those moments when you feel the future so much that it humbles the present. Her absence was palpable, even though she was still in the room.

"I'm going to miss you, too," she said. And then she slipped out of the moment, slipped out of the *us*, by adding, "I'm going to miss everyone."

We had never lied to each other (at least not to my knowledge). But we had never gone out of our way to reveal ourselves, either. Instead, we'd let the facts speak for themselves. *I think I'm in the mood for Chinese food. I have to go now so I can finish my homework. I really enjoyed that movie.* My *family is moving back to Spain, so I guess that means we're going to be apart.*

We hadn't vowed to write every day, and we hadn't written every day. We hadn't sworn to be true to each other, because there hadn't been much to be true to. Every now and then I would picture her there, in a country I'd only seen in her photo albums. And every now and then I'd write to say hello, to get the update, to stay in her life for no real reason beyond fondness. I told her things she already knew about our mutual friends and she told me things I didn't really need to know about her friends in Spain. At first, I'd asked her when she was going to come back to visit. Maybe she'd even said the holidays were a possibility. But I'd forgotten. Not because there was now an ocean between us, but because there had always been something in the way. Lily probably knew more about me in five days of back-and-forth than Sofia had known in our four months of dating.

Maybe, I thought, *it's not distance that's the problem, but how you handle it.*

When Dov, Yohnny, and I arrived at Boomer's place a little after six-thirty, we found him dressed like a prizefighter.

"I figured this was a good way to celebrate Boxing Day!" he said.

"It's not a costume party, Boomer," I pointed out. "You don't even have to bring boxes."

"Sometimes, Dash, you take the fun out of fun," Boomer said with a sigh. "And you know what's left then? *Nothing*." He trooped off to his room, came back with a Manta Ray T-shirt and a pair of jeans, and proceeded to put his jeans on right over his prizefighter shorts.

As we headed down the sidewalk, our own rock-bottom Rocky acted out his approximation of a boxer's moves, punching wildly into the air until he accidentally connected with the side of an old lady's grocery cart, toppling both of them. While Dov and Yohnny helped them back up, Boomer kept saying, "I'm so sorry! I guess I don't know my own strength!"

Luckily, Priya didn't live that much farther away. While we waited to be buzzed in, Dov asked, "Hey, did you bring the boot?"

I had not brought the boot. I figured if I saw some girl limping around the city wearing only one boot, I had enough of a recollection of the item to attempt a mental match.

"What boot?" Boomer asked.

"Lily's," Dov explained.

"You met Lily!" Boomer nearly exploded.

"No, I did not meet Lily," I replied.

"Who's Lily?" Priya asked. I hadn't even seen her appear in the doorway.

"A girl!" Boomer answered.

"Well, not really *a girl*," I corrected.

Priya raised an eyebrow. "A girl who's not really a girl?"

"She's a drag queen," Dov said.

"Lily Pad," Yohnny chimed in. "She does the most amazing version of 'It's Not Easy Being Green.' It reduces me to tears *every time*."

"Tears," Dov said.

"And Dash has her boot!" Boomer said.

"Hi, Dash."

Here she was. Over Priya's shoulder. A little hidden in the hallway light.

"Hi, Sofia."

Now, when I would have loved an interruption from Boomer, he fell silent. Everyone fell silent.

"It's good to see you."

"Yeah, it's good to see you, too."

It was like the full amount of time we'd been apart was falling between each sentence. There, on the front stoop, it was months of us looking at each other. Her hair was longer, her skin a little darker. And there was something else, too. I just couldn't figure it out. It was something in her eyes. Something in the way she was looking at me that wasn't like the way she'd looked at me before.

"Come in," Priya said. "There are some people here already."

It was peculiar—I wanted Sofia to hold back, to wait for me, like she would have when we'd been going out. But instead she led us into the party, with Priya, Boomer, Dov, and Yohnny between us.

Inside, it was hardly a rager. Priya's parents were not the type to leave the apartment while their daughter had a party. And they were of the mind that the strongest beverage offered should be sugared soda, and only that in moderation.

"I'm so glad you could make it," Priya was saying to me. "And that you're not in Sweden. I know Sofia would have been disappointed."

There was no reason for Priya to impart this information to me, so I immediately suspected there was much more to it than was being said. *Sofia would have been disappointed*. Did that mean she really wanted to see me? That she would have been crushed if I hadn't shown? Was this in fact the reason Priya had thrown the party in the first place?

I knew this was quite a leap to make, but when I looked at Sofia again, I found some footing on the other side. She was laughing at something Dov was saying to her, but she was looking at me, like he was the distraction and I was the conversation. She gestured with her head over to the drinks counter. I moved to meet her there.

"Fanta, Fresca, or Diet Rite?" I asked.

"I'll have a Fanta," she said.

"Fan-tastic," I replied.

As I got some ice and poured some soda, she said, "So how have you been?"

"Good," I said. "Busy. You know."

"No, I don't know," she said, taking the plastic cup from my hand. "Tell me."

There was a slight challenge in her voice.

"Well," I said, pouring myself a Fresca, "I was supposed to go to Sweden, but that had to be canceled at the last minute."

"Yeah, Priya told me."

"This soda has a massive amount of carbonation, doesn't it?" I gestured to where the Fresca was foaming over. "I mean, when this all settles down, I'll end up with, like, a demitasse of soda. I'm going to be pouring this drink all night."

I took a sip just as Sofia said, "Priya also told me you were studying the joys of gay sex."

Fresca. Up. My. Nose.

After I was done coughing, I said, "I'll bet she didn't mention the French pianism, did she? I'll bet she left that out entirely."

"You are studying French penises?"

"*Pianism*. Good lord, don't they teach you anything in Europe?"

This was a joke, but it didn't come out sounding entirely like a joke. As a result, Sofia was miffed. And if American girls make being miffed a sweet-and-sour emotion, European girls always manage to add an undercurrent of murder to it. At least in my limited experience.

"I can assure you," I told her, "that while I believe gay sex to be a beautiful, joyful thing, I do not think that I myself would find it particularly joyful, and thus my reading about its joys was all a part of a greater pursuit."

Sofia looked at me archly. "I see."

"Since when do you have an arch expression?" I asked. "There is a certain feistiness in your voice, too, that heretofore has not been present. It's extremely attractive, but not really the Sofia I knew before."

"Let's go to the bedroom," she replied.

"WHAT?"

She gestured behind me, where there were at least half a dozen people waiting to get some soda.

"We're in the way," she said. "And I have a present for you."

The path to the bedroom was not a clear one. It felt like every two steps we took, someone stopped Sofia to welcome her back, to ask her how Spain was, to tell her how amazing her hair looked. I hovered on the side, in the boyfriend position once more. And it felt just as awkward now as it had when I'd really been her boyfriend.

After a while, it appeared that Sofia had abandoned the bedroom plan, but when I moved to get myself some more Fresca, she actually took hold of my sleeve and extricated us from the kitchen.

Priya's door was closed, and when we opened it, we found Dov and Yohnny making out.

"Boys!" I cried.

Dov and Yohnny quickly refastened their jackets and put their hats back on over their yarmulkes.

"Sorry," Yohnny said.

"It's just that we haven't had a chance to . . . ," Dov continued.

"You spent all day in bed!"

"Yeah, but we were exhausted," Dov said.

"Completely wiped out," Yohnny echoed.

"And—"

"—it was *your mom's* bed."

They scooted past us, through the doorway.

"That happen a lot in Spain?" I asked Sofia.

"Yes. Only they're Catholic."

She went over to what I assumed to be her bag and took out a book.

"Here," she said. "This is for you."

"I didn't really get you anything," I sputtered. "I mean, I didn't know that you were going to be here, and—"

"Don't worry. It's your embarrassment at not having the thought that counts."

I was completely disarmed.

Sofia smiled and handed over the book. Its cover screamed *LORCA!* Literally, that was the title: *LORCA!* Which wasn't very *SUBTLE!* I started to thumb through.

"Oh, look," I said. "It's poetry! And in a language I don't speak!"

"I know you'll go out and buy a translation, just to make me believe you've read it."

"Touché. Absolutely true."

"But really, it's just a book that means a lot to me. He is a beautiful writer. And I think you'd like him."

"You'll have to give me Spanish lessons."

She laughed. "Just like you gave me English lessons?"

"Why did you just laugh?"

She shook her head. "No, it was sweet when you did that. Well, sweet *and* condescending."

"Condescending?"

She began to mimic my voice—inadequately, but enough so that I knew she was mimicking my voice. " 'What, you don't know what a *pizza bagel* is? Do you need me to explain the derivation of the word *derivation*? Is everything *copacetic*—I mean, *all right*?' "

"I never said that. I never said any of that."

"Maybe, maybe not. That's just how it felt. To me."

"Wow," I said. "You could've said something."

"I know. But it wasn't my thing, to 'say something.' And I liked that you never minded explaining things. I felt there was a lot that needed to be explained to me."

"And now?"

"Not as much."

"Why?"

"Do you really want to know?"

"Yes."

Sofia sighed and sat down on the bed.

"I fell in love. It didn't work out."

I sat down next to her.

"All in the past three months?"

She nodded. "Yes, all in the past three months."

"You didn't mention . . ."

"In my emails? No. He didn't want me talking to you at all, not to mention talking to you about *him*."

"I was such a threat?"

She shrugged. "I exaggerated you a little at first. To make him jealous. It worked in making him jealous, but didn't work so much in making him love me more."

"Was that why you didn't tell me you were coming?"

She shook her head. "No. I only knew I was coming last week. I convinced my parents I missed New York so much that they had to take me here for the holidays."

"But really, you wanted to get away from him?"

"No, that wouldn't work. I just thought it would be nice to see people. Anyway, what about you? Are you in love with anybody?"

"I'm not sure."

"Ah. Then there *is* someone. *The Joy of Gay Sex?*"

"Yes," I said. "But not in the way you're thinking."

So I told her. About the notebook. About Lily. Sometimes I looked at her while I was talking. Sometimes I was talking to the room, to my hands, to the air. It was too much at once to be so close to Sofia, yet also trying to conjure some closeness to Lily.

"Oh my," Sofia said when I was through. "You think you've finally found the girl in your head."

"What do you mean?"

"I mean, like most guys, you carry around this girl in your head, who is exactly who you want her to be. The person you think you will love the most. And every girl you are with gets measured against this girl in your head. So this girl with the red notebook—it makes sense. If you never meet her, she never has to get measured. She can be the girl in your head."

"You make it sound like I don't want to get to know her."

"Of course you want to get to know her. But at the same time, you want to feel like you already know her. That you will know her instantly. Such a fairy tale."

"A fairy tale?"

Sofia smiled at me. "You think fairy tales are only for girls? Here's a hint—ask yourself who wrote them. I assure you, it wasn't just the women. It's the great male fantasy—all it takes is one dance to know that she's the one. All it takes is the sound of her song from the tower, or a look at her sleeping face. And right away you know—this is the girl in your head, sleeping or dancing or singing in front of you. Yes, girls want their princes, but boys want their princesses just as much. And they don't want a very long courtship. They want to know immediately."

She actually put her hand on my leg and squeezed. "You see, Dash—I was never the girl in your head. And you were never the boy in my head. I think we both knew that. It's only when we try to make the girl or boy in our head real that the true trouble comes. I did that with Carlos, and it was a bad failure. Be careful what you're doing, because no one is ever who you want them to be. And the less you really know them, the more likely you are to confuse them with the girl or boy in your head."

"Wishful thinking," I said.

Sofia nodded. "Yes. You should never wish for wishful thinking."

ten

(Lily)

December 26th

"You're grounded."

Grandpa stared at me in all seriousness. I couldn't help but burst out laughing.

Grandpas give out dollar bills and bicycles and hugs. They don't give punishments to grandchildren! Everybody knows that.

Grandpa had unexpectedly driven back to NYC, all day and night, all the way from Florida! Once he got home, he immediately went looking for me and my brother to check on us, only to find my brother passed out in bed, lost under a sea of blankets and snotty tissues, and worse, his Lily Bear not only not upstairs in her Lily pad but nowhere to be found in her own family's apartment.

Luckily, I arrived home around three-thirty in the morning, within minutes of Grandpa's discovery of my disappearance. He'd only had enough time to nearly have a heart attack, and to search for me inside every closet and cabinet in the apartment. Before Grandpa had a chance to call the police, along with my parents and several thousand other relatives to instigate a full-on worldwide panic, I waltzed in the door, still breathless and flushed from the night's club scene excitement.

Grandpa's first words to me when he caught sight of me were not "Where have you been?" That came second. First was "Why are you only wearing one boot? And dear God, is that my sister's old majorette boot from high school on your foot?" He spoke from the kitchen floor in my apartment, where he was lying down, trying to determine, I believe, if I was hiding beneath the sink.

"Grandpa!" I cried out. I ran to smother him in day after Christmas kisses. I was so happy to see him, and exhilarated from the night out, despite how I'd ended it by sacrificing one of my great-aunt's shoes to the gumshoes and neglecting to return the notebook for Snarl.

Grandpa wasn't having my affection. He turned his cheek to me, then went for the "you're-grounded routine." When I failed to meet his pronouncement with fear, he frowned and demanded, "Where have you been? It's four in the morning!"

"Three-thirty," I corrected him. "It's three-thirty in the morning."

"You're in a world of trouble, young lady," he said.

I giggled.

"I'm serious!" he said. "You'd better have a good explanation."

Well, I've been corresponding with a complete stranger in a notebook, telling him my innermost feelings and thoughts and then blindly going to mystery places where he dares me to go. . . .

No, that wouldn't go over so well.

For the first time in my life, I lied to Grandpa.

"This friend from my soccer team had a party where her band played a Hanukkah show. I went to hear them."

"THIS MUSIC REQUIRES YOU TO GET HOME AT FOUR IN THE MORNING?"

"Three-thirty," I said again. "It's, like, a religious thing. The band's not allowed to play before midnight on the night after Christmas Day."

"I see," Grandpa said skeptically. "And don't you have a curfew, young lady?"

The invocation not once, but twice, of the dreaded *young lady* term of endearment should have put me on high fear alert, but I was too giddy from the night's adventures to care.

"I'm pretty sure my curfew is suspended on holidays," I said. "Like alternate side of the street parking rules."

"LANGSTON!" Grandpa yelled. "GET IN HERE!"

It took a few minutes, but my brother finally moped into the kitchen, trailing a comforter, looking like he'd been woken from a coma.

"Grandpa!" Langston wheezed, surprised. "What are you doing home?" I knew Langston was relieved now to be sick, because if he wasn't, Benny would surely have spent the night, and overnight companions of the romantic sort have not yet been authorized by the designated authority figures. Langston and I both would have been busted.

"Never mind me," Grandpa said. "Did you allow Lily to go out on Christmas night to hear her friend's music?"

Langston and I shared a knowing glance: Our secrets needed to stay just that, secrets. I initiated our covert code from childhood, batting my eyelids up and down, so Langston would know to confirm what had just been asked of him.

"Yes," Langston coughed. "Since I'm sick, I wanted Lily to go out and try to have some fun on the holiday. The band was playing in, like, the basement of someone's brownstone on the Upper West Side. I arranged a car service to take her home. Totally safe, Grandpa."

Quick thinking for a sickie. Sometimes I really love my brother.

Grandpa eyed the two of us suspiciously, not sure whether he'd been caught in a siblings' web of deceit and got-your-back-yo.

"Go to bed," Grandpa barked. "Both of you. I'll deal with you in the morning."

"Why *are* you home, Grandpa?" I asked.

"Never mind. Go to bed."

I couldn't fall asleep after the klezmer night, so I wrote in the notebook instead.

I'm sorry I didn't return our notebook to you. It was such a simple task, I mean. Yet I botched it. Why I'm writing to you now even though I have no idea how to return this to you, I don't know. There's just something about you—and this notebook—that gives me faith.

Were you even at the club tonight? At first I thought you might have been one of those gumshoe boys, but I quickly realized that was impossible. For one thing, those boys seemed too upbeat. It's not that I imagine you to be a miserable person, by the way. But I don't see you as the grinning type, either. Also, I feel like I would have known, like a sensory perception, if you had been standing there near me. For another thing, even though I don't know how to picture you yet (every time I try, you seem to be holding up a red Moleskine notebook to cover your face), I have a solid feeling you don't have hair ringlets dangling from your temples. Just a hunch. (But if you do, could I braid them sometime?)

So I left you with a boot and no notebook. Or, rather, I left it with two complete strangers.

You don't feel like a stranger to me.

I'll be wearing the spare boot at all times, just in case you happen to be looking for me.

Cinderella was such a dork. She left behind her glass slipper at the ball and then went right back to her stepmonster's house. It seems to me she should have worn the glass slipper always, to make herself easier to find. I always hoped that after the prince found Cinderella and they rode away in their magnificent carriage, after a few miles she turned to him and said, "Could you drop me off down the road, please? Now that I've finally escaped my life of horrific abuse, I'd like to see something of the world, you know? Maybe backpack across Europe or Asia? I'll catch back up with you later, Prince, once I've found my own way. Thanks for finding me, though! Super-sweet of you. And you can keep the slippers. They'll probably cause bunions if I keep wearing 'em."

I might have liked to share a dance with you. If I may be so bold to say.

Neither rain, nor sleet, nor gloom of the day after Christmas could keep Grandpa from meeting his buddies for coffee the following afternoon.

I went along, feeling like Grandpa needed the moral support.

While Grandpa was in Florida, where he usually spends the winters, he had indeed proposed on Christmas Day to Mabel, who lives in his complex down there. I have never liked Mabel. Aside from her always telling me and my brother to call her Glamma, her list of step grandmother-to-be infractions is long. Here's just a sampling: (1) The candies in the bowl in her living room are always stale. (2) She tries to put lipstick or rouge on me even though I don't like makeup. (3) She's a terrible cook. (4) Her vegetarian lasagna, which she made sure to mention a million times she made because I'm such a pain that I won't eat meat, tastes like glue with grated zucchini. (5) She kind of makes me want to barf. (6) So does her lasagna. (7) And the candies in her living room.

Shockingly, Mabel turned down Grandpa's proposal! I thought *my* Christmas morning had been sucky—but Grandpa's had been way worse. When Grandpa presented her with a ring, Mabel told Grandpa she likes the single life and likes having Grandpa as her winter fella, but she's got other fellas during the rest of the year, just like he has other gals during the non-winter months! She told him to get his money back for the ring and use it to take her on a swell vacation somewhere grand.

Grandpa never imagined she would turn down his proposal, so rather than consider the logic of Mabel's answer, he typically returned home to New York a few hours later, totally heartbroken! Especially when he came home to find his sweet little Lily bear was out having a wild night on the town. Like, in twenty-four hours, his whole world turned upside down.

It's good for the old fella, I think.

However, Grandpa seems, like, genuinely depressed. So that afternoon, I stayed close to Grandpa's side as he met with his buddies, all of them retired business owners from around the neighborhood who've been meeting regularly for coffee since my mom was a baby, so they could weigh in with their opinions about Grandpa's Christmas misadventure. Most of his buddies' names are complicated and involve many syllables, so Langston and I have always referred to them by the names of their former businesses.

The roundtable discussion of Mabel proceeded like this:

Mr. Cannoli told Grandpa, "Arthur, give her time. She'll come around."

Mr. Dumpling said, "You virile man, Arthur! This lady not have you, someone better will!"

Mr. Borscht sighed, "This woman who turns down a marriage proposal on a day that's sacred to you gentile people is worthy of your heart, Arthur? I think not."

Mr. Curry exclaimed, "I will find you another lady, my friend!"

"He *has* plenty of other lady friends here in New York," I reminded the group. "He just"—this killed me to say, I want to note—"seems to want Mabel for keeps."

Amazingly, I did not choke on my Lilyccino (foamed milk with shaved chocolate on top, courtesy of Mr. Cannoli's son-in-law, who now runs Mr. Cannoli's bakery) when I said this. Grandpa's face—always so chipper and eager—looked so uncharacteristically downcast. I couldn't stand it.

"This one!" Grandpa said to his buddies, pointing at me sitting next to him. "Do you know what she did? Went to a party last night! Stayed out past her curfew! As if my

Christmas hadn't been lousy enough, I come home and panic because Lily bear's nowhere to be found. She strolls in a few minutes later—*at four in the morning!*—seemingly without a care in the world."

"Three-thirty," I stated. Again.

Mr. Dumpling said, "Were there boys at this party?"

Mr. Borscht said, "Arthur, this child should be out so late at night? Where boys might be?"

Mr. Cannoli said, "I'll kill the kid who . . ."

Mr. Curry turned to me. "A nice young lady, she does not . . ."

"Time for me to walk my dogs!" I said. If I spent any more time with these old men in their House of Coffee Woe, they'd conspire to have me locked in my room away from boys till I was thirty years old.

I left the gentlemen to their kvetching so I could play some catching with my favorite dog-walking clients.

I had my two favorite dogs with me in the park—Lola and Dude, a little pug-Chi mix and a giant chocolate Lab. It's true love between them. You can tell by how eagerly they sniff each other's butts.

I called Grandpa from my cell phone.

"You need to learn to compromise," I said.

"Excuse me?" he said.

"Dude used to hate Lola because she was so little and cute and took all the attention. Then he learned to play nice with her so he could have the attention, too. Dude compromised, like you should. Just because Mabel turned down your proposal doesn't mean you should break up with her over it!"

This concession was very big of me, I agree.

"I'm supposed to take love advice from a sixteen-year-old girl?" Grandpa said.

"Yes." I hung up before he could point out how completely not qualified I was to dole out such advice.

I've got to learn to stop being so Lily sweet and transition myself into a hard bargainer.

For instance.

If I am forced to move to Fiji next September, which is when Langston said Dad's new job would start if Dad decides to take it, I am going to demand a puppy. I'm realizing there is a lot of parental guilt to be mined from this situation, and I plan to use it to my animal kingdom benefit.

I sat down at a bench while Lola chased Dude in the dog park. From the next bench, I noticed a teenage boy wearing an argyle print beret tilted backward, squinting at me like he knew me. "Lily?" he asked.

I stared at him more closely.

"Edgar Thibaud!" I growled.

He came over to my bench. How *dare* Edgar Thibaud recognize me and have the audacity to approach me, after the living hell he made my elementary school years at PS 41?

Also.

How *dare* Edgar Thibaud have used the past few years to grow so . . . tall? And . . . good-looking?

Edgar Thibaud said, "I wasn't sure it was you, then I noticed the weird boot on one foot and the beat-up Chuck on the other, and I remembered that red pom-pom hat. I knew it could only be you. 'Sup?"

'*Sup?* he wanted to know? So casually? Like he hadn't ruined my life and killed my gerbil?

Edgar Thibaud sat down next to me. His (deep green, and rather beautiful) eyes looked a little hazy, like perhaps he'd been smoking from the peace pipe.

"I'm the captain of my soccer team," I announced.

I don't really know how to talk to boys. In person. Which is probably why I've become dependent on a notebook for creative expression of a potentially romantic nature.

Edgar laughed at my idiotic response. But it wasn't a mean laugh. It sounded like an appreciative one. "Of course you are. Same old Lily. You've even got the same black-rimmed glasses like you wore in elementary school."

"I heard you got kicked out of high school for some conspiracy plot."

"Just suspended. It was like a vacation, actually. And check you out, keeping tabs on me all this time." Edgar Thibaud leaned into my ear. "Anyone tell you that you grew up to be sort of cute? In, like, a misfit type of way?"

I didn't know whether to be flattered or outraged.

I did know his breath in my ear sent very unfamiliar shivers through my body.

"What are you doing here?" I asked him, needing trivial conversation to distract me from the sordid thoughts my mind was starting to spin about Edgar Thibaud . . . with his shirt off. I could feel my face turning hot, blushing. And yet my dialogue was no racier than: "You didn't go away for Christmas like everybody else?"

"My parents went skiing in Colorado without me. I annoyed them too much."

"Oh, that's too bad."

"No, I did it on purpose. A week without their bourgeois hypocrisy is a week of paradise."

Was Edgar Thibaud even speaking? I couldn't stop staring at his face. Just how exactly had it turned so handsome in the intervening years?

I said, "I think that's a girl's beret you're wearing."

"Is it?" Edgar asked. "Cool." He cocked his head to the side, pleased. "I like girls. And their hats." He reached to grab my hat from my head. "May I?"

Edgar Thibaud had obviously evolved over the last few years if he had the decency to ask for my hat, rather than snatch it off my head and then probably throw it to the dogs to play with, as the old Edgar on the school yard would have done.

I moved my head down so he could take my hat. He placed my red pom-pom hat on his head, then put his beret on mine.

His beret on my head felt so warm and . . . forbidden. I liked it.

"Want to go to a party with me tonight?" Edgar asked.

"Grandpa probably won't let me go!" I blurted out.

"So?" Edgar said.

Exactly!

Clearly, it was time for Lily to have the kind of boy adventures that would allow her to give legitimate love advice, later in the future.

I might have arrived in Tompkins Square Park with my heart still intent on a Snarl, but right in front of me, I had a real, live Edgar Thibaud.

The secret tactic of a good hard bargainer is to know when to compromise.

For instance.

I will demand a puppy if I am forced to move to Fiji.

But I will settle for a bunny.

eleven

–Dash–

December 27th

So I found myself once again at the Strand.

It hadn't been a late night—Priya's parties tended to fizzle before the Cinderella hour, and this was no exception. Sofia and I stayed together most of the evening, but once we emerged from the bedroom and started to mingle with everyone else, we stopped talking to each other and instead talked as two parts of the larger group. Yohnny and Dov left to see their friend Matthue slam some poetry, and Thibaud never showed. I might have lingered until Sofia and I were almost alone again, but Boomer had consumed about thirteen too many cups of Mountain Dew and was threatening to make holes in the ceiling with his head. Sofia was going to be around until New Year's, so I said we had to get together, and she said yeah, that'd be good. We left it at that.

Now it was eleven the next morning and I was back in the bookstore, resisting the siren call of the stacks in order to find and, if necessary, interrogate Mark. I was walking with a lady's boot under my arm, like some pallbearer for the post-melt Wicked Witch of the West.

The guy at the information desk was thin and blond, bespectacled and tweeded. In other words, not the guy I was looking for.

"Hey," I said. "Is Mark here?"

The guy barely looked up from the Saramago novel in his lap.

"Oh," he said, "are you the stalker?"

"I have a question to ask him, that's all. That hardly makes me a stalker."

Now the guy looked at me. "It depends on the question, doesn't it? I mean, I'm sure stalkers have questions, too."

"Yes," I conceded, "but their questions usually run along the lines of 'Why won't you love me?' and 'Why can't I die by your side?' I'm more along the lines of 'What can you tell me about this boot?' "

"I'm not sure I can help you."

"This is the information desk, isn't it? Aren't you obligated to give me information?"

The guy sighed. "Fine. He's shelving. Now let me finish this chapter, okay?"

I thanked him, though not profusely.

The Strand proudly proclaims itself as home to eighteen miles of books. I have no idea how this is calculated. Does one stack all the books on top of each other to get the eighteen miles? Or do you put them end to end, to create a bridge between Manhattan and, say, Short Hills, New Jersey, eighteen miles away? Were there eighteen miles of shelves? No one knew. We all just took the bookstore at its word, because if you couldn't trust a bookstore, what could you trust?

Whatever the measurement, the applicable fact was that the

Strand had lots of aisles to shelve. Which meant that I had to weave in and out of dozens of narrow spaces—dodging disgruntled and pregruntled patrons, ladders, and haphazardly placed book cairns in order to find Mark in the Military History section. He was buckling a little under the weight of an illustrated history of the Civil War, but otherwise his appearance and demeanor were similar to that of when we first met.

"Mark!" I said in a tone of holiday camaraderie, as if we were members of the same eating club who had somehow found ourselves in the lobby of the same brothel.

He looked at me for a second, then turned back to the shelf.

"Did you have yourself a merry little Christmas?" I continued. "Did you make the yuletide gay?"

He brandished a volume of Winston Churchill's memoirs and pointed it accusingly at me. The jowly prime minister stared from the jacket impassively, as if he were the judge of this sudden contest.

"What do you want?" Mark asked. "I'm not going to tell you anything."

I took the boot from under my arm and placed it on Churchill's face.

"Tell me whose boot this is."

He (Mark, not Churchill) was surprised by the appearance of footwear—I could tell. And I could also glean from the knowledge he was trying to hide that he knew the identity of its owner.

Still, he was obstinate, in the way that only truly miserable people can be obstinate.

"Why should I tell you?" he asked, with no small amount of petulance.

"If you tell me, I will leave you alone," I said. "And if you don't tell me, I am going to grab the nearest ghostwritten James Patterson romance novel and I am going to follow you through this store reading it out loud until you relent. Would you prefer me to read from *Daphne's Three Tender Months with Harold* or *Cindy and John's House of Everlasting Love?* I guarantee, your sanity and your indie street cred won't last a chapter. And they are very, *very* short chapters."

Now I could see the fright beneath the defiance.

"You're evil," he said. "You know that?"

I nodded, even though I usually saved the word *evil* for perpetrators of genocide.

He continued, "And if I tell you, you'll stop calling and coming by. Even if you don't like what you find?"

That seemed uncharitable to Lily, but I would not let my pique peak.

"I will stop calling," I said calmly. "And while I will never allow myself to be banned from the Strand, I promise not to seek information when you are sitting at that particular desk, and if you are ever working the cash register, I will make sure to maneuver so that you are not the clerk who rings me up. Will that suffice?"

"There's no need to snarl," Mark said.

"That wasn't snarling," I pointed out. "Not even remotely. If you're planning to make it in the bookselling arena, I would advise you to learn to make the distinction between a snarl and a well-placed bon mot. They are not one and the same."

I took out a pen and offered him the inside of my arm.

"Just write down the address and we'll be squared away."

He took the pen and wrote down an address on East Twenty-second Street, pressing down a little too hard on my skin.

"Thank you, sir," I said, reclaiming the boot. "I'll be sure to put in a good word with Mr. Strand for you!"

As I exited the aisle, I felt a treatise on American naval misadventure shot-put past my head. I left it on the ground for the shot-putter to reshelve.

I will admit: There was a part of me that wanted to wash my arm. Not because of Mark's handwriting, which was the kind of chicken scratch more associated with death row convicts than bookstore clerks. No—it wasn't the handwriting I was tempted to erase, but the information it conveyed. Because here was the key to meeting Lily . . . and I wasn't sure I wanted to put it in the lock.

Sofia's words were nagging at me: Was Lily the girl in my head? And if she was, wasn't reality bound to be disappointing?

No, I had to reassure myself. *The words in the red Moleskine were not written by the girl in your head. You have to trust the words. They do not create anything more than themselves.*

When I rang the doorbell, I could hear it chime throughout the brownstone, the kind of intonation that lets you believe a servant will be answering the door. For at least a minute, there was a responding silence—I shifted the boot from hand to hand and debated whether to ring again. My restraint was a rare victory of politeness over expediency, and I was rewarded eventually by a shuffle of feet and a maneuvering of locks and bolts.

The door was answered by neither a butler nor a maid. Instead, it was answered by a museum guard from Madame Tussauds.

"I know you!" I sputtered.

The old woman gave me a long, hard look.

"And I know that boot," she replied.

"Yes," I said. "There's that."

I had no idea whether she remembered me from the museum. But then she opened the door a little wider and motioned for me to come in.

I half expected to be greeted by a waxwork statue of Jackie Chan. (In other words, I expected her to have taken some of her work home with her.) But instead, the foyer was an antechamber of antiques, like suddenly I had stepped back into a dozen decades at once, and none of them were later than 1940. Next to the door was a stand filled with umbrellas—at least a dozen of them, each with its own curved wood handle.

The old woman caught me staring.

"You've never seen an umbrella stand before?" she asked haughtily.

"I was just trying to imagine a situation where one person would need twelve umbrellas. It seems almost indecent to have so many, when there are so many people who don't have any."

She nodded at this, then asked, "What's your name, young man?"

"Dash," I told her.

"Dash?"

"It's short for Dashiell," I explained.

"I never said it wasn't," she replied flatly.

She led me into a room that could only be called a parlor. The drapery was so thick and the furniture so cloaked that I half expected to find Sherlock Holmes thumb-wrestling with Jane Austen in the corner. It wasn't as dusty or smoky as one expects a parlor to be, but all the wood had the weight of card catalogs and the fabric seemed soaked in wine. Knee-high sculptures perched in corners and by the fireplace, while jacketless books crowded on shelves, peering down like old professors too tired to speak to one another.

I felt very much at home.

Following a gesture from the old woman, I settled on a settee. When I breathed in, the air smelled like old money.

"Is Lily home?" I asked.

The woman settled down across from me and laughed.

"Who's to say I'm not Lily?" she asked back.

"Well," I said, "a few of my friends have actually met Lily, and I like to think they would've mentioned if she were eighty."

"Eighty!" The old woman feigned shock. "I'll have you know I'm not a year over forty-three."

"With all due respect," I said, "if you're forty-three, then I'm a fetus."

She leaned back in her chair and examined me like she was contemplating a purchase. Her hair was fastened tightly in a bun, and I felt fastened just as tightly into her scrutiny.

"Seriously," I said. "Where's Lily?"

"I need to gauge your intentions," she said, "before I can allow you to dillydally with my niece."

"I assure you I have neither dillying nor dallying on my mind," I replied. "I simply want to meet her. In person. You see, we've been—"

She raised her hand to cut me off. "I am aware of your epistolary flirtation. Which is all well and good—as long as it's well and good. Before I ask you some questions, perhaps you would like some tea?"

"That would depend on what kind of tea you were offering."

"So diffident! Suppose it was Earl Grey."

I shook my head. "Tastes like pencil shavings."

"Lady Grey."

"I don't drink beverages named after beheaded monarchs. It seems so *tacky*."

"Chamomile?"

"Might as well sip butterfly wings."

"Green tea?"

"You can't be serious."

The old woman nodded her approval. "I wasn't."

"Because you know when a cow chews grass? And he or she chews and chews and chews? Well, green tea tastes like French-kissing that cow after it's done chewing all that grass."

"Would you like some mint tea?"

"Only under duress."

"English breakfast."

I clapped my hands. "Now you're talking!"

The old woman made no move to get the tea.

"I'm afraid I'm out," she said.

"No worries," I replied. "Do you want your boot back in the meantime?"

I handed it her way and she took it for a moment before handing it back to me.

"This was from my majorette days," she said.

"You were in the army?"

"An army of cheer, Dash. I was in an army of *cheer*."

There was a series of urns on the bookshelf behind her. I wondered if they were decorative or if they contained some of her relatives' remains.

"So what else can I tell you?" I asked. "I mean, to get you to reveal Lily to me."

She triangled her fingers under her chin. "Let's see. Are you a bed wetter?"

"Am I a . . . ?"

"Bed wetter. I am asking if you are a bed wetter."

I knew she was trying to get me to blink. But I wouldn't.

"No, ma'am. I leave my beds dry."

"Not even a little drip every now and then?"

"I'm trying hard to see how this is germane."

"I'm gauging your honesty. What is the last periodical you read methodically?"

"*Vogue*. Although, in the interest of full disclosure, that's mostly because I was in my mother's bathroom, enduring a rather long bowel movement. You know, the kind that requires Lamaze?"

"What adjective do you feel the most longing for?"

That was easy. "I will admit I have a soft spot for *fanciful*."

"Let's say I have a hundred million dollars and offer it to you. The only condition is that if you take it, a man in China will fall off his bicycle and die. What do you do?"

"I don't understand why it matters whether he's in China or not. And of course I wouldn't take the money."

The old woman nodded.

"Do you think Abraham Lincoln was a homosexual?"

"All I can say for sure is that he never made a pass at me."

"Are you a museumgoer?"

"Is the pope a churchgoer?"

"When you see a flower painted by Georgia O'Keeffe, what comes to mind?"

"That's just a transparent ploy to get me to say the word *vagina*, isn't it? There. I've said it. Vagina."

"When you leave a public bus, is there anything special that you do?"

"I thank the driver."

"Good, good," she said. "Now—tell me your intentions regarding Lily."

There was a pause. Perhaps too long a pause. Because, to be forthright, I hadn't really thought about my intentions. Which meant I had to think aloud while answering.

"Well," I said, "it's not as if I've come to take her to the sock hop, or ask her to go double-spooning in some tapioca, if that's what you mean. We've already established my position on dillying and dallying, which right now is chaste with a chance for inveterate lust, depending on the ripeness of our first interactions. I have been told by a source of surprising trustworthiness that I must not paint her too much with my ideas of her, and my intention is to follow that advice. But really? Completely uncharted territory here. *Terra enigma*. It could be a future or it could be a folly. If she's cut from your cloth, I have a sense we might get along."

"I think she's still figuring out her pattern," the woman told me. "So I won't comment on the cloth. I find her to be a delight. And while sometimes delights can be tiresome, mostly they are . . ."

"Delightful?" I offered.

"*Pure*. They're burnished by their own hopes."

I sighed.

"What is it?" the old woman asked.

"I'm persnickety," I confessed. "Not, incidentally, to the point of being snarly. But still. Delightful and persnickety are not a common blend."

"Do you want to know why I never married?"

"The question wasn't at the top of my list," I admitted.

The old woman made me meet her eye. "Listen to me: I never married because I was too easily bored. It's an awful, self-defeating trait to have. It's much better to be too easily interested."

"I see," I said. But I didn't. Not then. Not yet.

Instead, I was looking around the room and thinking: *Of all the places I've been, this is the one that seems the most like a place that a red notebook would take me.*

"Dash," the old woman said. A simple statement, like she was holding my name in her hand, holding it out to me like I'd held out her boot.

"Yes?" I said.

"Yes?" she echoed.

"Do you think it's time?" I asked.

She got up from her chair and said, "Let me make a phone call."

twelve

(Lily)

December 26th

"Do you still kill gerbils?" I asked Edgar Thibaud.

We were standing outside the brownstone apartment building of some girl he goes to school with who was having a party that night.

From the street, we could see the party through the living room window. The scene looked very polite. No wild noises that one would expect to come from a teenager's party boomed down to the street. We could see two parental types wandering through the living room, offering juice boxes and Mountain Dews on silver trays, which may have explained the lack of noise, and the open curtains.

"This party's gonna suck," Edgar Thibaud said. "Let's go somewhere else."

"You didn't answer my question," I said. "Do you still kill gerbils, Edgar Thibaud?"

If he gave me a sarcastic answer back, our newly discovered truce would end as abruptly as it had started.

"Lily," Edgar Thibaud said, oozing sincerity. He took my hand in his. My hand, now oozing sweat, quivered from his touch. "I'm so sorry about your gerbil. Truly. I would never knowingly harm a sentient being." His lips placed a contrite peck on my knuckles.

I happen to know that Edgar Thibaud graduated from killing gerbils in first grade to becoming one of those fourth-grade boys who use magnifying glasses to direct the sun to fry worms and other random insects in alleyways.

It is possibly true what Grandpa's buddies have repeatedly told me: Teenage boys cannot be trusted. Their intentions are not pure.

This must be part of Mother Nature's master plan—making these boys so irresistibly cute, in such a naughty way, that the purity of their intentions becomes irrelevant.

"Where would you rather go instead?" I asked Edgar. "I have to be home by nine or my grandpa will freak."

I'd lied to Grandpa a second time. I'd told him an emergency holiday soccer practice had been convened because our team was on a massive losing streak. Only because he was moping over that Mabel lady did he fall for it.

Edgar Thibaud answered in a baby voice. "Gwanpaah won't wet wittle Wily stay up wate?"

"Are you being mean?"

"No," he said, his face turning serious. "I salute you and your curfews, Lily. With apologies for the brief and unnecessary foray into baby talk. If you have to be home by nine, that probably only leaves us enough time for a movie. Have you seen *Gramma Got Run Over by a Reindeer*?"

"No," I said.

I'm getting good at this lying.

* * *

I am trying to embrace danger.

Once again, I found myself locked in a bathroom, communing with Snarl. The movie theater's bathroom was a bit cleaner than the previous night's music club's, and the evening show meant the cinema wasn't brimming with toddlers. But once again, life and action brimmed all around me, yet all I wanted to do was write in a red notebook.

Danger comes in many forms, I suppose. For some people, it might be jumping off a bridge or climbing impossible mountains. For others, it could be a tawdry love affair or telling off a mean-looking bus driver because he doesn't like to stop for noisy teenagers. It could be cheating at cards or eating a peanut even though you're allergic.

For me, danger might be getting out from under the protective cloak of my family and venturing into the world more on my own, even though I don't know what—or who—awaits me. I wish you were part of this plan. But are you dangerous? Somehow I doubt it. I'm scared you're just a figment of my imagination.

I think it's time to experience life outside the notebook.

Edgar Thibaud whooped with laughter at fat Gramma on the screen as I returned to my seat. The movie was so stupid I had no choice but to fixate my stare away from the screen and onto Edgar Thibaud's biceps. He has some kind of magical muscle arms—not too bulky, not too skimpy. They're cut just right. I was rather mesmerized.

The hand attached to the end of Edgar's arm decided to get frisky. His eyes never left the screen, but his hand discreetly landed on my thigh, while Edgar's mouth continued to guffaw over the macabre massacre that was befalling

Gramma on the screen as the reindeer's tusks once again ran her over.

I couldn't believe the boldness of the maneuver. (Reindeer's *and* Edgar's.) I was all for danger, but we hadn't even kissed yet. (I mean, me and Edgar, not me and Reindeer. I love animals, but not that much.)

I've waited all my life for that first kiss. I wasn't going to ruin it by allowing whole bases to be skipped.

"Ruff ruff," I barked at Edgar Thibaud as his hand drew circles over the embroidered poodle on my poodle skirt. I returned his hand to the armrest, the better perch from which I could return to admiring his bicep.

In the backseat of the cab home, I let Edgar unbutton my sweater and take it off me. I pulled my skirt down myself.

I was wearing my soccer shorts and shirt underneath the sweater and skirt in case Grandpa was waiting for me when I got home. I took a water bottle from my purse and wet my face and hair so I'd appear sweaty.

The meter on the cab read $6.50 and 8:55 p.m. as we pulled up to the curb in front of my building.

Edgar leaned into me. I knew it could be about to happen.

I don't delude myself that the first real kiss I experience will lead to a happily ever after. I don't believe in any of that Prince Charming nonsense. I also don't delude myself that I'd wish for it to happen in the backseat of a smelly taxi.

Edgar whispered in my ear, "Do you have money for your half of the fare? I'm kind of broke and won't have enough for the driver to drop me off after you otherwise." His index finger quickly brushed across my neck.

I shoved him away, even though I longed for more of his touch. But not in a taxi, for goodness' sake!

I gave Edgar Thibaud five dollars, and a million silent curses.

Edgar's mouth moved *thisclose* to mine. "I'll get the fare next time," he murmured. I turned my cheek to him.

"You're not going to make this easy for me, are you, Lily?" Edgar Thibaud said.

I ignored his sleek bicep peeking at me from under his snug sweater.

"You did kill my gerbil," I reminded him.

"I love a hunt, Lily."

"Good."

I stepped out of the cab and shut the door.

"Just like that reindeer loved a hunt!" Edgar called out to me from the window as the cab moved toward its next destination.

December 27th

Where ARE you?

It seemed I was destined to commune by notebook with Snarl most frequently while I was lodged in bathrooms.

This day's bathroom was at an Irish pub on East Eleventh Street in Alphabet City. It was one of those pubs that are more family places during the day and become watering holes at night. I was there during the day, so Grandpa could relax.

I hadn't wanted to lie to Grandpa again, so I'd told him the truth—that I was meeting my Christmas caroling group for a reunion. We were going to sing "Happy Birthday" to angry Aryn, the vegan riot grrrl, whose twenty-first birthday was December 27.

I didn't mention the part to Grandpa about how I'd texted Edgar Thibaud to meet me there, too. Grandpa hadn't asked me whether Edgar Thibaud would be at the birthday party; therefore, I had not lied to him.

Since it was Aryn's twenty-first birthday, my caroling troupe had taken up drinking songs instead of traditional Christmas hymns to usher in her legal drinking age. The group was on its fourth round of beers by the time I arrived. *And Mary McGregor / Well, she was a pretty whore,* they sang. Edgar had yet to appear. When I heard the dirty words being sung, I quickly excused myself to the bathroom and opened the familiar red notebook to write a new entry.

But what was there left to say?

I still wore the one boot and one sneaker, just in case Snarl should find me, but if I was going to face danger head-on, I probably had to acknowledge that in forgetting to return the red notebook, I'd blown it with Snarl. I'd have to settle on the brand of danger Edgar Thibaud offered as my most promising consolation prize.

My phone rang, displaying a photo of a certain house in Dyker Heights decked out in celestial orbit Christmas lights. I answered. "Happy two days after Christmas, Uncle Carmine." I realized I'd taken the notebook back from him on Christmas Day, and yet never asked him for any clues about Snarl. "Did you ever get a look at the boy who returned the red notebook at your house?"

"I might have, Lily bear," Uncle Carmine said. "But that's

not what I called to talk to you about. I heard your grandpa came back from Florida early and that things didn't go so well down there. Is this true?"

"True. Now, about that boy . . ."

"I didn't get any information about him, sweetheart. Although the kid did do a curious thing. You know the giant nutcracker we place on the lawn, near the fifteen-foot red soldier?"

"Lieutenant Clifford Dog? Sure."

"Well, when your mystery friend left behind the red notebook, he also deposited something else. The most butt-ugly puppet I've ever seen."

Snarl couldn't have. Did he?

"Did it look like an early Beatle who'd gotten a makeover for a Muppet movie?"

Uncle Carmine said, "You could say that. A really *bad* makeover."

Another call rang on my cell, this time displaying my favorite picture of Mrs. Basil E. sitting in the grand library of her brownstone, legs crossed, drinking from a teacup. What could Great-aunt Ida want to discuss right now? She probably also wanted to talk about Grandpa, when I had much more important things on my mind—like that I'd just learned Snarly Muppet, whom I had personally, *lovingly,* crafted for Snarl, had been recklessly abandoned by him inside a nutcracker!

I ignored Mrs. Basil E.'s phone call and said to Uncle Carmine, "Yeah. Grandpa. Depressed. Please visit him and tell him to stop asking me where I'm going all the time. And could you return the *beautiful* puppet to me next time you come into the city?"

"'I love you, yeah yeah yeah,'" Uncle Carmine responded.

"I'm very busy," I told Uncle Carmine.

"'She's got a ticket to ride,'" Uncle Carmine sang. "'But she don't care!'"

"Call Grandpa. He'll be glad to hear from you. Mwah and goodbye." I couldn't help but add one last thing. "'Good day, sunshine,'" I sang to Uncle Carmine.

"'I feel good in a special way,'" he answered.

And with that, our call ended. I saw that Mrs. Basil E. had left me a voice mail, but I didn't feel like listening. I needed to mourn the end of the notebook, and of idealizing a Snarl who'd tossed aside my Snarly. Time to move on with my life.

I wrote a final entry in the notebook and closed it, perhaps for good.

I'm gripped by a cherishing so deep.

The party had moved to a garden table outside, at the back of the pub. The late-December day had finally turned appropriately wintry and chilly, and the group huddled now with hot toddies as their drinks of choice.

I'm dreaming of a white Christmas, they sang. It was an especially nice song to sing—a soft, sweet one that matched the feeling in the air like when snow's about to fall and the world feels quieter, and lovelier. Content.

Edgar Thibaud had arrived and joined the group while I was in the bathroom. As they sang "White Christmas," he placed his fist to his mouth and made a beat box of sound with it, rapping in "Go . . . snow . . . snow that Mary MacGregor ho," over the carolers' song. When he saw me approach the table, Edgar transitioned to join the carolers in their song, improvising, "Just like the Lily-white one I used to know . . ."

When the song ended, angry Aryn said, "Hey, Lily. Your chauvinist, imperialist friend Edgar Thibaud?"

"Yes?" I asked, about to cover my ears with the red pom-poms on my hat in expectation of an epithet-laden rant from Aryn about one Edgar Thibaud.

"He's got a decent baritone. For a man."

Shee'nah, Antwon, Roberta, and Melvin raised their glasses to Edgar Thibaud. "To Edgar!" They clinked.

Aryn raised her glass. "It's *my* birthday!"

The group raised glasses again. "To Aryn!"

Edgar Thibaud did the Stevie Wonder version of "Happy Birthday." As he sang "Happy birthday to you! Happy biiiiiirrrrrrthdayyyy . . . ," Edgar closed his eyes, nodded aimlessly, and placed his hands on the table to pretend he was a blind guy playing piano.

Aryn was surely wasted by this point, because the political incorrectness of such a performance normally should have made her insane. Instead, she bellowed, "I want *my* birthday to be a national holiday." She stood up on her chair and announced to everyone within earshot, "Everybody, I give you the day off today!"

It seemed silly to remind her that most people already had the day off, since it was the week between Christmas and New Year's.

"What are you drinking?" I asked Aryn.

"A candy cane!" she told me. "Try some!"

Since I was flirting with danger, I took a sip of her drink.

It *did* taste like a candy cane . . . only better! I could understand why my carolers had made a habit of passing the peppermint schnapps flask when we'd made our rounds in the weeks before Christmas.

Tasty.

I looked over to Edgar. He was taking a picture with his cell phone of my feet: one part majorette boot, one part sneaker. "I'm sending out an all points bulletin to find your other boot," Edgar said. He hit Send on the picture like he was a regular Gossip Girl.

The carolers laughed. "To Lily's boot!" Glasses again clinked.

I wanted more Tasty. And Dangerous.

"I want to toast, too," I said. "Who wants to let me sip their hot toddy?"

As I reached over for Melvin's glass, the red notebook fell out of my purse, which was still slung over my shoulder.

I left the notebook on the floor.

Why bother?

"Lil-eee! Lil-eee!" the group—and by now, the whole bar—cheered.

I danced on the table and sang out a punkier-than-Beatles line o' lyric, gesturing a defiant fist in the air: "'It's! Been! A! Long! Cold! Lonely! Winter!'"

"'Here comes the sun,'" sang back dozens of bar voices.

All it had taken was three sips of peppermint schnapps, four hot toddy sips, and five sips of Shee'nah's drink of choice, the Shirley Temple—not!—to turn me into a veritable party girl. I felt changed already.

Since Christmas, so much had happened, all started by the notebook I'd decided to leave discarded on the barroom floor. I was now a girl—no, a *woman*—transformed.

I had become a liar. A Lily bear who flirted with a gerbil killer. A Mary MacGregor who after only six random sippies unbuttoned the top two pearl buttons on her sweater to allow a glimpse of her cleavage.

But the real Lily—the way-too-tipsy-and-needing-to-nap-and/or-barf sixteen-year-old one—was also way out of her element in this birthday-party-turned-full-on-bash with party girl Lily at its center.

Winter's early darkness had fallen; it was only six o'clock, but dark outside, and if I didn't get home soon, Grandpa would come looking for me. But if I did go home, Grandpa would know I was mildly . . . *mildly* . . . inebriated. Even if I hadn't ordered or been knowingly served alcohol in the pub—I had only taken sips of others' drinks. Grandpa might also find out about Edgar Thibaud. What to do?

A new group of people arrived in the bar and I knew I had to stop singing and dancing on the table before they, too, joined the party. I was in way over my head already.

The clock was running out. I jumped off my chair and pulled Edgar over to a secluded corner in the outdoor garden. I wanted him to explain how he was going to get me home, and not in trouble.

I wanted him to kiss me.

I wanted the snow to finally start falling, as the crisp night air and gray skies indicated would happen at any moment.

I wanted my other boot because my sneaker foot was getting really, really cold.

"Edgar Thibaud," I murmured, trying to sound sexy. I pressed myself up against his warm, rock-solid body. I parted my mouth to his approaching lips.

This was *It.*

Finally.

I was about to close my eyes for *It* when, from the corner of my eye, I noticed a teenage boy standing nearby, holding something I needed.

My other boot.

Edgar Thibaud turned to the boy. "Dash?" he asked, confused.

This boy—Dash, apparently—looked at me strangely.

"Is that our red notebook on the floor over there?" he asked me.

Could this be *him*?

"Your name is *Dash*?" I said. I burped. My mouth had one more nugget of wisdom to offer. "If we got married, I'd be, like, Mrs. Dash!"

I cracked myself up laughing.

Then I'm pretty sure I passed out in Edgar Thibaud's arms.

thirteen

–Dash–

December 27th

"How do you know Lily?" Thibaud asked me.

"I'm not really sure I do," I said. "But, really, what was I expecting?"

Thibaud shook his head. "Whatever, dude. You want something from the bar? Aryn's hot, she's twenty-one, and she's buying for *everybody*."

"I think I'm a teetotaler tonight," I said.

"I think the only kind of tea they have at this place is *Long Island*. You're on your own, my friend."

So, presumably, was Lily. Thibaud placed her conked-out self on the nearest bench.

"Are you kissing me?" she murmured.

"Not so much," he whispered back.

I stared up at the sky, trying to search out the genius who coined the term *wasted*, because she or he deserved mad props for nailing it so perfectly. What a wasted girl. What a wasted hope. What a wasted evening.

The proper response for a lout in this situation would be to walk away. But I, who had such anti-loutish aspirations, couldn't muster up the bad taste to do that. So instead, I found myself taking off Lily's sneaker and slipping her aunt's second boot onto her foot.

"It's back!" she muttered.

"Come on," I said lightly, trying to disguise the crushing weight of my disappointment. She was in no state to hear it.

"Okay," she said. But then she didn't move.

"I need to take you home," I told her.

She started to flail. Eventually I realized she was shaking her head.

"Not home. I can't go home. Grandpa will kill me."

"Well, I have no desire to accessorize your murder," I said. "I'll take you to your aunt's."

"That's a good good good idea."

To give them credit, Lily's friends at the bar were concerned about her and wanted to be sure we'd be okay. To give him discredit, Thibaud was too busy trying to get the birthday girl to try on her birthday suit to notice our departure.

"Drosophila," I said, remembering the word.

"What?" Lily asked.

"Why do girls always fall for guys with the attention span of drosophila?"

"What?"

"Fruit flies. Guys with the attention span of fruit flies."

"Because they're hot?"

"This," I told her, "is not the time for being truthful."

Instead, it was the time for us to hail a cab. More than a few of them saw the way Lily was leaning—somewhat like a street sign after a car had crashed into it—and drove right on by. Finally, a decent man pulled over and picked us up. A country song was playing on his radio.

"East Twenty-second, by Gramercy Park," I told him.

I thought Lily was going to fall asleep next to me. But what happened instead was invariably worse.

"I'm sorry," she said. And it was like a faucet had been turned, and only one sentiment could come gushing out. "I'm *so* sorry. Oh my God, I can't believe how sorry I am. I didn't mean to drop it, Dash. And I didn't mean—I mean, I'm just so sorry. I didn't think you were going to be there. I was just there. And, God, I am *so* sorry. I am really, really sorry. If you want to get out of the cab right this minute, I will completely understand. I will definitely pay for all of it. *All* of it. I'm sorry. You believe me, right? I mean it. I am so, so, SO sorry."

"It's okay," I told her. "Really, it's okay."

And, strangely, it was. The only things I blamed were my own foolish expectations.

"No, it's not okay. Really, I'm sorry." She leaned forward. "Driver, can you tell him that I'm sorry? I wasn't supposed to be like this. I swear."

"The girl's sorry," the driver told me, with no shortage of sympathy shot my way in the rearview mirror.

Lily sat back in the seat. "You see? I'm just so—"

I had to tune out then. I had to stare at the people on the street, the cars going by. I had to tell the cabbie when to turn, even though I was sure he knew perfectly well when to turn. I was still tuning out when we pulled over, when I paid for the cab (even though this got me more apologies), when I carefully maneuvered Lily out of the cab and up the stairs. It became a physics problem—how to prevent her from hitting her head on the cab as she got out, how to get her up the stairs without dropping her sneaker, which I still held in my hand.

I only tuned back in when the lock on the front door turned before I had a chance to ring the bell. Lily's aunt took one look and said a simple, "Oh my." Suddenly the torrent of apologies was directed at her; had I not been holding Lily up, I might have chosen this as my opportunity to leave.

"Follow me," the old woman said. She led us to a bedroom at the back of her house and helped me sit Lily down on the bed. For her part, Lily was near tears now.

"This wasn't what was supposed to happen," she told me. "It wasn't."

"It's okay," I told her again. "It's all okay."

"Lily," her aunt said, "you should still have pajamas in the second drawer. I'm going to walk Dash out while you change. I'll also call your grandfather and let him know you're safe with me, no harm done. We'll concoct your alibi in the morning, when you're much more likely to remember it."

I made the mistake of turning back to look at her one last time before I left the room. It was heartbreaking, really—she just sat there, stunned. She looked like she was waking up in a strange place—only she knew she hadn't gone to sleep yet, and that this was actually life.

"Really," I said. "It's okay."

I took the red notebook out of my pocket and left it on the dresser.

"I don't deserve it!" she protested.

"Of course you do," I told her gently. "None of the words would have existed without you."

Lily's aunt, watching from the hall, motioned me out of the room. When we were a safe distance away, she said, "Well, this is quite uncharacteristic."

"The whole thing was silly," I said. "Please tell her there's no need to apologize. We set ourselves up for this. I was never going to be the guy in her head. And she was never going to be the girl in mine. And that's okay. Seriously."

"Why don't you tell her that yourself?"

"Because I don't want to," I said. "Not because of the way she is now—I know that's not what she's like. There was no way it was going to be as easy as the notebook. I get that now."

I got to the door.

"It was a pleasure to meet you," I said. "Thank you for the tea you never served me."

"The pleasure was mine," the old woman replied. "Come back again soon."

I didn't know what to say to that. I think we both knew I wouldn't.

Back on the street, I wanted to talk to someone. But who? It's moments like this, when you need someone the most, that your world seems smallest. Boomer would never in a million years understand what I was going through. Yohnny and Dov might, but they were in such couple mode that I doubted they could see the forest because they'd be too busy pairing up the trees. Priya would just stare at me strangely, even over the phone. And Sofia didn't have a phone. Not anymore. Not in America.

Either of my parents?

That was a laughable idea.

I started to walk home. The phone rang.

I looked at the screen:

Thibaud.

Despite my deeper reservations, I picked up.

"Dash!" he cried. "Where are you guys?"

"I took Lily home, Thibaud."

"Is she okay?"

"I'm sure she would appreciate your concern."

"I just looked up and you guys were gone."

"I don't even know how to begin to address that point."

"What do you mean?"

I sighed. "I mean—that is to say, what I really don't understand is how you get away with being such a lout."

"That's not fair, Dash." Thibaud actually sounded hurt. "I totally care. That's why I called. Because I care."

"But, you see, that's the luxury of being a lout—you get to be selective about when you care and when you don't. The rest of us get stuck when your care goes shallow."

"Dude, you think too much."

"Dude, you know what? You're right. And you don't think enough. Which makes you the perennial screwer and me the perennial screwee."

"So she's upset?"

"Really, does it matter to you?"

"Yes! She's grown up a lot, Dash. I thought she was cool. At least until she passed out. You can't really try to get with a girl once she passes out. Or even when she's coming close."

"That's mighty chivalrous of you."

"God, you're pissed! Were the two of you dating or something? She didn't mention you once. If I'd known, I promise I wouldn't have been flirting with her."

"Again, chivalry. You're almost up to a knighthood."

Another sigh. "Look, I just wanted to make sure she was okay. That's it. Just tell her I'll catch her later, right? And that I hope she doesn't feel too bad in the morning. Tell her to drink lots of water."

"You're going to have to tell her yourself, Thibaud," I said.

"She didn't answer."

"Well, I'm not there now. I'm gone, Thibaud. I've left."

"You sound sad, Dash."

"One of the failures of cellular communication is that tiredness often comes across as sadness. But I appreciate your concern."

"We're still here, if you want to come back."

"I'm told there's no going back. So I'm choosing forward."

I hung up then. The exhaustion of living was just too much for me to talk any longer. At least to Thibaud. And, yes, there was sadness in that. And anger. And confusion. And disappointment. All exhausting.

I kept walking. It wasn't too cold for December 27, and all the holiday-week visitors were out in force. I remembered where Sofia had said her family was staying—the Belvedere, on Forty-eighth Street—and walked in that direction. Times Square sent its glow into the air, blocks before it actually began, and I walked heavily into the light. The tourists still crowded into a thronging pulse, but now that Christmas was over, I wasn't as repelled. Especially in Times Square, everyone was enraptured by the simple act of *being here*. For every exhausted soul like myself, there were at least three whose faces were lifted in absurd wonder at the neon brightness. As much as I wanted to have the hardest of hearts, such plaintive joy made me feel what a leaky, human vessel it really was.

When I got to the Belvedere, I found the house phone and asked to be connected to Sofia's room. It rang six times before an anonymous voice mail picked up. I returned the receiver to its cradle and went to sit on one of the couches in the lobby. I wasn't waiting, per se—I simply didn't know where else to go. The lobby was full of hustling and bustling—guests negotiating each other after negotiating the city, some about to plunge back in. Parents dragged vacation-tired children. Couples sniped about what they'd done or hadn't done. Other couples held hands like teenagers, even when they hadn't been teenagers for over half a century. Christmas music no longer wafted in the air, which allowed a more genuine tenderness to bloom. Or maybe that was just in me. Maybe everything I saw was all in me.

I wanted to write it down. I wanted to share it with Lily, even if Lily was really just the idea I'd created of Lily, the *concept* of Lily. I went to the small gift shop off the lobby and bought six postcards and a pen. Then I sat back down and let my thoughts flow out. Not directed to her this time. Not directed at all. It would be just like water, or blood. It would go wherever it was meant to go.

Postcard 1: Greetings from New York!

Having grown up here, I always wonder what it would be like to see this city as a tourist. Is it ever a disappointment? I have to believe that New York always lives up to its reputation. The buildings really are that tall. The lights really are that bright. There's truly a story on every corner. But it still might be a shock. To realize you are just one story walking among millions. To not feel the bright lights even as they fill the air. To see the tall buildings and only feel a deep longing for the stars.

Postcard 2: I'm a Broadway Baby!
Why is it so much easier to talk to a stranger? Why do we feel we need that disconnect in order to connect? If I wrote "Dear Sofia" or "Dear Boomer" or "Dear Lily's Great-Aunt" at the top of this postcard, wouldn't that change the words that followed? Of course it would. But the question is: When I wrote "Dear Lily," was that just a version of "Dear Myself"? I know it was more than that. But it was also less than that, too.

Postcard 3: The Statue of Liberty
For thee I sing. What a remarkable phrase.

"Dash?"

I looked up and found Sofia there, holding a *Playbill* from *Hedda Gabler*.

"Hi, Sofia. What a small world!"

"Dash—"

"I mean, small in the sense that right at this moment, I'd be happy if it only had the two of us in it. And I mean that in a strictly conversational sense."

"I always appreciate your strictness."

I looked around the lobby for a sign of her parents. "Mom and Dad leave you alone?" I asked.

"They went for a drink. I decided to come back."

"Right."

"Right."

I didn't stand up. She didn't sit down next to me. We just

looked at each other and saw each other for a moment, and then held it for another moment, and another moment. There didn't seem to be any question about what was going to happen. There didn't seem to be any doubt about where this was going. We didn't even need to say it.

fourteen

(Lily)

December 28th

> **fan•ci•ful**\fan(t)si-fəl*adj* (ca. 1627) 1. marked by fancy or unrestrained imagination rather than by reason and experience.

According to Mrs. Basil E., *fanciful* is the adjective for which Snarl—I mean Dash—feels the most longing. Certainly it explained why he'd answered the call of the red notebook at the Strand to begin with and played along, for a while, until he discovered that the real Lily, as opposed to his imagined one, would turn him less *fanciful* and more *dour* (3. gloomy, sullen).

What a waste.

Although, *fanciful*'s origin circa 1627 made me still love the word, even if I'd ruined its applicability to my connection with Snarl. (I mean *DASH*!) Like, I could totally see Mrs. Mary Poppencock returning home to her cobblestone hut with the thatched roof in Thamesburyshire, Jolly Olde England, and saying to her husband, "Good sir Bruce, would it not be wonderful to have a roof that doesn't leak when it rains on our green shires, and stuff?" And Sir Bruce Poppencock would have been like, "I say, missus, you're very *fanciful* with your ideas today." To which Mrs. P. responded, "Why, Master P., you've made up a word! What year is it? I do believe it's circa 1627! Let's carve the year—we *think*—on a stone so no one forgets. *Fanciful!* Dear man, you are a genius. I'm so glad my father forced me to marry you and allow you to impregnate me every year."

I placed the dictionary back on the shelf, next to a hardcover edition of *Contemporary Poets,* as Mrs. Basil E., who is keen on reference books, returned to the parlor with a silver tray bearing a pot of what smelled like very strong coffee.

"What have we learned, Lily?" Mrs. Basil E. asked me as she poured me a cup.

"Taking too many sips of other people's drinks can lead to disastrous consequences."

"Obviously," she said imperiously. "But more importantly?"

"Don't mix drinks. If you're going to sip peppermint schnapps, only sip peppermint schnapps."

"Thank you."

Her calm observation was what I appreciated best about that small degree of separation between a parent or grandparent and a great-aunt. The latter could react sensibly, pragmatically, to the situation, without the complete and wholly unnecessary hysteria that would have befallen the former.

"What did you tell Grandpa?" I asked.

"That you came over last night to have dinner with me, but I asked you to stay over to shovel the snow from my sidewalk in the morning. Which is entirely true, even if you slept through dinner."

"Snow?" I pulled back the heavy brocade drapery and looked out the front window to the street.

SNOW!!!!!!!!!!!!!

I had forgotten about the previous evening's promise of snow. And darned if I hadn't slept through it, conked out on too many sips and too many hopes—dashed (so to speak). All my own fault.

The morning's view onto the street of Gramercy town houses was blanketed with snow, at least two inches deep—not a lot, but enough for a good snowman. The accumulation still appeared gloriously new, the street a blanket of white, with cottony tufts heaped on cars and sidewalk railings. The snow had yet to lose its luster to multiple foot tramplings, yellow dog markings, and the scars of engine fumes.

My cluttered brain formed a vague idea.

"May I build a snowman in the back garden?" I asked Mrs. Basil E.

"You may. Once you shovel my front sidewalk. Good thing you got my other boot returned to you, eh?"

I sat down opposite my great-aunt and took a sip of coffee.

"Do pancakes come with this coffee?" I asked.

"I wasn't sure whether you'd be hungry."

"Starving!"

"I thought you might have woken up with a headache."

"I did! But the good kind!" My head was pounding, but it was a light, giddy tap in my temples as opposed to a thunderous roar across my whole head. For sure some pancakes doused in maple syrup would do the job of relieving the headache, and the hunger. Since I'd skipped dinner the previous night, I had lots of eating to make up.

Despite the minor headache and hungry tummy, I couldn't help but feel a bit of satisfaction.

I had done it. I had embraced danger.

The experience might have been an epic disaster, but it was still . . . an *experience.*

Cool.

"Dash," I murmured over a heaping pile of pancakes. "Dash Dash Dash." I needed to absorb his name while the pancakes absorbed the butter and syrup. As it was, I could barely recall what he looked like; my memory's image of him was shrouded in a champagne-colored mist, sweet and woozy, unclear. I remembered that he was on the tall side, his hair looked neat and freshly combed, he wore regular jeans and a peacoat, possibly vintage, and he smelled like boy, but in the nice and not gross way.

Also he had the bluest eyes ever, and long black lashes almost like a girl's.

"Dash, short for Dashiell," Mrs. Basil E. said, passing me a glass of OJ.

"Why wouldn't it be?" I asked.

"Precisely."

"I guess it's not going to be true love between him and me," I realized.

"True love? Pish posh. A concept manufactured by Hollywood."

"Ha-ha. You said *pish posh*."

"Mish mosh," she added.

"Put a kibosh on that nosh."

"Enough, Lily."

I sighed. "So I guess I blew it with him?"

Mrs. Basil E. said, "I think it will be hard to recover from that first impression you made on him. But I'd also say if anyone deserves a second chance, it's you."

"But how do I get him to give me a second chance?"

"You'll figure something out. I have faith in you."

"You like him," I teased.

Mrs. Basil E. pronounced, "I find young Dashiell to be not contemptible, for a specimen of teenage male. His persnicketiness is not nearly as delightful as he'd have one believe, but he has his own charm nonetheless. Articulate to a fault, perhaps—but a forgivable and, dare I say, an admirable misdemeanor."

I had no idea what she just said.

"So he's worth a second shot, then?"

"The more apt question, my dear, is: Are you?"

She had a good point.

Just as much, if not more than, a hero as that stapler in *Collation,* Dash had not only brought me my other boot when my toes were wanting to turn frostbitten, he'd placed that boot on me when I'd passed out, and he'd made sure I got home safely. What had I done for him, except probably dashed his hopes, too?

I hoped I'd apologized to him.

I texted that rascal of a gerbil killer, Edgar Thibaud.

```
Where can I find Dash?

R U a stalker?

Possibly.

Awesome. His mom's place is at E Ninth &
University.
```

```
Which building?

A good stalker doesn't need to ask.
```

I did want to ask Edgar: Did we kiss last night?

I licked my morning lips. My mouth felt very full and untouched by luscious matter other than pancakes and syrup.

```
Wanna get wasted again tonight?
```

From Edgar Thibaud.

Suddenly I recalled Edgar hitting on Aryn as Dash had helped my unfortunately wasted self out of the pub.

```
1. No. Retiring from that game.  2. And
especially not with you. Regards, Lily
```

The snow crunched beneath my boots as I made my way home that afternoon. East Ninth Street at University Place was a not totally inconvenient stop between Mrs. Basil E.'s in Gramercy Park and my apartment in the East Village, and I reveled in the winter's walk along the way. I love snow for the same reason I love Christmas: It brings people together while time stands still. Cozy couples lazily meandered the streets and children trudged sleds and dogs chased snowballs. No one seemed to be in a rush to experience anything other than the glory of the day, with each other, whenever and however it happened.

There were four different apartment buildings at each corner of East Ninth and University. I approached the first one and asked the doorman, "Does Dash live here?"

"Why? Who wants to know?"

"I'd like to know, please."

"No Dash lives here that I know of."

"Then why did you ask who wanted to know?"

"Why are you asking for Dash if you don't know where he lives?"

I took a spare Baggie of lebkuchen spice cookies out of my bag and handed it to the doorman. "I think you could use some of these," I said. "Merry December 28."

I walked across the block to the next building. There was no uniformed doorman, but a man sat behind a desk in the lobby as some elderly people using walkers strolled the hallway behind him. "Hello!" I greeted him. "I'm wondering if Dash lives here?"

"Is Dash an eighty-year-old retired cabaret singer?"

"I'm pretty sure not."

"Then no Dash here, kiddo. This is a nursing home."

"Do any blind people live here?" I asked.

"Why?"

I handed him my card. "Because I would like to read to them. For my college applications. Also, I like old people."

"How generous of you. I'll hold on to this just in case I hear of anything." He glanced down at my card. "Nice to meet you, Lily Dogwalker."

"You too!"

I crossed the street to the third building. A doorman was outside shoveling snow. "Hi! Would you like some help?" I asked him.

"No," he said, eyeing me suspiciously. "Union rules. No help."

I gave the doorman one of the Starbucks gift cards one of my dog-walking clients had gifted me with before Christmas. "Have a coffee on me on your break, sir."

"Thanks! Now whaddya want?"

"Does Dash live here?"

"Dash. Dash who?"

"Not sure of his last name. Teenage boy, on the tall side, dreamy blue eyes. Peacoat. Shops at the Strand near here, so maybe he carries bags from there?"

"Doesn't sound familiar."

"Seems sort of . . . snarly?"

"Oh, that kid. Sure. Lives at that building."

The doorman pointed to the building on the fourth corner.

I walked over to that building.

"Hi," I said to the doorman, who was reading a copy of the *New Yorker.* "Dash lives here, right?"

The doorman looked up from his magazine. "16E? Mom's a shrink?"

"Right," I said. Sure, why not?

The doorman tucked the magazine into a drawer. "He went out about an hour ago. Want to leave a message for him?"

I took a package from my bag. "Could I leave this for him?"

"Sure."

"Thanks," I said.

I handed the doorman my card also. He glanced at it. "No pets allowed in this building," he said.

"That's *tragic,*" I said.

No wonder Dash was so snarly.

The package I'd left for Dash contained a gift box of English breakfast tea and the red notebook.

Dear Dash:

Meeting you through this notebook meant a lot to me. Especially this Christmas.

But I know I botched its magic, big-time.

I'm so sorry.

What I'm sorry about is not being a tipsy idiot when you found me. I'm sorry about that, obviously, but more sorry that my stupidity caused us to lose a great opportunity. I don't imagine you would have met me and fallen crazy in love with me, but I would like to think that if you'd had a chance to meet me under different circumstances, something just as nice could have happened.

We could have become friends.

Game over. I get that.

But if you ever want a (sober) new Lily friend, I'm your girl.

I feel like you may be a special and kind person. And I would like to make it my business to know special and kind people. Especially if they are boys my age.

Thank you for being a real stapler of a hero guy.

There is a snowman in the garden at my great-aunt's house who'd like to meet you. If you dare.

Regards,
Lily

PS I'm not going to hold it against you that you associate with Edgar Thibaud, and I hope you will extend me the same courtesy.

Below my dare, I'd stapled my Lily Dogwalker business card. I didn't hold out hope that Dash would take me up on the snowman offer, or try to call me ever, but I figured if he did want to get directly in touch with me again, the least

I could do was not make him go through several of my relatives.

After my last entry in the notebook, I'd cut out and pasted a section of a page I'd photocopied of the *Contemporary Poets* reference book in Mrs. Basil E.'s parlor library.

Strand, Mark

[Blah blah blah biographical information, crossed out with Sharpie pen.]

We are reading the story of our lives
As though we were in it,
As though we had written it.

fifteen

–Dash–

December 28th

I woke up next to Sofia. At some point in the night, she'd turned away from me, but she'd let one hand linger, reaching back to rest on my own hand. A border of sunlight ringed the curtains of the hotel room, signaling morning. I felt her hand, felt our breathing. I felt lucky, grateful. The sound of traffic climbed from the street, mingled with parts of conversations. I looked at her neck, brushed back her hair to kiss it. She stirred. I wondered.

Our clothes had stayed on the whole time. We'd cuddled together, looking not for sex but comfort. We'd sailed to sleep together, with more ease than I ever would have imagined.

Knock. Knock. Knock.

POUND. POUND. POUND.

The door. Three pounds on the door.

A man's voice. "*Sofia? ¿Estás lista?*"

Her hand grabbed for mine. Squeezed.

"*Un minuto, Papa!*" she called out.

As it happened, the maids at the Belvedere did a fine job of vacuuming, so when I hid under the bed, I was attacked by neither rats nor dust mites. Just the general fear of a vengeful father storming into a hotel room.

More knocking. Sofia headed for the door.

Too late, I realized my shoes were lollygagging on the floor about an arm's length away from me. As Sofia's father lumbered in—he was a sizable man, roughly the shape of a school bus—I made a desperate grab, only to have my hand kicked away by Sofia's bare feet. My shoes followed in quick succession—Sofia shooting them right into my face. I let out an involuntary cry of startled pain, which Sofia covered by telling her father loudly that she was almost ready to go.

If he noticed she was wearing yesterday's clothes, he didn't say anything. Instead, he came closer and closer to the bed. Before I could maneuver, he let his weight fall onto the mattress, and I found myself cheek to cheek with the indentation of his sizable behind.

"*¿Dónde está Mamá?*" Sofia asked. When she bent down to pick up her shoes, she shot me a stern *Stay put* look. As if I had a choice. I was basically pinned to the floor, my forehead bleeding from being attacked by my own shoe.

"*En el vestíbulo, esperando.*"

"*¿Por qué no vas a esperar con ella? Bajo en un segundo.*"

I wasn't really following this exchange, just praying it would be a quick one. Then the weight above me shifted, and Sofia's father was once more floor-based. Suddenly the space under the bed seemed the size of a downtown loft. I wanted to roll over, just because I could.

As soon as her father was gone, Sofia climbed under the bed with me.

"That was a fun wake-up call, was it not?" she asked. Then she pushed back my hair to look at my forehead. "God, you're hurt. How did that happen?"

"Bumped my head," I replied. "It's an occupational hazard, if your occupation happens to be sleeping over with ex-girlfriends."

"Does that occupation pay well?"

"Clearly." I made a move to kiss her—and hit my head again.

"Come on," Sofia said, starting to slide away from me. "Let's get you somewhere safer."

I stomach-crawled out after her, then went to the sink to clean myself up. Meanwhile, in the other room, she changed her clothes. I sneaked peeks in the closet mirror.

"I can see you as well as you can see me," Sofia pointed out.

"Is that a problem?" I asked.

"Actually," she said, lifting her shirt over her head, "no."

I had to remind myself that her father was no doubt waiting for her. Now was not the time for canoodling, no matter how much the canoodling impulse was striking.

A new shirt went on, and Sofia walked over to me, putting her face next to mine in the bathroom mirror reflection.

"Hello," she said.

"Hello," I said.

"It was never this fun when we were actually going out, was it?" she asked.

"I assure you," I replied, "it was never this fun."

I knew she was leaving. I knew we were never going to date long-distance. I knew that we wouldn't have been able to be like this back when we were dating, so there was no use in regretting what hadn't happened. I suspected that what happens in hotel rooms rarely lasts outside of them. I suspected that when something was a beginning and an ending at the same time, that meant it could only exist in the present.

And still. I wanted more than that.

"Let's make plans," I ventured.

And Sofia smiled and said, "No, let's leave it to chance."

It was snowing outside, anointing the air with a quiet wonder shared by all passersby. When I got back to my mother's apartment, I was a mixture of giddy thrill-happiness and muddled gut-confusion—I didn't want to leave anything regarding Sofia to chance, and at the same time I was enjoying this step away from it. I hummed my way into the bathroom, checked on my shoe-inflicted wound, then headed to the kitchen, where I opened the refrigerator and found myself yogurtless. Quickly I bundled myself up in a striped hat and striped scarf and striped gloves—dressing for snow can be the keenest, most allowable kindergarten throwback—and traipsed down University and through Washington Square Park to the Morton Williams.

It was only on my way back that I encountered the ruffians. I have no knowledge of what I did to provoke them. In fact, I like to believe there was no provocation whatsoever—their target was as arbitrary as their misbehavior was focused.

"The enemy!" one of them cried. I didn't even have time to shield my bag of yogurts before I was being bombarded by snowballs.

Like dogs and lions, small children can sense fear. The slightest flinch, the slightest disinclination, and they will jump atop you and devour you. Snow was pelting my torso, my legs, my groceries. None of the kids looked familiar—there were nine, maybe ten of them, and they were nine, maybe ten years old. "Attack!" they cried. "There he is!" they shouted, even though I'd made no attempt to hide. "Get 'im!"

Fine, I thought, bending over to scoop up some snow, even though this left my backside ripe for an offensive.

It is not easy to hurl snowballs while holding on to a plastic bag of groceries, so my first few efforts were subpar, missing their mark. The nine maybe ten nine-maybe-ten-year-olds ridiculed me—if I turned to aim at one, four others outflanked me and shot from the sides and the back. I was, in the parlance of an ancient day, cruising for a bruising, and while a more disdainful teenager would have walked away, and a more aggressive teenager would have dropped the bag and kicked some major preteen ass, I kept fighting snowball with snowball, laughing as if Boomer and I were playing a school yard game, flinging my orbs with winter abandon, wishing Sofia were here by my side. . . .

Until I hit the kid in the eye.

There was no aim involved. I just threw a snowball at him and—pow!—he went down. The other kids unleashed the last of their snowballs and ran to him to see what had happened.

I walked over, too, asking if he was okay. He didn't look concussed, and his eye was fine. But now vengeance was spreading across the faces of the nine/tens, and it wasn't a cute little vengeance. Some took out cell phones to take pictures and call their mothers. Others began to reload on snowballs, making sure to create them from patches where the snow mixed with gravel.

I bolted. I ran down Fifth Avenue, skirted onto Eighth

Street, hid in an Au Bon Pain until the elementary school mob had passed.

When I got back to my mom's building, the doorman had a package for me. I thanked him, but decided to wait until I got to the apartment before opening it, because this was the doorman who was notorious for "tithing" the residents by stealing one out of every ten of our magazines and I didn't want to share any potential goodies.

As I was letting myself back into the apartment, the phone rang. Boomer.

"Hey," he said after I answered. "Do we have plans for today?"

"I don't think so."

"Well, we should!"

"Sure. What are you up to?"

"Tracking your celebrity! I'll send you a link!"

I took off my boots and mittens, unwrapped my scarf, set my hat aside, and headed to my laptop. I opened up Boomer's email.

"WashingtonSquareMommies?" I asked, picking the phone back up.

"Yeah—click it!"

The site was a mommy blog, and on the front page a headline screamed:

CRIMSON ALERT!
ATTACKER IN PARK
Posted 11:28 am, December 28
by **elizabethbennettlives**

I am activating the crimson alert because a young man—late teens, early twenties—

assaulted a child in the park ten minutes ago. Please study these photos, and if you see him, alert the police immediately. We know he shops at Morton Williams (see bag) and was last seen on Eighth Street. ***He will not hesitate to use force against your children, so be alert!!!***

maclarenpusher adds:
people like this should be shot.

zacephron adds:
purvurt

christwearsarmani adds:
remind me the difference between a crimson alert and a fuchsia one? i can never keep them straight!

The photos attached to the posting showed much more of my hat and scarf than anything else.

"How did you know it was me?" I asked Boomer.

"It was a mixture of your clothes, your brand of yogurt, and your piss-poor aim—well, at least until you clobbered that kid."

"And what were you doing on WashingtonSquareMommies, anyway?"

"I love the way they're so mean to each other," Boomer said. "I have it bookmarked."

"Well, if you don't mind hanging out with the source of a crimson alert, come on over."

"I don't mind. In fact, I find it a little exciting!"

As soon as we were off the phone, I unwrapped the package (brown paper, tied up in string) and found the red Moleskine had come back to me.

I knew Boomer wouldn't take long to get here, so I dove right back in.

I'm sorry I didn't return our notebook to you.

That already seemed like so long ago.

You don't feel like a stranger to me.

I wanted to ask her, *What does a stranger feel like?* Not to be snarky or sarcastic. Because I really wanted to know if there was a difference, if there was a way to become truly knowable, if there wasn't always something keeping you a stranger, even to the people you weren't strange to at all.

I always hoped that after the prince found Cinderella and they rode away in their magnificent carriage, after a few miles she turned to him and said, "Could you drop me off down the road, please? Now that I've finally escaped my life of horrific abuse, I'd like to see something of the world, you know?"

Maybe the prince would be relieved. Maybe he was tired of being asked who he was going to marry. Maybe all he wanted to do was go back to his library and read a hundred books, only everyone kept interrupting him, telling him he couldn't ever let himself be alone.

I might have liked to share a dance with you. If I may be so bold to say.

I thought:

But isn't this a dance? Isn't all of this a dance? Isn't that what we do with words? Isn't that what we do when we talk, when we spar, when we make plans or leave it to chance? Some of it's choreographed. Some of the steps have been done for ages. And the rest—the rest is spontaneous. The rest has to be decided on the floor, in the moment, before the music ends.

I am trying to embrace danger. . . .

I am not dangerous. Only the stories are dangerous. Only the fictions we create, especially when they become expectations.

I think it's time to experience life outside the notebook.

But don't you see—that's what we were doing.

I'm so sorry.

No need to apologize. No need to say *Game over*. Your disappointment makes me sad.

Then Mark Strand:

We are reading the story of our lives
As though we were in it,
As though we had written it.

Mark Strand, whose three most famous lines are:

In a field
I am the absence
of field

So I took out my fourth postcard and wrote:

Postcard 4: Times Square on New Year's Eve
In a field, I am the absence of field. In a crowd, I am the absence of crowd. In a dream, I am the absence of dream. But I don't want to live as an absence. I move to keep things whole. Because sometimes I feel drunk on positivity. Sometimes I feel amazement at the tangle of words and lives, and I want to be a part of that tangle. "Game over," you say, and I don't know which I take more exception to—the fact that you say that it's over, or the fact that you say it's a game. It's only over when one of us keeps the notebook for good. It's only a game if there is an absence of meaning. And we've already gone too far for that.

Only two postcards left.

Postcard 5: The Empire State Building at Sunrise
We ARE the story of our lives. And the red notebook is for our storytelling. Which, in the case of lives, is the same as truth telling. Or as close to it as we can get. I don't want the notebook or our friendship to end just because we had an ill-advised encounter. Let's label the incident minor, and move on from it. I don't think we should ever try to meet again; there's such freedom in that. Instead, let our words continue to meet. (See next postcard.)

The last postcard I saved for the notebook's next destination. The doorbell rang—Boomer—and I scribbled down some hasty instructions.

"Are you in there?" Boomer yelled.

"No!" I yelled back, Scotch-taping each postcard onto its own page of the notebook.

"Really—are you in there?" Boomer said, knocking again.

It hadn't been my intention when I'd asked him over, but already I knew I'd be sending Boomer on another assignment. Because as curious as I was to see Lily's snowman, I knew that if I started talking to her great-aunt again, or stepped inside that house again, I would likely end up staying for a very long time. Which was exactly what the notebook didn't need.

"Boomer, my friend," I said, "would you be willing to be my Apollo?"

"But don't you have to be black to sing there?" was Boomer's response.

"My messenger. My courier. My proxy."

"I don't mind being a messenger. Does this have to do with Lily?"

"Yes, indeed it does."

Boomer smiled. "Cool. I like her."

After the contretemps with Thibaud last night, it was refreshing to have one of my male friends beam with niceness.

"You know what, Boomer?"

"What, Dash?"

"You restore my faith in humanity. And lately I've been thinking that a guy can do far, far worse than surrounding himself with people who restore his faith in humanity."

"Like me."

"Like you. And Sofia. And Yohnny. And Dov. And Lily."

"Lily!"

"Yes, Lily."

I was attempting to write the story of my life. It wasn't so much about plot. It was much more about character.

sixteen

(Lily)

December 29th

Males are the most incomprehensible species.

The Dash fellow never showed up to see his snowman. *I* would have shown up if someone had built me a snowman, but *I* am a female. Logical.

Mrs. Basil E. called to tell me the snowman melted. I thought, *Sucks to be you, Dash. A girl made a snowman using lebkuchen spice cookies to shape the snowman's eyes, nose, and mouth, just for you. You don't even know what you missed.* Although, according to Mrs. Basil E., the snowman's demise should not be a cause for concern. "If the snowman melts," she said, "you simply build another." Ladies represent: logical.

Illogical Langston woke up from his flu and promptly broke up with Benny, because Benny left for Puerto Rico to visit his *abuelita* for two weeks. Langston and Benny decided their relationship was still too new and fragile to survive a two-week absence, so breaking up entirely was their compromise. They did so with the promise that they might get back together when Benny gets back home, but if either of them should meet someone else in that two-week window, they had the green light to pursue. Makes no sense to me whatsoever. With that kind of logic, they deserve each other—or not to have each other, as the case may be. Boys are crazy—so much drama.

The worst male offender? Grandpa. He goes down to Florida for Christmas to propose marriage to Mabel, who turns him down, so he drives all the way back to New York on Christmas Day in a huff, convinced the relationship is over. Four days later, December 29, and he's driving back down to Florida, with a complete change of heart.

"Gonna work this thing out with Mabel," Grandpa announced over breakfast to me and Langston. "I'm leaving in a few hours." Even if I wasn't thrilled by the idea of Grandpa and Mabel forming a more permanent union, I guessed I could get used to the union, if it made the old fella happy. And from a practical point of view, removing Grandpa from our city would serve the added bonus of preventing him from asking where I was going all the time, just when things were starting to get interesting in the Lilyverse.

"How do you propose to work things out?" Langston asked. His face was still pale, his voice hoarse and nose runny, but my brother was eating his second scrambled egg and had already devoured a stack of toast with jam, clearly feeling much better.

"What was I thinking with that we-have-to-get-married business?" Grandpa said. "Outdated concept. I'm going to propose that Mabel and I just be exclusive to one another.

No ring, no wedding, just . . . partnership. I'd be her only boyfriend."

"Guess who has a boyfriend, Grandpa?" Langston asked menacingly. "Lily!"

"I do not!" I said, but in a quiet, not Shrilly-like tone.

Grandpa turned to me. "You're not allowed to date for another twenty years, Lily bear. In fact, your mother still isn't allowed to date, according to my recollection. But somehow she slipped away anyway."

At the mention of her name, I realized I missed Mom. Fiercely. I'd been too busy the last week with the notebook and other random misadventures to remember to miss my parents, but suddenly I wanted them home *right now.* I wanted to hear why they thought moving to Fiji was a good idea, I wanted to see their unfortunately tanned faces, and I wanted to hang out with them telling stories and laughing together. I wanted TO OPEN MY CHRISTMAS PRESENTS ALREADY.

I bet they were starting to miss me just as much. I bet they were feeling truly awful with missing me, and for abandoning me at Christmas, and for possibly making me move to a remote corner at the farthest end of the world when I've been perfectly content living right here in the center of the world that is the island of Manhattan.

(But maybe trying a new place could be interesting. Maybe.)

I held the truth to be self-evident: There was no way I wouldn't be able to mine a puppy out of this situation. So much parental guilt, so much Lily need for a dog. And I believed I could make the case that I'd evolved as a human and as a personal dog owner rather than just walker. I could handle pet ownership this time around.

Merry Christmas, Lily.

Practically speaking, no way would I settle for a bunny.

I barely had time to search dog shelter sites in Fiji for an appropriate adoptable pooch when I received a text from my cousin Mark.

> `Lily Bear: My co-worker Marc needs to go upstate to tend to his mother, who's been felled by eggnog poisoning. Do you have room in your client list for his dog, Boris? Needs to be fed and walked twice a day. Just for a day or two.`

`Sure,` I texted back. Admittedly, part of me had been hoping Mark's text would involve a Dash sighting, but a new dog job was adequate distraction.

> `Can you come by the store and pick up his keys?`

> `Be there in a few.`

The Strand was its usual mix of bustling people and laconic aisle readers. Mark wasn't at the information desk when I arrived, so I decided to do a little browsing. First I went to the animals section, but I'd read almost every book there, and I could only look at puppy pictures so many times without needing to pet one instead of just coo at its picture.

I wandered and found myself in the basement, where a sign on a bookcase in the deepest trenches at the back announced SEX & SEXUALITY BEGINS ON LEFT SHELF. The sign made me think of *The Joy of Gay Sex* (third edition), which in turn, of course, made me blush, and then think of J. D. Salinger. I returned upstairs to Fiction and there found a most curious male depositing a familiar red notebook in between *Franny and Zooey* and *Raise High the Roof Beam, Carpenters and Seymour: An Introduction.*

"Boomer?" I said.

Startled, and looking guilty, as if he'd been caught shoplifting, Boomer clumsily grabbed the red notebook back from the shelves, causing several hardcover editions of *Nine Stories* to noisily tumble to the floor. Boomer clutched the red notebook to his chest as if it were a Bible.

"Lily! I didn't expect to see you here. I mean, I kinda hoped to, but then I didn't, so I got used to that, but then here you are, just when I'm thinking about not seeing you, and—"

I reached my hands out. "Is that notebook for me?" I asked. I wanted to snatch the notebook from Boomer and read it posthaste, but I tried to sound casual, like, *Oh, yeah, that old thing. I'll read it whenever I get to it. It might be a while. I'm super-busy, not thinking about Dash or the notebook or anything.*

"Yes!" Boomer said. But he made no movement to hand it to me.

"Can I have it?" I asked.

"No!"

"Why not?"

"Because! You have to discover it on the shelves! When I'm not here!"

I hadn't realized there was a rule book for the notebook exchange. "So how about if I leave, and you put the notebook back on the shelves and walk away, and then when you're gone, I'll return and pick it up?"

"Okay!"

I started to turn around to execute the plan, but Boomer called after me.

"Lily!"

"Yes?"

"Max Brenner is across the street! I forgot about that!"

Boomer referred to a restaurant a block away from the Strand, a Willy Wonka–esque chocolate-themed eating extravaganza place—a tourist trap for sure, but of the best kind, not unlike Madame Tussauds.

"Want to split a chocolate pizza?" I asked Boomer.

"Yes!"

"I'll meet you there in ten minutes," I said, walking away.

"Don't forget to come back for the notebook when I'm not looking!" Boomer said. It both mystified and intrigued me that such a seemingly dour person as Dash was great friends with an extremely exclamation-pointed person as excitable Boomer. I suspected this spoke well for Dash, that he could appreciate this brand of Boomer dude.

"I won't," I called back.

I enlisted my cousin Mark to join us at Max Brenner, since bringing along an adult meant Mark would pick up the check, even if he likely would just bill it back to Grandpa.

Boomer and I ordered the chocolate pizza—a warm, thin pastry shaped like a pizza, with double-melted chocolate as the "sauce," topped with melted marshmallows and candied hazelnut bits, then carved into triangle slices like a real pizza. Mark ordered the chocolate syringe, which was exactly what it sounded like—a plastic syringe filled with chocolate that you could shoot straight into your mouth.

"But we could share our pizza with you!" Boomer told Mark after Mark ordered the syringe. "It's more fun when the sugar infusion is a truly communal experience."

"Thanks, kid, but I'm trying to reduce my carbs," Mark said. "I'll stick with shooting up straight chocolate. No need to add more dough to my waistline." The waitress left us and Mark turned to Boomer in all seriousness. "Now, tell us everything about your little punk friend Dash."

"He's not a punk! He's pretty square, actually!"

"No criminal record?" Mark said.

"Not unless you count the crimson alert!"

"The what?" Mark and I both said.

Boomer took out his phone and displayed a website called WashingtonSquareMommies.

Mark and I read through the crimson alert posting, inspecting the evidence on the site.

"He eats *yogurt*?" Mark asked. "What kind of teenage boy is he?"

"Lactose tolerant!" Boomer said. "Dash loves yogurt, and anything with cream in it, and he especially likes Spanish cheeses."

Mark turned to me consolingly. "Lily. Sweetie. You realize this Dash may not be straight?"

"Dash is for sure straight!" Boomer announced. "He has a super-pretty ex-girlfriend named Sofia, who I think he still has a thing for, and also, in seventh grade, there was a game of spin the bottle and it was my turn and I spun and it landed at Dash, but he wouldn't let me kiss him."

"Proves nothing," Mark muttered.

Sofia? *Sofia?*

I needed a bathroom break.

I don't think we should ever try to meet again; there's such freedom in that.

And now, for his final trick, Dash had insulted me.

Postcard 6: The Metropolitan Museum of Art

met past and past part of **MEET** *meet\mēt\1 a : to come into the presence of:* **FIND** *b : to come together with esp. at a particular time or place c : to come into contact or conjunction with :* **JOIN** *d : to appear to the perception of . . .*

"Are you okay, Lily?" a voice at the bathroom sink next to me asked as I read through Dash's latest inexplicable (to make no sense; *see:* ***BOYS***) message.

I shut the red notebook and looked up. In the mirror, I saw Alice Gamble, a girl from my school who was also on my soccer squad.

"Oh, hey, Alice," I said. "What are you doing here?" I half expected her to turn around and leave me standing there since I was not part of the "cool crowd" at school. Maybe because it was the holidays, she didn't.

"I live around the corner," Alice said. "My younger twin sisters love this place, so I get dragged here anytime the grandparents are in town."

"Boys make no sense," I told her.

"For sure!" Alice said, looking happy to have a topic on hand more interesting than younger siblings and grandparents. She glanced at the red notebook curiously. "Do you have any particular boy in mind?"

"I have no idea!" And I really didn't. I couldn't understand from his last message whether Dash was saying we should meet again or we should just correspond through the notebook. I couldn't understand why I even cared. Especially if there was some other girl named Sofia in the picture.

"Do you want to go get coffee or something tomorrow and discuss and analyze the situation at length?" Alice asked.

"Are your grandparents really that bad?" I couldn't imagine Alice wanting to hang out and do girl stuff with me like talk about boys endlessly unless she was really desperate.

Alice said, "My grandparents are pretty cool. But our apartment is small, and cramped with too many people visiting for the holidays. I need to get out of the house. And it would be fun to, you know, finally get to know you."

"Really?" I asked. I wondered if these kinds of invitations had always been available to me and I just hadn't noticed before, too shrouded in Shrilly fear?

"Really!" Alice said.

"You too!" I said.

We made a coffee date for the next day.

Who needed Dash?

Not me, for sure.

When I returned to our table, my cousin Mark was shooting up his chocolate directly into his mouth from the large plastic syringe. "Fantastic!" he slurpily exclaimed.

"This is probably not fair-trade chocolate here, though!" Boomer explained.

"Did I ask your opinion?" Mark asked.

"No!" Boomer said. "But I don't mind that you didn't!"

There was a matter on which I wanted Boomer's opinion. "Did Dash like the Snarly Muppet I made him?"

"Not really! He said it looked like the spawn of if Miss Piggy and Animal had sex."

"My eyes!" Mark said. No, he hadn't shot chocolate into his eyes by mistake. "What a disgusting thought. You teenagers have such perverted ideas." Mark set down his chocolate syringe. "You've made me lose my appetite, Boomer."

"My mom tells me that all the time!" Boomer said. He turned to me. "Your family must be just like mine!"

"Doubt that," Mark said.

My poor Snarly. I silently vowed to rescue my little felt darling and provide it the loving home that Dash never would.

"This Dash kid," Mark continued. "Sorry, Lily. I just don't like him."

"Do you even know him?" Boomer asked.

"I know enough about him to pass judgment," Mark said.

"Dash is a good guy, really," Boomer said. "I think the word his mom uses to describe him is *finicky,* which is kinda true, but trust me, he's good people. The best! Especially when you consider that his parents had a really nasty divorce and don't even talk to each other *at all* anymore. How weird is that? He probably wouldn't like me telling you this, but Dash got dragged through a terrible custody battle when he was a kid, with his dad trying to get full custody just to spite his mom, and Dash having to go in to have all these talks with lawyers and judges and social workers. It was *awful.* If you got caught in the middle of that, would you manage to be a super-friendly person after? Dash is the kind of guy who's always had to figure out everything for himself. But you know what's so cool about him? He always does! He's totally the most loyal friend a person could ever have. Takes a lot to earn his trust, but once you do, there's nothing he won't do for you. Nothing you can't depend on him for. He can sometimes act a bit loner-ish, but I think that's not because he's some serial killer waiting to happen; he's just his own best company sometimes. And he's comfortable with that. I guess there's nothing wrong with that."

I admit I was moved by Boomer's heartfelt defense of Dash, even if I was still mad about Snarly, but Mark shrugged. "Pshaw," he said.

I asked my cousin, "Do you not like Dash because you genuinely think he's unlikable or because there's a bit of Grandpa in you, who doesn't want me to have new friends who are boys?"

"I'm your new friend who's a boy, Lily," Boomer stated. "You like me, don't you, Mark?"

"Pshaw," Mark repeated. The answer was clear: Mark liked Dash just fine, so long as Dash wasn't someone I could potentially be interested in. Boomer too.

Boris the dog who needed walking turned out to be more like a pony who needed sprinting. He was a bullmastiff who came up to my waist, a young buck with tons of energy who literally tried to drag me through Washington Square Park. Boris barely gave me time to tape the sign I'd created to the tree. The sign had the crimson alert photo in the middle with a message that said: *WANTED—this teenage boy, not a pervert, not a hoodlum, simply a boy who likes yogurt. WANTED—this boy to explain himself.*

I need not have posted the sign, however.

Because five minutes after I posted it, Boris started loudly barking at a teenage boy who approached me as I scooped up the biggest piece of dog dung I'd ever seen.

"Lily?"

I looked up from my plastic bag filled with giant poo.

Of course.

It was Dash.

Who else would find me at just this moment? First he found me drunk, now he found me cleaning up poo from a barking pony who was about to go into attack mode.

Perfect.

No wonder I'd never had a boyfriend.

"Hi," I said, trying to sound super-casual, but aware that my voice was coming out super-high-pitched and, indeed, somewhat Shrilly.

"What are you doing here?" Dash asked, stepping back a few feet farther from me and Boris. "And why do you have so many keys?" He pointed to the huge key ring clasped to my purse, which had the keys for all my dog-walking clients attached to it. "Are you a building super or something?"

"I WALK DOGS!" I shouted over Boris's barking.

"CLEARLY!" Dash shouted back. "But it looks like he's walking you!"

Boris leapt back into action, dragging me behind him,

with Dash running to our side—far to our side, as if not quite sure he wanted to participate in this spectacle.

"What are you doing here?" I asked Dash.

"I ran out of yogurt," Dash said. "Went out to get more."

"And to defend your good name?"

"Oh, dear. You heard about the crimson alert?"

"Who didn't?" I said.

He must not have seen my posted sign yet. Could I take it down before he reached that tree?

I tugged on Boris's leash to turn us in the opposite direction, away from the Washington Square arch and toward downtown. For some unknown reason, the direction change calmed Boris down, and he switched from his full-on gallop to a mild trot.

Logically, based on what I knew of boys generally and specifically of Dash, I would have expected Dash to bolt in the opposite direction at this point.

Instead, he asked, "Where are you going?"

"I don't know."

"Can I come with?"

Seriously?

I said, "That'd be awesome. Where do you think we should go?"

"Let's just wander and see what happens," Dash said.

seventeen

–Dash–

December 29th

It was rather awkward, insofar as we were both teetering between the possibility of something and the possibility of nothing.

"So which way should we go?" Lily asked.

"I don't know—which way do you want to go?"

"Either way."

"You sure?"

She was definitely more attractive sober, as most people are. She had a winsome quality now—but smartly winsome, not vacuously winsome.

"We could go to the High Line," I said.

"Not with Boris."

Ah, Boris. He seemed to be losing patience with us.

"Is there a certain dog-walking route you take?" I asked.

"Yes. But we don't have to take it."

Stasis. Total stasis. Her sneaking peeks at me. Me sneaking peeks at her. Teeter teeter teeter.

Finally, one of us was decisive.

And it wasn't me or Lily.

It was as if a dog-whistle orchestra had suddenly struck up the *1812 Overture*. Or a parade of squirrels had marched into the other side of Washington Square Park and started to rub themselves with oil. Whatever the provocation, Boris was off like a shot. Lily was caught off balance, dragged onto a sleety patch, and knocked from her footing entirely. The bag of poop went flying in the air. Much to my deep delight, as Lily fell, she let out a raucous "MOTHERSUCKER!"—a curse I had not heretofore heard.

She landed gracelessly, but without injury. The bag of poop narrowly missed popping her on the temple. Meanwhile, she had let go of Boris's leash, which I foolishly grabbed for and caught. Now I was the one who had the sensation of water-skiing over pavement.

"Stop him!" Lily yelled, as if there were some button I could press that would shut the dog down. Instead, I simply added worthless ballast as he charged forth.

It was clear he had a target in mind. He was storming toward a group of mothers, strollers, and kids. With horror, I saw he'd zeroed in on the most vulnerable prey around—a kid wearing an eye patch, chomping on an oat bar.

"No, Boris. No!" I cried.

But Boris was going to go his own way, whether I was on board or not. The kid saw him coming and unleashed a shriek that was, frankly, more appropriate to a girl half his age. Before his mother could whisk him out of harm's way, Boris had barreled into him and knocked him down, pulling me in his wake.

"I'm so sorry," I said as I tried to pull Boris to a stop. It was like playing tug-of-war with a garden party of NFL linebackers.

"It's him!" the boy squealed. "IT'S THE ATTACKER!"

"Are you sure?" a woman I could only assume was his mother asked.

The boy lifted his eye patch, revealing a perfectly good eye.

"It's him. I swear," he said.

Another woman came over with what looked like a wanted poster with my face on it.

"CRIMSON ALERT!" she yelled into the air. "WE ARE UPGRADING FROM MANGO!"

Another mother, about to take her baby out of its stroller, let go in order to blow a whistle—four short bursts, which I had to imagine corresponded to crimson.

The whistle blowing was not a wise idea. Boris heard it, turned, and charged.

The woman jumped out of the way. The stroller could not. I flung myself to the ground, trying to make myself as heavy as possible. Boris, confused, crashed right into the stroller, dislodging the baby inside. In slow motion, I saw it fly up, a shocked expression on its docile face.

I wanted to close my eyes. There was no way I could get to the baby in time. We were all paralyzed. Even Boris stopped to watch.

In the corner of my eye: movement. A cry. Then the most magnificent sight: Lily flying through the air. Hair streaming. Arms outstretched. Entirely unaware of how she looked, only aware of what she was doing. A flying leap. An honest, bona fide flying leap. There wasn't any panic on her face. Only determination. She got herself under that baby, and she caught it. As soon as it landed in her arms, it started to wail.

"My God," I murmured. I had never seen anything so transfixing.

I thought the crowd would break into applause. But then Lily, recovering from her flying leap, took a few extra steps, and a mother behind me yelled, "Child stealer! Stop her!"

Mothers and other bystanders all had their cell phones out. Some in the mommy circle were arguing over who would send out the crimson alert and who would call the police. Lily, meanwhile, was still in her golden moment, unaware of the fuss. She was holding on to the baby, trying to calm it down after its traumatic flight.

I tried to get up from the ground, but suddenly there was a formidable weight on my back.

"You're not going anywhere," one of the mothers said, sitting on me firmly. "Consider this a citizen's arrest."

Two more mothers and the eye-patched kid piled on. I almost let go of the leash. Luckily, Boris seemed to have had enough excitement for the day, and was now barking out orders to no one in particular.

"The police are coming!" someone yelled.

The baby's mother ran over to Lily, who had no idea that it was the baby's mother. I saw her say, "One sec," as she tried to get the baby to stop crying. I think the mother was thanking her—but then a few other mothers descended and boxed Lily in.

"I saw this on *Dateline*," one of the louder mothers was saying. "They create a diversion, then steal the baby. In broad daylight!"

"This is absurd!" I yelled. The kid started bouncing up and down on my tailbone.

Two police officers arrived and were immediately besieged with versions of the story. The truth went vastly underrepresented. Lily looked confused as she handed the baby over—hadn't she done the right thing? The police asked her if she knew me, and she said of course she did.

"You see!" one mother crowed. "An accomplice!"

The ground was cold and slushy, and the weight of the mothers was starting to rupture some of my choicer internal organs. I might have confessed to a crime I hadn't committed in order to get out of there.

It was unclear whether we were being arrested or not.

"I think you should come with us," one of the officers said. It didn't seem like *Actually, I'd rather not* was an appropriate answer to give.

They didn't cuff us, but they did march us to the squad car and make us sit in the back with Boris. It wasn't until we were back there, with some mommies calling for vengeance and the flying baby's mother concentrating on making sure her baby was okay, that I got a chance to actually say something to Lily.

"Nice catch," I told her.

"Thanks," she said. She was in shock, staring out the window.

"It was beautiful. Really. One of the most beautiful things I've ever seen."

She looked at me for what felt like the first time. We held like that for a few heartbeats. The squad car pulled away from the park. They didn't bother with the sirens.

"I guess we know where we're going now," she said.

"Fate has a strange way of making plans," I agreed.

Lily had relatives all across the five boroughs, but unfortunately none of them were in law enforcement.

She listed many of them for me, trying to figure out who would be best suited to get us out of this jam.

"Uncle Murray got indicted, which is pretty much the opposite of what we need. Great-aunt Mrs. Basil E. dated someone in the district attorney's office for a while . . . but I don't think it ended well. One of my cousins went into the CIA, but I'm not allowed to say which one. This is so frustrating!"

We weren't, thankfully, locked in a cell. Instead, we'd been marched into an interrogation room, although nobody had thought to interrogate us yet. Maybe they were just watching through the mirror to see if we'd confess something to each other.

I was surprised by how well Lily was taking our incarceration. She was far from a wee timorous beastie—if anything, I was the one who was jangled as we were ramrodded into custody. None of the police officers seemed particularly impressed that neither of us had parents who were currently within bailing-out distance. Lily ended up calling her brother. I ended up calling Boomer, who happened to be with Yohnny and Dov at the time.

"It's all over the news!" Boomer told me. "Some people are calling you heroes and others are saying you're criminals. The videos are all over the Web. I think you might even make the six o'clock news."

This was not how I'd seen the day going.

Lily and I hadn't been read our rights or offered a lawyer, so I was guessing we hadn't actually been charged with anything yet.

Meanwhile, Boris was getting hungry.

"I know, I know," Lily responded to his whining. "Hopefully your daddy doesn't have Internet where he is."

I tried to think of interesting conversational topics to bring up. Had she been named after the flower? How long had she been dog walking? Wasn't she relieved that none of the officers had thought to use a billy club against us?

"You're uncharacteristically quiet," she said, sitting down at the interrogation table and taking the red notebook from her jacket pocket. "Do you want to write something down and pass it over to me?"

"Do you have a pen?" I asked.

She shook her head. "It's in my bag. And they took my bag."

"I guess we'll have to talk, then," I said.

"Or we could take the Fifth."

"Is this your first time in prison?" I asked.

Lily nodded. "You?"

"My mom once had to bail my father out, and there wasn't anybody at home to watch me. So I came along. I must've been seven or eight. At first she told me he'd had a little accident, which made me think he'd peed himself somewhere inconvenient. Then I was told it had been 'disorderly conduct'—it never went to trial, so there's no paper trail."

"That's awful," Lily said.

"I guess it is. At the time, it just seemed normal. They got divorced soon after."

Boris started to bark.

"Not a fan of divorce, I see," I observed.

"His treats are also in my bag," Lily said with a sigh.

For a minute or two, she closed her eyes. Just sat there and let everything else drift away, become beside the point. I didn't mind that I, too, was disappearing. She looked like she needed a break, and I was willing to give it to her.

"Here, Boris," I said, attempting to be friendly with the beast. He looked at me warily, then started licking the floor.

"I guess I'm nervous to be meeting you," Lily said at long last, eyes still closed.

"Likewise," I assured her. "I find I very rarely live up to my words. And since you know me primarily through my words, there are oh so many ways I can disappoint."

She opened her eyes. "It's not just that. It's just the last time you saw me—"

"—you weren't yourself. Don't you think I know that?"

"Sure. But isn't it possible that I *was* myself then? Maybe that's who I'm supposed to be, only I don't let her out a lot."

"I think I like the dog-walking, baby-catching, truth-telling Lily better," I said. "For what it's worth."

And that was the question, wasn't it? What was it worth?

"That Lily landed us in jail," Lily pointed out.

"Well, you wanted danger, right? And, really, it was Boris who landed us in jail. Or the red notebook that landed us in jail. The red notebook was a great idea, by the way."

"It was my brother's," Lily admitted. "Sorry."

"Well, you're the one who stuck with it, aren't you?"

Lily nodded. "For what it's worth."

I pulled my chair over so we were next to each other at the interrogation table.

"It's definitely worth something," I said. "A lot. We still don't know each other, right? And I'll admit—I thought it might be best if we kept it all to the page, passed that notebook back and forth until we were ninety. But clearly that wasn't meant to be. And who am I to blow against the wind?"

Lily blushed. "'And what did you do on your first date, Lily?' 'Well, we went down to the precinct house and grabbed two Styrofoam cups of water.' 'That seems very romantic.' 'Oh, it *was*.'"

"'So what did you do for a second date?'" I continued. "'Well, we figured we'd have to rob a bank. Only it ended up being a sperm bank, and we were accosted by angry mommies-to-be in the waiting room. So it was back to the jailhouse for us.' 'That sounds exciting.' 'Oh, it was. And it went on. Now when I have to remember a date, all I have to do is consult my rap sheet.'"

"'And what drew you to her?'" she asked.

"'Well,'" I answered the phantom interviewer, "'I'd have to say it was the way she catches babies. Exquisite, really. And you? What made you think, *Wow, this gent's a keeper?*'"

"'I love a man who doesn't let go of the leash, even when it leads him to ruin.'"

"Well done," I said. "Well done."

I thought Lily would be happy with this compliment. But instead she sighed and slumped down in her chair.

"What?" I asked.

"What about Sofia?" she said.

"Sofia?"

"Yes. Boomer mentioned Sofia."

"Ah, Boomer."

"Do you love her?"

I shook my head. "I can't love her. She lives in Spain."

Lily laughed. "I guess you get points for truthfulness."

"No, really," I said. "I think she's great. And I honestly like her about twenty times more now than I did when we were dating. But love needs to have a future. And Sofia and I don't have a future. We've just had a good time sharing the present, that's all."

"You really think love needs to have a future?"

"Absolutely."

"Good," Lily said. "So do I."

"Good," I echoed, leaning in. "So do you."

"Don't repeat what I say," she told me, swatting at my arm.

"Don't repeat what I say," I murmured, smiling.

"You're being silly," she said, but the silliness was falling out of her voice.

"*You're* being silly," I assured her.

"Lily is the greatest girl who ever was."

I drew closer. *"Lily is the greatest girl who ever was."*

For a moment, I think we'd forgotten where we were.

And then the officers returned, and we were reminded once again.

"Well," said Officer White, who was black, "you'll be happy to know that the videos of your exploits this afternoon have already garnered two hundred thousand hits on YouTube. And you were captured at pretty much every angle possible—it's impressive that the statue of George Washington didn't whip out an iPhone and email the photos to his friends."

"We've looked at all the footage closely," said Officer Black, who was white, "and have come to the conclusion that there's only one guilty party in this room."

"I know, sir," I stepped in. "It was all my fault. Really, she had nothing to do with it."

"No, no, no," Lily disagreed. "I was the one who hung that poster. It was a joke. But that made the mommies go a little crazy."

"Seriously," I said, turning to Lily, "you did nothing but help. It's me they wanted."

"No, I'm the one they thought was stealing the baby. And believe me, I don't even *want* a baby."

"Neither of you is to blame," Officer White interrupted.

Officer Black pointed her finger at Boris. "If there's anyone at fault, it's the one on all fours."

Boris shuffled back guiltily.

Officer White looked at me. "As for Johnny One-Eye, we can't find anything actually wrong with him. So even if you happened to hit him with a snowball in the middle of a snowball fight—and I'm not saying you did or didn't—no harm, no foul."

"Does that mean we're free to go?" Lily asked.

Officer Black nodded. "You've got quite a posse waiting for you outside."

Officer Black wasn't kidding. Boomer was there with not only Yohnny and Dov but Sofia and Priya as well. And it looked like Lily's whole family was waiting in the wings, presided over by Mrs. Basil E.

"Take a look!" Boomer said, holding up two printouts, one from the *Post* website, one from the *Daily News*.

Both had a dazzling photo of the baby falling into Lily's arms.

OUR HERO! shouted the *Daily News*.

BABY STEALER! cried the *Post*.

"There are reporters outside," Mrs. Basil E. informed us. "Most of them quite indecent."

Officer Black turned to us.

"Well, then—do you want to be celebrities or not?"

Lily and I looked at each other.

The answer was pretty clear.

"Not," I said.

"Definitely not," Lily added.

"The back door it is, then!" Officer Black said. "Follow me."

With the crowds that had come to fetch us, Lily and I lost

each other in the shuffle. Sofia was asking if I was okay, Boomer was enthusing that Lily and I had finally met, and the rest were just taking it all in.

We didn't even have a chance to say goodbye. The doors opened and the police told us to move quickly, because the reporters would catch on quick.

She went her way with her people, and I went my way with mine.

I felt a weight in my pocket.

Sly girl, she'd slipped me the notebook.

eighteen

(Lily)

December 30th

The news of the world travels fast and far. Even to Fiji.

They didn't know it, but I was intermittently muting my computer speakers while my parents ranted from their side of our video chat. Occasionally I'd click the speakers back on to hear snippets of their tirade:

"How are we supposed to trust you on your own, Lily, if—"

Mute.

Their hands flailed madly about from across the world while my hands concentrated on my new knitting project.

"Who is this Dash? Does Grandpa know about—"

Mute.

I watched as Mom and Dad furiously tried to pack luggage while yelling at their computer.

"We're late for our flight! We'll be lucky to make it. Do you know how many calls we've—"

Mute.

Dad appeared to be yelling at his cell phone for ringing again. Mom peered into the computer screen.

"*Where* has Langston been all this time—"

Mute.

I continued working on my newest creation: a pin-striped, jail-uniform-themed doggy sweater for Boris. I looked up to see Mom's index finger wagging at me.

Un-mute.

"And one more thing, Lily!" Mom's face peered as close as she possibly could to her computer screen. I'd never noticed before, but she had truly excellent pores, which could only bode well for my own aging process.

"Yes, Mommy?" I asked as Dad sat on their hotel bed behind her, flailing his arms around again, explaining the situation again to someone calling his phone again.

"That was a marvelous catch, darling."

Grandpa was driving through Delaware (the toll capital of the highway world, he says) when Mr. Borscht called his cell to tell him about the headline, followed by calls from scandalized Messrs. Curry and Cannoli. First Grandpa almost had a heart attack while driving. Then he went to McDonald's for a Big Mac to calm himself down. Then he called Langston and yelled at him for allowing me to become a jailbird and an international celebrity in the few hours since Langston was supposed to be in charge after Grandpa left back for Florida. Grandpa then turned around and returned to Manhattan, arriving home just in time for Langston and Mrs. Basil E. to bring me home from the police station.

"You're grounded until your parents get home to take care

of this mess!" Grandpa screeched at me. He pointed at poor little Boris. "And keep that terror dog away from my cat upstairs!" Boris barked loudly and appeared poised to topple Grandpa, too.

"Sit, Boris," I told the beast.

Boris plopped down onto the floor and placed his head across my feet. He hissed a low growl in Grandpa's direction.

"I don't think Boris and I agree about being grounded," I told Grandpa.

"This is nonsense, Arthur," Mrs. Basil E. chimed in. "Lily didn't do anything wrong. It was all a big misunderstanding. She saved a baby! It's not like she stole a car and went out joyriding."

"It's common knowledge that no good comes to a young lady appearing on the cover of the *New York Post*!" Grandpa bellowed. He pointed at me. "Grounded!"

"Go to your room, Lily bear," Mrs. Basil E. whispered in my ear. "I'll take care of this from here. Take that pony with you."

"Please don't tell Grandpa about Dash," I whispered back.

"Can't keep a lid on that one," she said aloud.

The upshot of all the parental and grandparental hysteria was that I did not technically get grounded. Instead, I was told, most affirmatively, to lay low until Mom and Dad got home from Fiji on New Year's Day. It was *recommended* that I stay home and chill for the time being.

Not that I wanted to anyway, but I've been instructed I'm not allowed to talk to the press, all my trash must go through a shredder, I'm not to plan how I'd look on the cover of *People* magazine (an exclusive, which could potentially pay for my whole college education in one fell swoop), and if Oprah calls, she talks to my mom first, and not to me. Quite frankly, the family are all hoping some celebrity dies or is exposed in a tawdry scandal ASAP so the tabloids can move on from Lily Dogwalker.

For my own emotional well-being it has been suggested that I not Google myself.

There aren't many people you can trust in this world who aren't related to you, according to the familial overseers. Better to stay within your own family's tender bosom till all this blows over.

What I know for certain is: You can always trust a dog.

Boris liked Dash.

You can tell a lot about a person by the way they treat animals. Dash never hesitated to grab for Boris's leash when crisis struck. He's one stand-up (or sat-upon, in the case of the crimson alert mommies) kind of dude, for sure.

Boomer, who's rather like a dog, also likes Dash.

Dog instincts are always right.

Dash must be very likable.

There are just lots of possibilities in the world, I've decided. Dash. Boris. I need to keep my mind open for what could happen and not decide that the world is hopeless if what I want to happen doesn't happen. Because something else great might happen in between.

The verdict on Boris, therefore, is unequivocal: He's a keeper.

Boris's owner, my cousin Mark's co-worker Marc from the Strand, had been illegally harboring Boris at his own studio apartment, in a no-pets building. He'd been able to get away with it before, because his building was run by an off-site management company with no super or owner living there, but now that Boris is so famous (according to a *New York Post* online poll, 64 percent of respondents think Boris is a menace to society, 31 percent think he's an unwitting victim of his own strength, and 5 percent think Boris should meet his maker in an unmentionable way), Marc obviously can't bring Boris "home."

That's okay, because I've made the executive decision that my home is now Boris's home. In the less than twenty-four hours since he's been under my care, Boris has learned to Sit, to Heel, to Not Beg for Food at the Dinner Table, and to Drop It (meaning Grandpa's shoes about to be chewed to oblivion). Clearly the problem all along was that Boris's owner was not giving him the proper attention and guidance he needed to flourish and become an upstanding member of society. Also, according to the Internet, Marc was not a reliable pooper-scooper and only used Boris as a pawn to meet girls. More disturbingly, Marc has texted me several times that he doesn't mind me keeping Boris as long as I want. That's one high-maintenance dog. Obviously Marc never deserved Boris to begin with.

Boris and I spent a night at the jailhouse together. We are bonded for eternity. Well, we spent a few hours in an interrogation room at the police precinct together, with an extremely cute boy. Close enough. Boris's home is with me now, and Mom and Dad and everyone else will just have to get used to that. Family takes care of family, and Boris is family now.

My crisis management team turned out to be Alice Gamble, along with Heather Wong and Nikesha Johnson, two other girls from my soccer team.

As we hung out in my room, Alice said, "So, Lily. Even

though we've known you for a long time, we've never, like, really gotten to *know* you, know you, right? So since your grandpa invited us over for this slumber party to keep you from going outside—"

"The slumber party was my idea," I interrupted. "Grandpa just had conveniently hidden my phone before I had a chance to ask you myself."

"Where'd you find your phone?" Alice asked.

"The cookie jar. So. Obvious. It's like he wasn't even trying."

Alice smiled. "The girls and I, we conjured up something sweet for you, too." She sat over my laptop and called up a video clip on YouTube. "Since you're not available to the media to defend yourself, we decided your soccer could do it for you."

"Huh?" I said.

Nikesha said, "You're a mad good goalie! And who but a mad good goalie could make a baby catch like that? A goalie catches babies by natural instinct. Not because they're trying to steal it! They're trying to save it."

Heather said, "Behold," and started the YouTube video.

And there it was. To the tune of "Stop," by the Spice Girls, my teammates had assembled a series of photos and video clips showing me in soccer goalie motion—running, grunting, kicking, leaping, jumping, soaring.

I had no idea I was that good a player.

I had no idea my teammates had ever noticed, or cared.

Maybe I'd never bothered to think of them as my teammates before. Maybe I myself had been the biggest part of the friendship impasse.

There's no *i* in *team,* as the saying goes.

When the clip ended, the girls wrapped me in a victory

huddle in my bedroom such as we'd never shared together on the field. I couldn't help it. I was crying—not a full-on embarrassing sobfest, but silly yet profound tears of joy and gratitude.

"Wow, guys. Thank you" was all I could blubber to say.

"We chose the 'Stop' song because that's what you do—stop the other team from scoring," Heather said. "Just like you stopped that baby from hitting the pavement."

Nikesha said, "And as a Beckham homage, too."

"Obvs," Alice and I both said.

Heather said, "If you read the comments—I mean, there are 845 of them so far, so maybe don't. But I perused them when we first put this up to defend your good name, and, Lily, you totally already have five proposals of marriage in there, at least until I stopped reading. I mean, 95,223 views—no, just jumped to 95,225 as of this second. I could only read so many of the marriage offers and other indecent proposals. There are a few college recruiters who posted that you should try out for their teams, too."

Boris barked approvingly from his new dog bed at the corner of my room.

December 31st

"Benny and I are back together," Langston announced over lunch. The slumber party girls had all gone home to prepare for their own New Year's Eve celebrations, and Grandpa was upstairs negotiating on the phone with Mabel to forsake Miami to visit him in New York—in *January*!—so he wouldn't have to drive down to Florida again, return to New York again, turn around back to Florida again, then return to New York again, all within a matter of days.

Men just can't make up their minds about what they want.

"A couple of days apart was just too much for you and Benny?" I asked my brother.

"That, yes. But also, we figured, you know, we started that whole red notebook thing for you. We have kismet together."

"And you really missed each other! And hopefully decided to just admit that and see each other exclusively?"

"I wouldn't go *that* far," Langston said. "Let's just say Benny and I have a behind-closed-doors Skype date for New Year's Eve tonight while he's in Puerto Rico. No babysitting you and your hijinks."

"Gross. And you never babysat me."

"I know. And believe me, I'll be blamed for everything that's happened for the rest of my life."

"Thanks for doing a terrible job being in charge, Brother. I had a blast." Something about the red notebook's origins still bothered me, though. "Langston?" I asked.

"Yes, Lily celebrity-bear? Oh, Celebri-bear! That's going to be my new name for you."

I ignored that last bit. "What if it's really you he likes?"

"Who? What do you mean?"

"Dash. Finding the red notebook. That was your idea. I wrote the first messages in my own handwriting, but the words and ideas were yours. Maybe the person Dash asked out for New Year's Eve is based on some figment of his imagination that you created?"

"So what if it is? You kept on with the notebook. You

continued the adventure. And look what it turned into! I coughed away in my bedroom and mistakenly broke up with my boyfriend. You went out and made your own destiny with that notebook!"

He didn't get it.

"But, Langston. What if . . . Dash ends up not really liking me? *Me*-me, not his *idea* of me."

"So what if he doesn't?"

I'd been expecting my brother to jump to my defense and proclaim his certainty in Dash's certain liking of me. "What?" I said, offended.

"I mean, if Dash doesn't like you once he gets to know you, so what?"

"I don't know if I want to take that risk." Get hurt. Be rejected. Like Langston once was.

"The reward is in the risk. You can't stay hidden inside Grandpa's overprotective cloak forever. You've seemed like you needed to grow out of that for a while. Mom and Dad going away, and the red notebook, these things just helped. Now it's up to you to figure out how Dash figures into the picture. How *you* fit into this picture. Take the risk."

I wanted so badly to believe, but the fear felt as great and overwhelming as the desire. "What if this all has been a dream? What if we're just wasting each other's time?"

"How can you know if you don't try?" Langston then quoted the poet he'd been named after, Langston Hughes. "'A dream deferred is a dream denied.'"

"Are you over him?" I asked.

We both knew the him I referred to was not Benny, but the him who broke Langston's heart so devastatingly. Langston's first love.

"In some ways, I think I'll never be over him," Langston said.

"That is such an unsatisfying answer."

"That's because you're interpreting it the wrong way. I don't mean it as a wistful, overdramatic declaration. I meant that the love I felt for him was huge and real, and, while painful, it forever changed me as a person, in the same way that being your brother reflects and changes how I evolve, and vice versa. The important people in our lives leave imprints. They may stay or go in the physical realm, but they are always there in your heart, because they helped form your heart. There's no getting over that."

My heart undoubtedly wanted to embrace and/or be trampled upon by Dash. That much was sure. The risk would have to discover its own reward.

From under the table, Boris licked at my ankles. I said, "Boris is staying and he has imprinted on my heart and Mom and Dad are just going to have to live with that."

"Joke's on you, Celebri-bear. Your big Christmas present on New Year's Day was going to be Mom and Dad finally giving you permission again to have your own pet."

"Really? But what if we move to Fiji?"

"The parents will figure it out. If they do decide to go, they'll keep this apartment, where I'm going to stay living while I'm at NYU. I don't think Mom and Dad are planning to live in Fiji year-round—just during the school terms. I'll take care of Boris when you're away, if you end up going with them and it turns out Boris isn't allowed past customs in Fiji. How about if that's my Christmas present to you?"

"Because you were too busy being with Benny to get me something this year?"

"Yep. And how about in return, instead of the sweater you've undoubtedly knit me, and the umpteen cookies you've undoubtedly baked me for Christmas on New Year's, if you just tell Grandpa not to blame me for all your hijinks and get him off my case?"

"Okay," I agreed. "Let the girl call the rules, as it should be."

"Speaking of rules . . . what *are* you doing for New Year's, Lily? Surely you'll be let back outside again? Will Monsieur Dashiell be squiring you around our fair town tonight?"

I sighed and shook my head. There was nothing to do but admit it: "He hasn't called me or emailed me or notebooked me since the police station."

I abruptly stood up from my chair so I could return to my room and feel terribly sorry for myself and eat way too much chocolate in private.

I supposed I could text or email Dash (even *call* him—what?!?!?), but those options felt intrusive after all we'd been through. After the red notebook. Dash was a guy that appreciated his privacy and seemed to revel in solitude. I could respect that.

He should be the one to contact me.

Right?

What did it say about me that he hadn't?

That he couldn't possibly like me as much as I'd started to like him. That I would never be as pretty and interesting as that Sofia girl, while Dash's handsome face would continue to appear in my daydreams.

Unrequited.

It wasn't fair that I sort of missed him. Not his presence

so much—I barely knew him—but having that red notebook link to him. Knowing he was out there thinking or doing something that would be communicated to me in some surprising way.

I lay on my bed, daydreaming about Dash, and reached down to receive a reassuring lick from Boris, but he was not there. He was out on his walk.

Our apartment doorbell buzzed loudly and I jumped up and ran into the hallway to answer it. "Hello?" I said from the other side of the door.

"It's your favorite great-aunt. I left my key inside the apartment when I came to walk Boris."

Boris!

The twenty minutes since he'd been gone had nearly destroyed me. Boris never ignored me like that Dash guy.

I opened the door to let Mrs. Basil E. and Boris back inside.

I looked down at Boris, pawing at my ankles to get my attention.

Boris's mouth held not a doggy bone or a postman's jacket. From between his teeth, Boris slobberingly offered me a red-ribbon-wrapped red notebook.

nineteen

–Dash–

December 30th

We retreated to my mother's apartment after I was released from jail. The adrenaline in all of us was amazing—we alternated between bouncing and floating, as if the excitement of escape had turned the world into a giant trampoline.

As soon as we were in the door, Yohnny and Dov attempted to raid the refrigerator and were unsatisfied with what they found.

"Noodle pudding?" Yohnny asked.

"Yeah, my mom made it," I told them. "I always save it for last."

While Priya went to the loo and Boomer checked his email on his phone, Sofia stepped into my bedroom. Not for any lascivious reason—just to check it out.

"It hasn't changed much," she observed, staring at the quotes I'd thumbtacked to my walls.

"Little things have," I said. "There are some new quotes on the wall. Some new books on the shelves. Some of the pencils have lost their erasers. The sheets are changed every week."

"So even though it doesn't seem like anything's changed—"

"—things change all the time, mostly in little ways. That's how it goes, I guess."

Sofia nodded. "Funny how we say it *goes*. That's the way life *goes*."

"*That's the way life comes* just sounds so awkward."

"Well, sometimes you can see the future come, no? Sometimes it even, say, catches a baby."

I studied her face for any hint of sarcasm or meanness. And sadness—I was also looking for sadness, or regret. But all I found was amusement.

I sat down on my bed and held my head in my hands. Then, realizing this was way too dramatic, I looked up at her.

"I truly don't understand any of this," I confessed.

She stayed standing, facing me.

"I wish I could help you there," she told me. "But I can't."

So there we were. Once upon a time, during the storybook version of dating we'd gone through, I'd pretended that it was possible to love her when I only mildly liked her. Now I had no desire to pretend we'd ever be in love, and I liked her madly.

"Can we try to be wise with each other for a very long time?" I asked her.

She laughed. "You mean, can we share our fuckups and see if we can get any wisdom out of them?"

"Yeah," I said. "That would be nice."

I felt we needed to seal our new pact. Kissing was out. Hugging seemed peevish. So I offered her my hand. She shook it. And then we went to join the rest of our friends.

I couldn't help but wonder about what Lily was doing. How she was feeling. What she was feeling. Yes, it was confusing, but it wasn't a bad confusion. I wanted to see her again, in a way I'd never wanted to see her before.

I knew the notebook was in my hands. I just wanted to find the right thing to say.

My mother called to see how things were going. There was no Internet access at the spa, and she wasn't the type who turned on the TV when she wasn't home. So I didn't have to explain anything. I just said I had a few people over and we were all behaving ourselves.

My father, I couldn't help but note, usually checked the news every five minutes on his phone. He'd probably even seen the headline on the *Post* site, and the photos. He simply didn't recognize his own son.

Later that night, after a marathon of John Hughes movies, I kept Boomer, Sofia, Priya, Yohnny, and Dov in my mother's living room and brought out a dry-erase board from her home office.

"Before you leave," I told them, "I would like to conduct a brief symposium on love."

I took out a red marker—I mean, why not?—and wrote the word *love* on the board.

"Here we have it," I said. "Love." For good measure, I drew a heart around it. Not the ventricled kind. The made-up kind.

"It exists in this pristine state, upholding its ideals. But then . . . along come words."

I wrote *words* over and over again, all around the dry erase board, including over the word *love*.

"And feelings."

I wrote *feelings* in the same way, crisscrossing it on top of everything I'd already written.

"And expectations. And history. And thoughts. Help me out here, Boomer."

We wrote each of these three words at least twenty times each.

The result?

Pure illegibility. Not only was *love* gone, but you couldn't make out anything else, either.

"This," I said, holding up the board, "is what we're up against."

Priya looked disturbed—more by me than by what I was saying. Sofia still looked amused. Yohnny and Dov were curling closer together. Boomer, pen still in hand, was trying to work something out.

He raised his hand.

"Yes, Boomer?" I asked.

"You're saying that either you're in love or you're not. And if you are, it becomes like this."

"Something to that effect."

"But what if it's not a yes-or-no question?"

"I don't understand what you mean."

"I mean, what if love isn't a yes-or-no question? It's not either *you're in love* or *you're not*. I mean, aren't there different levels? And maybe these things, like words and expectations and whatever, don't go on top of the love. Maybe it's like a map, and they all have their own place, and then when you see it from the sky—whoa."

I looked at the board. "I think your map is cleaner than mine," I said. "But isn't this what the collision of the right two people at the right time looks like? I mean, it's a mess."

Sofia chuckled.

"What?" I asked her.

"*Right person, right time* is the wrong concept, Dash," she said.

"Totally," Boomer agreed.

"What does she mean by that?" I asked him.

"What I mean," Sofia said, "is that when people say *right person, wrong time*, or *wrong person, right time*, it's usually a cop-out. They think that fate is playing with them. That we're all just participants in this romantic reality show that God gets a kick out of watching. But the universe doesn't decide what's right or not right. You do. Yes, you can theorize until you're blue in the face whether something might have worked at another time, or with someone else. But you know what that leaves you?"

"Blue in the face?" I asked.

"Yup."

"You have the notebook, right?" Dov chimed in.

"I really hope you didn't lose it," Yohnny added.

"Yes," I said.

"So what are you waiting for?" Sofia asked.

"You all to leave?" I said.

"Good," she said. "You now have your writing assignment. Because you know what? It's up to you, not fate."

I still didn't know what to write. I fell asleep with the notebook next to me, both of us staring at the ceiling.

December 31st

The next morning, over breakfast, I had my grand idea.

I called Boomer immediately.

"I need a favor," I told him.

"Who is this?" he asked.

"Is your aunt in town?"

"My aunt."

I told him my idea.

"You want to go on a date with my aunt?" he asked.

I told him my idea again.

"*Oh*," he said. "That shouldn't be a problem."

I didn't want to give too much away. All I wrote is the time and the place to meet. When the hour dawned decent, I headed over to Mrs. Basil E.'s. I found her outside, taking Boris around the block.

"Your parents have let you run free?" Mrs. Basil E. inquired.

"So to speak," I said.

I offered her the notebook.

"Assuming she's up for the next adventure," I said.

"You know what they say," Mrs. Basil E. offered. "Dullness is the spice of life. Which is why we must always use other spices."

She went to take the notebook, but Boris beat her to it.

"Bad girl!" she chided.

"I'm pretty sure Boris is a boy," I said.

"Oh, I know," Mrs. Basil E. assured me. "I just like to keep him confused."

Then she and Boris headed off with my future.

When Lily arrived at five o'clock, I could tell she was a little bit disappointed.

"Oh, look," she said, gazing out at the Rockefeller Center ice rink. "Skaters. Millions of them. Wearing sweaters from all fifty states."

My nerves were whirling to see her. Because, really, this was our first shot at a semi-normal conversation, assuming no dogs or mothers intervened. And I wasn't as good at semi-normal conversations as I was at ones that were written down, or adrenalized in a surreal moment. I wanted to like her, and I wanted her to like me, and that was more want than I'd saddled myself with in many a moon.

It's up to you, not fate.

True. But it was also up to Lily.

That was the trickiest part.

I pretended to be hurt by her unenthusiastic reaction to my cliché destination. "You don't want to hit the ice?" I said, pouting. "I thought it would be so *romantic*. Like in a *movie*. With Prometheus watching over us. Because, you know, what's more fitting than Prometheus *over an ice rink*? I'm sure that's why he stole the fire for us in the first place—so we could make ice rinks. And then, when we're done skating on that traffic jam of an ice rink, we could go to Times Square and be surrounded by *two million people* without *any bathrooms* for the next seven hours. C'mon. You know you want to."

It was funny. She clearly hadn't known what to dress for, so she'd given up and just dressed for herself. I admired that. As well as the revulsion she couldn't hide at the thought of us being not-at-all-alone in a crowd.

"Or . . . ," I said. "We could go with Plan B."

"Plan B," she said immediately.

"Do you like to be surprised, or would you rather anticipate?"

"Oh," she said. "Definitely surprised."

We started walking away from Prometheus in his ring. After about three steps, Lily stopped.

“You know what,” she said. “That was a total lie. I would much rather anticipate.”

So I told her.

She slapped me on the arm.

“Yeah, right,” she said.

“Yeah,” I told her. “Right.”

“I don’t believe a word you’re saying . . . but say it again.”

So I said it again. And this time I took a key out of my pocket and dangled it in front of her eyes.

Boomer’s aunt is famous. I’m not going to name names, but it’s a name everyone knows. She has her own magazine. Practically her own cable network. Her own line of housewares at a major chain store. Her kitchen studio is world famous. And I happened to have the key for it in my hand.

I turned on all the lights, and there we were: in the center of the most glamorous baking palace in all of New York City.

“Now, what do you want to make?” I asked Lily.

“You’re kidding,” she said. “We can actually *touch things*.”

“This isn’t the NBC tour,” I assured her. “Look. Supplies. You are an ace baker, so you deserve ace raw material.”

There were copper pots and pans of all sizes. Every sweet and/or salty and/or sour ingredient that U.S. Customs would allow.

Lily could hardly contain her glee. After a split second more of reticence, she started opening drawers, sizing up her options.

“That’s the secret closet,” I said, pointing to an out-of-the-way door.

Lily went right over and opened it.

“Whoa!” she cried.

It had been the most magical place for me and Boomer growing up. Now it was like I was eight again, and Lily was eight again. We both stood, awed supplicants in front of the bounty before us.

"I don't think I've ever seen so many boxes of Rice Krispies," Lily said.

"And don't forget the marshmallows and the mix-ins. There's every kind of marshmallow, and every kind of mix-in."

Yes, for all of the floral arrangements Boomer's aunt got *just right*, and all the wine tours given in her name, her favorite food just happened to be the Rice Krispie treat, and her goal in life was to perfect the recipe.

I explained this to Lily.

"Well, let's get to it," she said.

Rice Krispies are designed to be a clean food to make—no flour, no sifting, no baking.

And yet Lily and I made the mother of all messes.

Partly, it was the trial and error with the mix-ins—everything from peanut butter cups to dried cherries to one ill-advised foray into potato chips. I let Lily take the lead, and she in turn let her inner-baking freak out. Before I knew it, marshmallows were melting everywhere, cereal boxes were toppled, and Rice Krispies were finding their way into our hair, our shoes, and—I had no doubt—our underwear.

It didn't matter.

I had thought Lily would be methodical—a checklist kind of baker. Much to my surprise—and delight—she was not like this at all. Instead, she was impulsive, instinctive, combining ingredients at whim. There was still a seriousness to her endeavor—she wanted to get this right—but there was also a playfulness. Because she realized that this *was* playing, after all.

"Snap!" Lily said, feeding me an Oreo Krispie treat.

"Crackle," I purred, feeding her a banana crème Krispie treat.

"Pop!" we said together, feeding each other from a pan of plum-and-Brie Krispie treats, which were gruesome.

She caught me looking at her.

"What?" she asked.

"Your lightness," I said, hardly knowing what I was saying. "It's disarming."

"Well," she said, "I have a treat for you, too."

I looked at the pans and pans we'd made.

"I'd say we have treats for everyone in your extended family," I told her. "And that's saying a lot."

She shook her head. "No. A different kind of treat. You're not the only one who can make secret plans, you know."

"What is it?" I asked.

"Well, do you like to be surprised, or do you like to anticipate?"

"Anticipate," I said. Then, when she opened her mouth to tell me, I jumped in with, "No no no—I like to be surprised."

"Okay then," she said, smiling in a way that was almost devilish. "Let's pack up these treats, clean up this kitchen, and take this show on the road."

"Somewhere there are babies to catch," I said.

"And words to find," she added mischievously. But she wouldn't say anything more.

I readied myself for the surprise.

twenty

(Lily)

December 31st

Imagine this:

You may not own the claim to a friend called Boomer who can get the key to his famous aunt's cooking studio.

But you are more than delighted to be a beneficiary of said key's treasures.

Snap. Crackle. Dash yum.

In exchange for said privilege, perhaps the opportunity exists for you to call upon a great-aunt nicknamed Mrs. Basil E. and ask that she telephone a cousin named Mark to harangue this cousin into giving you the key to a very different kind of kingdom.

What do you do?

The answer is obvious:

You get that key.

"Cheap shot, Lily," my cousin Mark said as he stood at the entrance to the Strand. "Next time, just ask me yourself."

"You would have said no if I'd asked you."

"True. Trust you to manipulate what a sucker I am for Great-aunt Ida." Mark eyed poor Dash, then pointed a finger warily at him. "And you! No funny stuff in here tonight, you understand?"

Dash said, "I assure you I could not contemplate any of your so-called funny stuff seeing as how I have no idea why I'm even here."

Mark scoffed. "You bookish little pervert."

"Thank you, sir!" Dash said brightly.

Mark turned the key to the front door and opened the store to us. It was 11 p.m. on New Year's Eve. Revelers streamed by along Broadway and we could hear loud, festive gatherings a couple blocks up at Union Square.

This quiet bookstore, our evening's destination, had closed hours before.

For us, and us alone, it had opened on New Year's Eve.

It pays to know people.

Or it pays to know people who will call certain cousins and remind them who put aside a trust fund many years ago for their college education and all that's asked in return is one teensy little favor for a Lily bear.

Dash and I stepped inside the Strand as Mark closed and locked the door behind us. He said, "Management has requested that in exchange for this privilege, you two pose for some publicity shots, wearing Strand T-shirts and holding Strand bags. We'd like to capitalize on your fame before the tabloids forget all about you."

"No," Dash and I both said.

Mark rolled his eyes. "You kids today. Think everything's a handout."

He waited, as if expecting us to change our minds.

He waited a few more seconds before throwing up his hands.

To me, Mark said, "Lily, lock up behind you when you leave." To Dash, Mark said, "Try anything with this precious baby girl and—"

"STOP DOTING ON ME!" Shrilly let out.

Oops.

Quietly, I added, "We'll be fine, Mark. Thank you. Please leave. Happy new year."

"You won't change your minds about those publicity shots?"

"No," Dash and I both proclaimed again.

"Baby stealers," Mark muttered.

"You're coming over tomorrow night for Christmas on New Year's Day dinner, right?" I asked Mark. "Mom and Dad get home in the morning."

"I'll be there," Mark said. He leaned in to kiss my cheek. "Love you, kid."

I kissed his cheek in return. "You too. Be careful you don't become a growly old man like Grandpa."

"I should be so lucky," Mark said.

He then unlocked the front door to the Strand and stepped back out into the New Year's Eve night.

Dash and I remained inside, staring at each other.

Here we were, alone together in our city's most hallowed ground of bookishness, on this city's night of biggest holiday anticipation.

"What now?" Dash asked, smiling. "Another dance?"

On the subway train from the cooking studio over to Union Square and the Strand, there had been a Mexican mariachi playing in our train car. A full five-piece band, no less, in traditional Mexican costumes, with a handsome, mustached singer who was wearing a sombrero and singing a most beautiful love song. I think it was a love song; he sang in Spanish, so I'm not sure (note to self: learn Spanish!). But two separate couples sitting nearby started randomly making out when the guy sang so beautifully, and I have to believe it's because the song's words were that romantic, and not because the couples didn't want to fork over some *dinero* to the musician passing round the donation hat.

Dash threw a dollar into the donation hat.

I took a risk and upped the ante. I said, "*Cinco* dollars if you'll share a dance with me." Dash had asked me out for New Year's Eve. The least I could do was return the favor and ask him for a dance. Someone had to step up already.

"Here?" Dash asked, looking mortified.

"Here!" I said. "I dare you."

Dash shook his head. His cheeks turned bright crimson.

A bum slumped in a corner seat called out, "Give the girl a dance already, ya bum!"

Dash looked at me. He shrugged. "Pay up, lady," he said.

I dropped a five-dollar bill into the musician's hat. The band played with renewed energy. Anticipation from the crowd of revelers on the train felt high. Someone muttered, "Isn't that the baby stealer?"

"Catcher!" Dash defended. He held out his hands to me.

I'd never imagined my dare would actually get called in. I leaned into Dash's ear. "I'm a terrible dancer," I whispered.

"Me too," he whispered in mine.

"Dance already!" the bum demanded.

The revelers applauded, goading us on. The band played harder, louder.

The train pulled into the Fourteenth Street Union Square station.

The doors opened.

I placed my arms on Dash's shoulders. He placed his hands around my waist.

We polkaed off the train.

The doors closed.

Our hands returned to their respective owners' sides.

We stood at the door to a special storage room in the basement of the Strand.

"Do you want to guess what's in here?" I asked Dash.

"I think I've got it figured out already. There's a new supply of red notebooks in there, and you want us to fill them in with clues about the works of, say, Nicholas Sparks."

"Who?" I asked. Please, no more broody poets. I couldn't keep up.

"You don't know who Nicholas Sparks is?" Dash asked.

I shook my head.

"Please don't ever find out," he said.

I took the storage room key from a hook beside the door.

"Close your eyes," I said.

I needn't have asked Dash to close his eyes. The basement was cold and dark and forbidding enough, except for the beautiful, musty scent of books everywhere. But it felt like there should be some element of surprise. Also, I wanted to remove some Rice Krispies lodged in my bosoms without him noticing.

Dash closed his eyes.

I turned the key and opened the door.

"Keep them closed just a little longer," I requested.

I removed one more Rice Krispie marshmallowed to my bra, then extracted a candle from my purse and lit it.

The cold, musty room glowed.

I took Dash's hand and guided him inside.

While his eyes were still closed, I took off my glasses so I'd seem, I don't know—sexier?—upon new reflection.

I let the door fall closed behind us.

"Now open your eyes. This isn't a gift for keeps. Just a visitation."

Dash opened his eyes.

He did not notice my new glasses-less look. (Or I may have been too blind to distinguish his reaction.)

"No way!" Dash exclaimed. Even with such dim visibility, he didn't need an explanation of the stacks of bound volumes piled up against the cement wall. He ran over to touch the books. "The complete volumes of the *Oxford English Dictionary*! Oh wow oh wow oh WOW!" Dash swooned, with the palpable bliss of Homer Simpson exalting, "Mmmm . . . donuts."

Happy new year.

Sorry to be so goofy and obvious about the declaration, but there was something just so . . . *dashing* about young Dashiell. It wasn't the fedora hat he was wearing or how nicely his blue shirt complemented his deep blue eyes; it was more the composition of his face, a mixture of handsome and sweet, young but wise, his expression arch yet kind.

I wanted to appear cool and indifferent, like this kind of thing happened to me all the time, but I couldn't. "Do you like it? Do you like it?" I asked, with all the eagerness of a five-year-old tasting the world's best cupcake.

"Fucking *love* it," Dash said. He took off his hat and tipped it to me in appreciation.

Ouch. Cursing—not so dashing.

I decided to pretend he'd said "*frocking* love it."

We sat down on the floor and chose a volume to explore.

"I like the etymology of words," I said to Dash. "I like to imagine what was happening when the word originated."

The red notebook was peeking out from my purse. Dash grabbed it, then looked up a word from the *R* volume of the *OED* and wrote it inside the red notebook.

"How about this one?" he asked.

He'd written *revel.* I took the *R* volume from Dash's lap and read up on the word. "Hmm," I said. "Revel. Circa 1300, 'riotous merry-making.' What else? As a verb, 'to feast in a noisy manner,' circa 1325."

Next to Dash's *revel* in the red notebook, I wrote, *Slop that trough, wench. 'Tis New Year's! We shall revel in slaughtering that there poor innocent pig and have bacon for breakfast! R-E-V-E-L.*

Dash read my entry and chuckled. "Now you choose a word."

I opened the *E* volume and chose a random word, writing down *epigynous.*

Only after I'd copied the word into the red notebook did I actually read what it meant. *Epigynous* (i-pi-jə-nəs): having floral parts attached to or near the summit of the ovary, as in the flower of the apple, cucumber, or daffodil.

Could I have chosen a more suggestive word?

Dash would think I was a trollop now.

I should have chosen the word *trollop.*

Dash's cell phone rang.

I think we were both relieved.

"Hi, Dad," Dash answered. His dashingness seemed to wither for a moment as his shoulders slumped and his voice became measured and . . . *tolerant* was the only word I could think of for the tone Dash used with his father. "Oh, it's my usual New Year's. Booze and women." Pause. "Ah, yes, you heard about that? Funny story . . ." Pause. "No, I don't want to talk to your lawyer." Pause. "Yes, I'm aware you'll be home tomorrow night." Pause. "Awesome. Nothing I love more than our father-son chats about important matters in my life."

I don't know what boldness came over me, but the resolute heaviness of Dash's demeanor threatened to crush my soul. My pinky finger crept over and nestled against his, for comfort. Like a magnet, his pinky finger latched onto and intertwined with mine.

I like magnets a whole lot.

"Now, about that word," Dash said after his call with his dad. *"Epigynous."*

I immediately jumped to my feet, in search of a new reference book with less embarrassing words. I picked up an edition of something called *The Speakeasy Urban Dickshun-yary.* I turned to a random page.

"'Running latte,'" I said aloud. "'When you're late because you stopped for a coffee.'"

Dash resumed writing in the red notebook.

Sorry I missed your bar mitzvah, I was running latte.

I took the pen and added *Sorry I just spilled coffee on your tux, too!*

Dash looked at his watch. "Almost midnight."

My epigynous zone worried. Would Dash think I trapped

him in the storage room to trap him into that awful (or wonderful?) midnight ritual of a New Year's kiss?

If we stayed in this room much longer, Dash might find out how completely inexperienced I was in the matters I was desperately wanting to experience. With him.

"There's something I need to tell you," I said quietly. *I don't know what I'm doing. Please don't laugh at me. If I'm a disaster, please be kind and let me down gently.*

"What?"

I meant to tell him, I really did. But what came out of my mouth was "Snarly Muppet has been returned to me by Uncle Carmine. It has asked to come live in this storage room, surrounded by reference books. It prefers these musty old tomes to suffocating inside a nutcracker."

"Smart Snarly."

"Do you promise to visit Snarly?"

"I can't make that promise. It's ridiculous."

"I think you should promise."

Dash sighed. "I promise to try. If your curmudgeon cousin Mark ever lets me back into the Strand."

I looked up to a clock on the wall behind Dash's head.

The midnight hour had passed.

Phew.

January 1st

"This is a rare opportunity we have, Lily. Alone in the Strand like this. I think we should take full advantage of it."

"How so?" Was it possible my heart was shaking as hard as my hands?

"We should dance around the aisles upstairs. Pore through volumes of books about circus freaks and shipwrecks. Pillage the cookbooks for that ultimate Rice Krispie treat recipe. Oh, and we must track down the fourth edition of *The Joy of—*"

"Okay!" I screeched. "Let's go upstairs! I love books about freaks." *Because I am one. You might be, too. Let's be freaks together?*

We walked to the storage room door.

Dash leaned in toward me mysteriously. Flirtatiously. He raised an eyebrow and declared, "The night is young. We have volumes and volumes of the *OED* to return to."

I reached for the doorknob and turned it.

The knob did not budge.

I noticed a handwritten sign next to the light switch I hadn't bothered to turn on when we first entered the room, so intent had I been on effecting a candle glow to our atmosphere. The sign read:

BEWARE!

In case you didn't read the huge sign on the wall
outside the door, please read this one:
DUDE! How many times do you have to be reminded?
The storage door locks from the OUTSIDE.
Be sure to keep the key on you to open it from the inside,
or you won't be able to get out.

No.

No no no no no no no.

NO!!!!!!!!!!!!!!!!!!!!!!!

I turned to face Dash.

"Um, Dash?"

"Um, yes?"

"I kind of locked us in here."

I had no choice but to call my cousin Mark for help. "You've awakened me, Lily Dogwalker," he barked into the phone. "You know it's my tradition to be asleep long before that stupid ball drops in Times Square."

I explained the predicament.

"Well, well," Mark said. "Great-aunt Ida can't save you from this one, now can she?"

"*You* can, Mark!"

"I might choose not to."

"You wouldn't."

"I would. For the emotional blackmail you placed upon me that got you and your punk friend into this situation."

He had a point.

I said, "If you don't come help us, I'll call the police to get us out."

"If you do that, the *Post* and *News* reporters will hear it on the police scanner. You'll be a headliner a second time. Just as Mommy and Daddy arrive home to the newsstands at JFK. I'm going to take a guess here and presume that they and Grandpa think you're spending the night at a girlfriend's and not out with a fella, and your cohorts Langston and Mrs. Basil E. are backing you up. This scandal gets out, and your folks will never leave you alone again. To say nothing of the fact that the media incident will ensure I lose my job. And, Lily? The worst part of all? Teenagers the world over will lose access to the secret stash of *OED*s in the basement at the Strand, all because of you and your bookish little pervert friend's reckless desire to peruse the volumes on New Year's Eve. Can you live with that, Lily? Oh, the horror!"

I paused before answering. Dash, who'd heard the conversation standing next to me, was laughing. That was a relief.

"I had no idea you were this evil, Mark."

"Sure you did. Now Markypoo wants to finish his sleep. Because he's such a sport, he's going to get up at seven a.m. and come rescue you two from your little predicament. But not before the sun rises."

I tried one last tactic. "Dash is getting very frisky in here with me, Mark." What I wanted to say was *I* wish *Dash was getting frisky in here with me.*

Dash raised an eyebrow at me again.

"No he's not," Mark said.

"How do you know?"

"Because if he was, you wouldn't be calling me to rescue you now, Googly Eyes. So here's the deal. You wanted to get to know this fellow. Here's your chance. You've got the night to yourselves. I'll be there after my good night's sleep. There's a toilet in a closet in the corner at the back of the storage room if you can't hold it. Might not be so clean. Probably no toilet paper."

"I really hate you right now, Mark."

"You can thank me in the morning, Lily bear."

Dash and I did what any two teenagers stranded in the Strand would do alone together in a basement storage room.

We sat side by side on the cold floor and played hangman in the red notebook.

S-N-A-R-L.

Q-U-I-E-S-C-E-N-T.

We talked. We laughed.

He made no untoward moves on me.

I thought about the bigger picture of my life, and about the people—and particularly the guys—I would encounter during my lifetime. How would I ever know when that moment was right, when expectation met anticipation and formed . . . connection?

"Lily?" Dash said at two in the morning. "Do you mind if we go to sleep? Also, I sort of hate your cousin."

"For imprisoning you here with me?"

"No, for imprisoning me here without any yogurt."

Food!

I'd forgotten I had some lebkuchen spice cookies inside my purse, along with an obscene amount of Rice Krispie treats. I couldn't eat another Rice Krispie treat or I'd surely turn into a human snap-crackle-pop, so I reached for the plastic bag of cookies.

As I fumbled inside my purse, I looked up once and saw that most dashing face just *looking* at me. In that certain way I knew had to mean something.

"You make really good cookies," Dash said, in that *Mmmm . . . donuts* voice.

Should I wait for him to make a move, or dare to make it myself?

As if he were wondering the same thing, he leaned down. And there it was. Our lips finally met—in a full-on head bang that wasn't anything close to a romantic kiss.

We both pulled back.

"Ouch," we both said.

Pause.

Dash said, "Try again?"

It had never occurred to me the matter would require conversation first. This lip-maneuvering business was complicated. Who knew?

"Yes, please?"

I closed my eyes and waited. And then I felt him. His mouth found mine, his lips grazing mine softly, playfully. Not knowing what to do, I mimicked his moves, exploring his lips with my own gently, happily. The honest-to-God smooching went on like that for a good minute.

There was no word in the dictionary adequate to describe the sensation other than *sensational.*

"More, please?" I asked him when we separated for air, our foreheads leaned in against one another.

"Can I be honest with you, Lily?"

Uh-oh. Here it was. All my hopes and fears about to be dashed by rejection. I was a bad kisser. Before I'd even gotten a good start.

Dash said, "I'm seriously so tired I feel like I'm going to pass out. Could we please sleep on this, and resume tomorrow?"

"With great frequency?"

"Yes, please."

I'd settle for one bang of a kiss followed by one sensational minute of kissing. For now.

I rested my head on his shoulder, and he rested his head on mine.

We fell asleep.

As threatened, my cousin Mark arrived after seven on New Year's morning to rescue us. My head was still nestled on Dash's shoulder when I heard Mark's footsteps coming downstairs and saw a light burst on underneath the doorway.

I needed to wake Dash. And believe that this hadn't all been a dream.

I looked down at the red notebook, sitting on Dash's lap. He must have woken up in the night while I was asleep and written in it. The pen was still in his hand and the notebook was open to a new page filled with his scrawl.

He'd written out the word and meaning for *anticipate,* next to which, in big block letters, he'd written: *DERIVATIVE: ANTICIPATOR.*

Below that, he'd drawn two figures who looked like action heroes in a cartoon. The sketch pictured two caped crusader teens, a fedora-wearing boy and a girl with black glasses and wearing majorette boots, passing a red notebook between them. *The Anticipators,* he'd labeled the drawing.

I smiled, and kept the smile on my face as I prepared to wake him. I wanted the first thing he saw when he opened his eyes to be the welcoming face of someone who liked him so much, someone who on this new morning, in this new year, was going to do her best to cherish this new person, whose name she finally knew.

I nudged his arm.

I said:

"Wake up, Dash."

Rachel Cohn & **David Levithan** have written three books together. Their first, *Nick & Norah's Infinite Playlist*, was made into a movie starring Michael Cera and Kat Dennings, directed by Peter Sollett. Their second, *Naomi and Ely's No Kiss List*, was named a New York Public Library Book for the Teen Age. For their third book, *Dash & Lily's Book of Dares*, David wrote Dash's chapters and Rachel wrote Lily's. Although they did not pass the chapters back and forth in a red Moleskine notebook, they did email them to each other without planning anything out beforehand. That's the way they work.

Rachel's previous books include *Gingerbread*, *Shrimp*, *Cupcake*, *You Know Where to Find Me*, and *Very LeFreak*. David's previous books include *Boy Meets Boy*, *The Realm of Possibility*, *Are We There Yet?*, *Wide Awake*, *Love Is the Higher Law*, and *How They Met, and Other Stories*.

For more information about Rachel and David, you can find them at rachelcohn.com and davidlevithan.com, respectively. You may also catch them in the aisles at the Strand.